Best wishes

Jo Sutton

2016.

The Apothecary's Daughter

Jo Sutton

GW00761135

Also by Jo Sutton

The Henrietta Trout Series:

Golden Shifter
The Mythic Encounter
The Island of Shrouds
Death at Stonehenge

Thank you.

*I would like to thank my family
for their encouragement and support.*

*A special thank you, too,
to Linda Harris and Jacqueline Abromeit
for their hard work on my behalf,*

*and to New Generation Publishing
for their guidance and patience.*

Jo Sutton 2016

1

1785

The doctor shuddered. The night was black, it felt black, a soft, clinging, sinister black. The fog had sidled in on the early tide, and the weak October sun had been unable to break its hold upon the city. All day voices had drifted in and out of the mist, a cold mist which had clung to clothes, settled on eyebrows and crept under doorways. It was no respecter of class or wealth, though as always, the poor suffered the most in their damp hovels. Hours earlier the tide had changed, but the fog refused to leave, and so a pale moon had no chance to shine a kindly light upon the city.

The doctor kept his eyes firmly fixed on the light of the link boy. He couldn't have been more than eight years old, such a responsible task for one so young. Even in these conditions he was very sure-footed and kept a steady pace, the doctor could only admire his confidence on such a night. He held his torch high, so that it burnt steadily in the still air, a soft glow encircled the flame as it cut a path through the fog. Occasionally a drunk would come staggering out of one of the many alehouses which they passed, and, momentarily, a yellow glow would filter out on to the road. One poor soul approached the doctor as if greeting a long-lost friend, only to be met by the cudgel of the burly manservant who had been sent as a bodyguard. The man was well armed and was obviously prepared to use force. The doctor did not stop, another cracked skull was of no concern to him, he had been summoned urgently. The manservant grunted something to the boy, and immediately they turned into a quiet side road. It was deserted. After a few yards they stopped in front of

1

large iron gates. The manservant produced a heavy key and unlocked the padlock.

"But I know this place," spluttered the doctor angrily. "Why wasn't the carriage sent? Why was I made to walk through the streets on such a night?"

The manservant merely pushed him through the gates, he passed something to the boy, which the doctor deduced from the clink must be a payment, then he locked the gates behind them. The boy disappeared swiftly into the fog to find another customer, whilst the doctor was half ushered and half pushed along the path, before being dragged up the few steps which led to the doors of a large mansion. The fog slid in over his feet as he stepped inside.

A magnificent oak staircase ascended the left-hand wall which was covered with portraits of the ancestors of this family. On either side of the hallway, great oak doors concealed the rooms beyond, though he remembered that the one on the right was used as the master's study. Was it only two days ago that he had been called here? He recalled with distaste the man who had required, no demanded, the bloodletting. The doctor didn't approve of this ancient medieval custom, but the man had insisted and had paid him well. If, since then, he had come down with a fever or some other malady, well, the doctor had no sympathy for him, he had been warned.

A heavy hand on his shoulder told him that he was not to ascend the staircase that night. For the first time he turned to look at the manservant. Dressed entirely in black, and still wearing his tricorn hat, he looked more like a coachman, or even a highwayman, than a manservant. A thin white scar ran down his right cheek and in his hand he still gripped the cudgel. Mercifully it had not been necessary for him to remove the pistol from his belt.

"This way," he said firmly, keeping his hand on the doctor's shoulder. He indicated a side passageway.

The doctor's face showed his contempt.

"Surely I haven't been called out on an emergency, on such a dreadful night, for a servant?" He sounded angry. "Others can deal with…" He stopped. The scream which came from the lower quarters tore through his soul. It was followed by a moaning such as someone might make in great distress. He looked at the manservant in horror before rushing towards the source.

*   *   *   *

It was several hours later, in the dark hours before the dawn, when the doctor burst into the master's study. He was angry, and tired, sweat poured down his face. There was no way the manservant, who had been his constant companion throughout his stay, could stop him.

The master of the house was seated at his desk writing in a ledger. An oil lamp and a few candles were the only source of light on this damp, cold October morning. Outside in the darkness the fog lingered like a waiting shroud. The doctor carried his own lantern, which in his haste was in danger of going out. After the chaos of below stairs, this room seemed a haven of tranquillity, another world. For a brief moment the doctor hesitated, it was just enough time to stop himself from shouting, just enough time to calm his voice.

"Sir," he said. "Your daughter is calling for you. She wishes to speak with you before…" He stopped.

The master continued his writing. He hadn't even looked up when the doctor, closely followed by the manservant, had burst into the room.

"I have no daughter," he answered coldly.

The doctor could not conceal his look of disgust. "Your daughter has given you a beautiful grandchild," he began, but was interrupted by a call from the hallway.

"Doctor, come quickly." It was the voice of the local midwife who had been responsible for calling him out.

"Sir?" The doctor hesitated expecting the master to at least look up.

"I have said, have I not, that I have no daughter. Good day to you, doctor," came the curt reply.

The doctor rushed from the room to assist his patient but, this time, the manservant remained.

"You can deal with all the necessary arrangements," said the master, sensing that his servant was still standing before him.

The man gave a short nod.

"And the baby, sir?"

"Get rid of it," came the answer.

This time there seemed a slight hesitation before the servant nodded and turned away. He quietly closed the heavy door behind him.

Not once, during all this time, did the master of the house look up. Not once did he stop writing in his book. Not once did he look up to see the boy hiding in the shadows and listening to all that was happening.

2

Mr Nimble was far from it. No one could have been more wrongly named. His portly body hurried along the passageway to his wife, Mrs Eliza Nimble. He burst into their parlour mopping his sweaty brow with his none-too-clean handkerchief as he did so.

"Mrs Nimble, my dearest, I have found the answer to our problem," he announced gleefully, as he sank into a chair.

"Which problem would that be, Mr Nimble?" asked his sour-faced wife. She wasn't portly like her husband, no, she was thin, wiry, and had a pinched face which in certain lights could appear almost evil. She never moved nimbly, but favoured stealth as her mode of movement, like a snake on a hunt.

"I have just admitted an apothecary and his daughter to our establishment," replied Mr Nimble triumphantly, as if that was the answer to everything.

"And?" His wife paused momentarily in her sewing.

"And he will save us money, my dear."

"How?" She put down her sampler, pursed her lips and glowered at him.

"Because, my dearest," explained her husband patiently, as though it was obvious and he couldn't understand why she was being so dull. "He will tend to our residents when they are sick or ill, for nothing! No payment, my petal. Nothing, except for his board and lodgings." He clapped his hands together like a little boy who has just been given some sweetmeats.

5

"And his daughter?" She knew there must be more to this.

"Ah," replied her husband. He had sensed this might be a difficult problem, but he knew he had to cut back on the fees which they had been paying the local doctor. They had to make a profit, even though they were a charity, the owner had made it abundantly clear. There would be no more money forthcoming now that the Trust had run out, unless... It was at this point that Mr Nimble had become a little confused, but it appeared that the owner would see it as a personal favour if the Nimbles were to take in the apothecary and his daughter for their lifetime. They were not to leave, and no one, not even Mrs Nimble, must know about this little arrangement.

Mr Nimble had asked if the workhouse was to act as a prison for these two persons.

"What a ridiculous idea," the owner had laughed. Not a very pleasant laugh as Mr Nimble had recalled. "Just make certain that the rest of their lifespan, however short or long, is spent with you."

"The daughter, Mr Nimble, the daughter."

His wife's rasping voice cut through his troubled thoughts.

"The apothecary will work for us only if his daughter remains with him. Apparently she's a bright little thing, nearly twelve years old. She helps him in his work, can recognise all the herbs which make up into his potions..."

"Mr Nimble!" shouted his wife. "You know that that is contrary to our regulations. We do not permit families to stay together, she must go to the women's quarters just like the other females. She..."

"No," returned Mr Nimble, very forcibly. His wife's jaw dropped in amazement at his tone. "No. They will stay together because we need this man to work for us. We cannot afford to constantly pay the doctor's fees, whereas the apothecary and his daughter will work for us for nothing

– for nothing, wife, except for their food which will be the same as every other resident here." He smiled because he knew he had won. "Bad times are coming, my dear," he said quietly. "I can feel it. He will get us out of a great deal of trouble. You mark my words."

Reluctantly his wife had to agree to his plan.

*   *   *   *

So it was that Amos and his daughter, Lucy, began their lives at Nimble's Workhouse, which lay on the outskirts of the city. As workhouses went, this was about average, neither too generous nor too meagre in their dealings with those unfortunate enough to be lodging with them. In fact, despite his wife's leanings towards the latter doctrine, Mr Nimble was a fair man and had a quiet sympathy for those who found themselves in such circumstances. He would often mutter to himself, "There but for the grace…" he never finished the saying, fearing that to do so might bring about that which he feared.

Lucy and her father worked hard for Mr Nimble, and in those early days even Mrs Nimble had to admit that the general health of their inmates seemed to improve. This she saw had a positive effect on the amount of work each one could achieve. She did not, however, approve of Amos having his own quarters, nor of his daughter remaining with him. Even more so, she did not approve of Lucy retaining her long fair hair, even though she kept it up under her little cap during the day or when working with her father.

"It should be cut short like the other women and girls," she constantly complained to her husband who just smiled and walked away. He relished his few moments of triumph. He knew he had won.

Several weeks passed by and all seemed well. In London the warm, wet summer had produced many cases of the fever, which some called cholera, and other diseases such as smallpox. Most of such cases were usually amongst the poorer folk, but that year the fever spread itself widely, creeping into the houses of the wealthier people. Mr Nimble congratulated himself that not one case of cholera had reared its ugly head in his workhouse. He was triumphant. It was all his doing, and nothing to do with the regime encouraged by Amos and his daughter. Mind you, both he and his wife thought that some of the precautions were ridiculous. All this washing of hands, scrubbing down of tables with soap and water, and even boiling water before use in cooking, it all seemed excessive.

As Mrs Nimble kept saying, "Ridiculous! Ridiculous! I've never done all this before and we ain't lost that many inmates in the past!"

Mr Nimble was inclined to agree but the owner had said follow the apothecary's instructions, so who was he to go against such rules. Whilst they kept Amos and Lucy close, there would be no trouble and Mr Nimble hated trouble.

*   *   *   *

After some time Lucy became aware that some of the younger and often fitter inmates would disappear. It always seemed to happen in the last week of the month, then at some stage during the first week of the new month others would arrive to take their place. There was a constant turnover, fit ones out, poorer ones in. One afternoon she decided to ask her father about this.

"Well," he answered. He was grinding some dried thyme leaves to make a potion for one of the elderly inmates who was suffering from a chest infection. "I have asked Mr Nimble this very question. He tells me that the owner of this charitable home finds employment for the young people in the factories of the Midlands and in the North. They are all found good homes and apprenticeships. This seems a most beneficial outcome to me, one which helps the young people, and one which will eventually benefit their country. What do you think, Lucy?"

Lucy didn't answer. It was one of the few times when she felt her father was very wrong. She'd seen the little ones crying when told they had to leave, she'd seen the look of horror on the women's faces when one of their own was forced to go. She could see nothing beneficial about it, and besides, she had recently met a little girl called Alice who had formed quite an attachment to her. She dreaded the thought that Alice would be made to leave.

Alice was five and looked up to Lucy as if she was her big sister. She had been found wandering the streets of London, begging for food wherever she could get any, doing little dances for odd coppers, singing for her supper. Her parents had both died of the cholera, somehow Alice had survived, but there was no one to care for her, so Alice was scooped up by a charity which then placed her with the Nimbles. When she arrived, Lucy had been given the task of cleaning Alice's cuts and bruises, which were many, and from that moment Alice had followed Lucy everywhere.

"What happens if the children don't want to leave?" she asked her father.

"Now why would they not want to leave for a better life and some independence?" asked her father.

Lucy looked at him and smiled. He was such a gentle man, how could she expect her father to harbour such harsh thoughts as those which she had gleaned from listening to the chatter amongst the women.

9

3

Children came and children left, but the cholera never arrived. So it seemed inevitable that as September slipped unseen into a new October, the Nimbles allowed some of Amos's safety precautions to fade away.

It was later in that month that Amos diagnosed the first case of cholera, followed almost immediately by a nasty case of diphtheria. Mrs Nimble had let the new entries bypass the usual washing and medical because she was in a hurry to get to her evening meal. Silently Amos cursed her.

The first case of diphtheria was a little girl, she reminded him so much of Lucy when she was younger. Those were dark days when his wife had died of smallpox and his Arab neighbour had shown him how to vaccinate Lucy against this dreadful disease. He had learnt much from Hassan, who had been a doctor in his own country and had travelled widely.

At first Amos didn't want Lucy anywhere near these cases, but as the numbers grew he was more than glad to have her help. It was during this time that Lucy lost contact with Alice, they were so busy cleaning their makeshift ward, caring for the sick, and comforting those who were so ill. Amos tried every potion he could think of, garlic, thyme, coltsfoot, honey, but nothing could stop the march of the disease.

On the fourth day he asked Mr Nimble, "Is there no doctor nearby who could come to help us?"

"None," came the reply. "The doctor in the next village died last year and there has been no replacement, besides he was very expensive, I doubt if we could find one now that would be cheaper. You're doing very well, only four died yesterday."

"But don't you see," replied a tired Amos. "It's growing. Two at the beginning of the week, now four. It's getting beyond us. If only you had kept to our plan, Mrs Nimble."

"It's not my fault," she shouted. "You goin' on about washin' this and washin' that. If you can't see it, then it ain't there. I don't believe in them things what you calls germs, ain't no such thing. I'm right ain't I?" she added every morning as the cases grew.

"It isn't just that," returned Amos angrily. "Didn't I say that you should keep the new intakes separate from the rest until I have judged their state of health. The last group of people were very sick and poorly, they have brought the diseases with them. It will be a miracle if more lives are not lost."

It was on the seventeenth night of October, when all was quiet in the home, that Lucy was woken by a dreadful screaming. Someone was shrieking her name, she ran to the window and there below was a dark carriage with its doors wide open. A tall man dressed in black was standing on the gravel path beside it. Several children were being loaded into the carriage, some were crying, most looked bemused, but to Lucy's horror, the small figure of Alice was being carried kicking and screaming by Mr Nimble. Suddenly he dropped her. That was when Alice looked up and seeing Lucy in the window shrieked her name, the man in black hit her hard and her body went limp. Lucy hastily picked up a shawl and flung it around her shoulders, she rushed from her room to the nearest staircase, but there at the top she met Mrs Nimble carrying a large lantern.

"Where are you going, Lucy, my dear?" she asked in barbed honey tones.

"It's Alice," Lucy replied. "She's crying, she needs me, she's…"

11

"Now, now, Lucy," said Mrs Nimble gently. "You've just had a bad dream, that's all. Come I'll take you back to your room." She gripped the girl's arm very tightly. "Just a bad dream. You've been working far too hard. Let's put you back in bed, shall we?"

Lucy had no chance of escaping that grip, and the noise of her own shouting had woken her father.

"Whatever is the matter?" Amos looked puzzled as he tried to make sense of the scene before him.

"It's alright, no need for concern," answered Mrs Nimble firmly. "Lucy's just had a bad dream, that's all." She thrust the girl straight at her father and left the room quickly, closing the door hard behind her.

But the next morning several children were missing again, including Alice.

When Lucy confronted Mr Nimble he just gave a sigh and looked at her long and hard. What could this poor, young child and her father have done which had caused him to become their jailer? For, in fact, that is what he was. They were not to leave, and yet here was this child, displaying such concern for her fellow beings that it made him feel ashamed.

"Lucy, my dear," he said kindly. "It is how we work. The poor children and some families come here, we make them fit and well, and then we send them off to a better life where they find work and employment befitting their talents. As some leave so others come in to take their place. It is the way of the world."

The new residents arrived much sooner than expected, much to Mrs Nimble's annoyance. They were very poorly, so once more, Amos and Lucy worked tirelessly helping these weak and frightened new arrivals.

It was a bitter November. No one could remember such cold winds and severe frosts.

"Perhaps this cold spell will drive away the sickness," said Mrs Nimble hopefully, for even she could now see that they were beginning to lose residents at an alarming rate.

No one, however, had bargained on Amos succumbing to bronchitis, and because he wouldn't rest it rapidly turned to pneumonia. Lucy did her best but she just could not keep up with the growing numbers of sick inmates. An outbreak of fevers began to run rampant through the workhouse.

"I can't arrange the burials fast enough," complained a frightened Mr Nimble one evening.

Mrs Nimble looked up from her knitting. This large house, which they ran as a charitable workhouse for the owner, had in its grounds a small church. Between the church and the house lay an even smaller storehouse made of solid stone, to give it the air of a chapel of rest.

"Put 'em in the chapel," she said.

"The chapel!" He looked at her in horror. "It's no more than a storeroom for logs and rubbish. I've seen rats in there. We can't put bodies in there."

"Yes we can," she answered, laying her knitting down carefully on the table.

"We'll get Thomas to tidy it up a bit tomorrow, and then I'll arrange with the vicar to have a pit dug."

"A pit!"

"Yes, a lime pit, like was done in plague times," Mrs Nimble's face was hard. "The vicar will agree for a little…" She rubbed the thumb and fingers of her left hand together. "They can all have a decent burial together. We ain't got time to sort 'em all out individually. The authorities won't know until it's too late, and then they'll be pleased as 'ow we've been able to sort it out without bothering any of them. The fever will have been contained, and not spread. The owner will be pleased too, you mark my words, Mr Nimble."

So Mr Nimble marked her words, whilst Lucy did her utmost to nurse her sick father and to look after the rest of the residents. It was all too much for her, and Mrs Nimble watched like a snake as the girl fought the deadly weariness which crept over her young body each day.

"When your father goes," she whispered on that fateful morning. "You can kiss goodbye to your special quarters and privileges. I'll cut your hair off personally and you can go and live with the other women, just as you should 'ave in the beginning."

"My father will not die," replied Lucy firmly.

Mrs Nimble just laughed, knowing that it was only a matter of time. Even she could see what Lucy refused to see. The apothecary was losing his battle with death, he was not long for this world.

4

It was much later that same day when Lucy returned to their room. It had been a hard morning, and despite Lucy's efforts a young mother had died. She had little hope for the woman's baby. How she wished her father had been with her, he was so calm and knowledgeable on these things. Exhausted as she was, Lucy had run to their room to see how her father was progressing. There she was confronted by Mrs Nimble. She was handing the bed sheets to another woman, and directing her to take them to the laundry. Amos's bed had been stripped.

"What are you doing?" shouted Lucy, rushing forward, her hands clenched into tight fists. "Where's my father?"

Mrs Nimble took hold of her wrists and laughed.

"He's dead. He went this morning just after you left. Called your name, he did, but you was too busy looking after the others, so I told him you couldn't come. He'll be in the lime pit tomorrow with the others, and you'll be out of this room and you'll have all this cut." She grabbed hold of Lucy's hair. "Should 'ave been cut a long time ago if I'd had my way. It'll fetch a good price I shouldn't wonder."

Lucy pulled away and gave Mrs Nimble such a sudden push, that she fell backwards onto the mattress, her legs up in the air, her skirt all askew and her bloomers showing for all to see.

"Mr Nimble! Mr Nimble! Come quick! I've been attacked!" she squealed. "I've been attacked!"

Lucy rushed from the room, down the long corridor, and round the sharp corner to the steep wooden staircase which led down to the back of the house. At the bottom of this was a door which led out to a gravel path. This would take

15

her to the storeroom where she knew the Nimbles were placing the bodies of the poor victims. She must reach her father before they put his body in the pit. How could they be so sure that he was dead? She had to see him. But Lucy didn't make it.

In her haste to reach her father, she tripped on the top step and fell headlong to the bottom, hitting the walls as she fell. With a sickening thud she hit the flagstone and a small trickle of blood slowly oozed its way onto the floor. She lay there quite still until Thomas found her.

*   *   *   *

Now Thomas was a strong, young man, the only child of Mr and Mrs Nimble. As a small baby he had suffered a terrible fall, and this had caused him a great deal of trouble as he grew up. His left leg had been damaged, and never given the chance to heal properly. His thoughts were slow and consequently his speech too. Many thought him silly, but this was not the case. He was a kind and caring person, the children of the workhouse loved him, and took great delight in helping him in the garden where Thomas was responsible for all their produce. He never complained about the sharp tongue of his mother, he accepted that, although his father loved him, Mr Nimble would never, could never, stand up for him when his mother punished him unjustly. Of one thing he was certain though, from the moment he first set eyes on Lucy, he loved her. He had never before met such a kind and beautiful young person. He thought she must be an angel sent down to help others. He would never have told her of his love, nor did anyone else know, but Lucy had been kind to him and had treated him like a real human being, and for that too, he loved her. So when he found Lucy's body at the bottom of the stairs he was horrified. He sat beside her and wept. He stroked her beautiful golden hair, which was slowly being stained with blood, and let his tears fall freely onto her lifeless face.

"You will want to be with your father, I know," he said quietly to her. "I shall take you there, so that you can be together."

He picked up her little body in his strong arms and carried her out into the bitter cold November air, ignoring all the screams and shouts coming from upstairs from his mother. No one saw him trudge along the gravel path, no one heard the heavy scrunch of his boots as he made his way to the stone storeroom which had been turned into a temporary mortuary. He knew exactly where the apothecary's body lay because he had placed it there only minutes previously. Carefully he laid her body down on the gravel path whilst he found the key to open the door. Once open, he reached for the lantern which he had left lit on the shelf just inside the room. A rat scuttled away into the darkness as the lantern swung a crazy light around the walls. There were three steps down to where several bodies lay waiting for the pit. The apothecary was on the right-hand side. Very carefully he picked up Lucy and laid her gently by the side of her father. There was an abandoned shawl on the floor, it had probably fallen from the shoulders of one of the poor victims, he placed this over Lucy, then he looked down, pleased with his work.

"There," he said. "You can sleep peacefully together."

With that he replaced the lantern on the shelf and closed the heavy door. He was just about to lock it when he heard his mother screaming his name.

"Thomas! Thomas! Are you out there? I need you now!"

He grunted as he began his slow journey back along the gravel path. There stood Mrs Nimble outside the house, all dishevelled and almost bouncing up and down with anger.

"Thomas! That wretched girl, that evil Lucy, has just attacked me. She's dangerous, Thomas. She's wicked. Go and find her, bring her back to me so that she can be

17

punished. When you've done that you can start digging the pit over there, by the stone wall. Now hurry, Thomas. Go on, go and find her before it gets too dark. Fetch her, Thomas. Fetch her!"

Thomas said nothing but stared at this awful woman. His mind told him, he wasn't a dog to be told to fetch and find. He certainly wasn't going to tell his mother where he had placed his beloved Lucy. As far as he was concerned, she was the angel who had lit his life and had given it some purpose, even if only for a short time.

No he wasn't going to tell Mrs Nimble anything.

"Go on, Thomas! Go on! Fetch her!" she was screaming again.

Thomas just grunted and shuffled away.

5

The sight which met Samuel's eyes filled him with horror. He peered down the stone steps searching for the disappearing figure of James who was swinging the lantern about as though inspecting his prize turnips. Then the stench hit him and Samuel was sick on the spot.

"Pull up your 'kerchief," grunted James. "It'll help with the smell and cover your face if anyone turns up."

Samuel did as he was told. "I thought you said it was alright. No one would want them, and that's why they've been put down here."

"True," replied James. "But tomorrow, so cook says, most of 'em are to be put in the lime pits. There's too many of 'em what 'as snuffed it. The sooner we get on with it, the sooner it'll be over."

All the most piteous creatures of humanity were piled high before Samuel's eyes. His lantern cast an eerie glow over their lifeless bodies. It sickened him to see the rats scurrying away from his lantern light. Predators of the dark. Silently the two men worked loading the bodies into their cart.

"The doctors'll pay good money for these," muttered James, pausing for breath. Despite the feebleness of the inmates, carrying their silent bodies was proving to be an exhausting task.

"Why so many?" asked Samuel. It was his first journey into this hell hole with James. If he had not been so desperate for money to keep his family out of the debtors' prison, if it had not been for the magistrate's threat of transportation, and if it had not been for lack of food for his children, he would never have agreed to come along.

"Don't sound so worried." James was grinning under his 'kerchief. "It's not as if we're like them what steals from graves. These poor sods have no one to mourn them. The workhouse has had a bit of a problem, a whole bunch of 'em went down with a sickness. They was already weak when they come in. We're doin' everyone a favour. We're 'elpin' to clean up the mess from the workhouse, we're 'elpin' the doctors in their experiments, and we're 'elpin' these poor souls to be useful at the end of their lives, so stop your worryin' and get on with the job."

Samuel sighed and thought of his own family. He vowed to kill them all before he ever allowed them to go to a workhouse such as this.

The nearby church clock struck 1 a.m.

"C'mon," urged James. "We've got to get a move on. We're to deliver these by two o'clock or the doctors'll be gone. These must be the last ones."

Samuel braced himself for the final descent into the vault. It was then that he saw her. No more than a heap of bones in a bundle of rags, the girl made a slight movement. She lay a little way past the main mound of corpses and next to a man. He gazed at her, not much older, he thought, than his eldest girl. Gently he lifted her up, despite the freezing temperatures he could tell the difference between this frail creature fighting for her life and the bodies of those who had long since expired. Blood was matted into her hair and on one side of her face dark bruises were beginning to form.

"Don't move," he whispered, as he carried her out into the freezing night air. Quietly he laid her behind a tombstone away from the eyes of James, and threw her shawl over her tiny body.

"When we have gone, you must leave this dreadful place. Go through the gate and make your way down the lane and into the woods. There is a path there which will lead you into the next village, someone there will surely help you. Take care little one."

"Hurry up, Samuel," whispered James, loudly. "What's 'oldin' you up?"

Samuel pretended to retch again behind the tombstone.

"Sorry, James," he replied. "My stomach ain't used to it like yours. I'll be better next time."

"If we don't get a move on," answered James, brusquely, "there won't be a next time. Close them doors, we must be away now."

'No there definitely wouldn't be a next time,' thought Samuel. 'None of this seems right.'

He glanced at the little bundle of humanity hidden behind the stone and secretly wished her well. He daren't tell James about her, in case James decided to end her days there. At least he'd given her a chance. He dreaded to think what might have happened if he hadn't spotted her. Quietly he closed the door saying a silent prayer for those left behind, then he hastily followed the horse and cart. Only the sound of the wheels slowly turning on the gravel could be heard, James had covered the horse's hoofs with thick sacking in order to muffle as much noise as possible.

*   *   *   *

Lucy lay behind the gravestone unable to decide whether she was shivering from the cold or from fear, the pain in her head was so terrible, it pulsated like an angry beast about to burst through her skull. She had no idea of the time nor of the day. Terrible things had happened, she knew that. Someone had just been talking to her. Was it her father? She tried hard to think as gradually some of the dreadful memories came creeping back. She had to get away, of that she was certain, but what of her father? Slowly she reached up to the top of the harsh grave stone, pulled herself upright and turned to look back at the heavy oak door of the store house. Amos, her father, was dead, and his last words must have been to get away from this place. Yes, it must have been his voice which she had heard in her head. But where? Where should she go? She gazed around the graveyard. The glow of the moon gave it a look of serenity and caused the frost to sparkle like a gentle blanket of silver diamonds. Lucy shivered. The cold was seeping into her bones, she had to get away. But where? The question came back again, and again. She looked to her left. The gaunt outline of the house towered over the scene. She had to escape. Carefully she made her way along the path towards the gate, pulling the shawl tightly around her shoulders. There was no one about, it was just after 3 a.m. on a bitterly cold November morning. What had the voice said? Go down the lane and into the wood, yes, that was it.

It was difficult to walk, her legs seemed to have a mind of their own but she made them follow the lane as it gently sloped away to her left. Sometimes the whole lane appeared to curve and sway like a river running to the sea. She began to realise that the stickiness in her hair must be blood and the lump, which was very tender, a large bruise. Her father had warned her of head injuries in the past, and had advised her on how to treat people who had such injuries. She smiled ruefully. Walking down lanes in the middle of the night was not recommended. Then, looking to her right, she saw a narrow path which led into some woodland.

'This must be the place,' she thought. 'I must lie down soon, Father, or I know I will collapse.'

It was as if Amos stood there before her, gently coaxing her along the pathway and into the shelter of the trees.

'No,' he seemed to say. 'Don't stop here on the path. Move into the wood, and away from the thoroughfare. You must hide amongst the bracken.'

She felt these words guiding her, and began following the path until she saw a gap in the undergrowth. Stumbling through this she made her way to a large oak tree and curled up at its base. Only then did she smile. She was free.

6

Mrs Nimble was scared. She was scared because she had searched the whole house from top to bottom, and there had been no sign of Lucy, she was scared because she had had the men searching the grounds, and they had found nothing, but most of all, she was scared because Mr Nimble had called her by her first name, Eliza. He had not used her first name since their wedding day. It was, she felt, an indication as to the seriousness of their situation. She sat by their fireside, wrapped in her shawl, slowly rocking herself backwards and forwards.

The door opened quietly, it was Mr Nimble clad in his nightshirt and carrying a lantern.

"Come to bed, Eliza, my dear," he said gently. "There is nothing to be gained by your sitting up all night, we will resume our search in the morning. The girl can't have gone far on such a cold night."

To his astonishment, Mrs Nimble gave out a loud howl at the sound of her name. He had imagined it would be a moment of comfort to her, but it seemed to make her even more agitated. He placed his lantern on the table and carefully approached her, he was only too aware that, as a woman prone to sudden tempers, she might still lash out at him despite her apparent torments. Gently he patted her hand, and to his amazement she suddenly flung both her arms around his shoulders, almost throttling him in her anxiety to bring him closer.

"What will happen to us when he finds out?" she sobbed into his ear, her tears flowing freely. "Oh, Horatio, what will happen?"

Mr Nimble was so taken aback by her sudden apparent dependence upon him, that he felt himself grow, six feet tall, the man of the house.

"We will go to bed, my love," he whispered. "In the morning all will seem much better, you'll see. Nothing bad will happen to us. Come along now."

He coaxed her from her chair and slowly led her to their bedroom, there he gently lay her on the bed. She was shaking too much to even consider undressing, and so he carefully placed the counterpane over her, making quiet comforting sounds as a parent might make for a sick child, then he went across to the fire, which was beginning to fade, and threw a log on to its dying embers. Slumping down in his chair, he knew her fears, he felt them running through his own body. The owner of the workhouse had been very explicit in his requirements. They were to keep Amos and his daughter until the end of their days. Amos had died, that was certain, but what had happened to Lucy? How would he explain to the owner that they had lost her? Sir Daniel Haggleton was not a man to be disobeyed. He fell into a troubled sleep.

*   *   *   *

Thomas was also a worried man. He had had to wake his parents, he couldn't remember a time when this had happened. His mother had been sleeping, fully clothed, on top of the bed, his father was slumped in the armchair by the fire, which had long since gone out. The room was cold, and Thomas set about coaxing a fire from the ashes before his father froze to death.

Suddenly his mother sat up and for a moment stared frantically around the room, there was a wild look in her eyes, but then she spotted Thomas. To his amazement she smiled.

24

"Thomas," she said brightly. "We must have some breakfast."

With that she left the room and proceeded to their private parlour. She made no attempt to tidy her hair or straighten her dishevelled appearance. His father began to stir as the flames of the fire reluctantly fluttered into life. Thomas patted his father's knee and followed his mother into the other room.

Breakfast was a strange affair. His parents hardly spoke. This was not that unusual for his father, but certainly each morning had always been punctuated by his mother's staccato tones, today she was silent. At the end of their meal Mr Nimble stood up, kissed Mrs Nimble on the cheek, and turning to Thomas said, with a rare air of authority, "Come, my son. We must search again for this missing child."

Well, this was all too much for Thomas. He had never before witnessed his father kiss his mother, and he could not recall when his father had last called him 'my son'. Yesterday he had been so angered by his mother's shouting and everyone yelling at him. "Go and look here. Go and look there. Haven't you searched there yet?" He had decided not to tell anyone of the whereabouts of Lucy, but now he could tell that her loss was affecting them too. Mistakenly he imagined their feelings to be of love, of mourning for her disappearance. He had no idea of their fear of Sir Daniel.

"Father," he mumbled.

"Not now, Thomas," said his father, as they made their way along the corridor. Although it was only 6 a.m. the house was already grumbling into the day's action.

Thomas tried again. "It's important," he said, clenching his fists and refusing to move.

Mr Nimble sighed, he remembered Thomas as a child, stamping his feet and throwing enormous tantrums. He turned to look at him, the expression on Thomas's face was just as it had been when a little boy, only now Mr Nimble was looking at a grown man.

"Lucy's dead," Thomas blurted out. "I put her with her father in the store shed."

Mr Nimble turned pale. "Show me," he answered hoarsely.

It was still dark when they made their way out into the freezing cold. A frost had wrapped itself about the world. The strange noise which Mr Nimble could hear was the sound of his own teeth chattering, it was impossible to stand still, the cold seemed to eat deep into his bones. Thomas led him to the store house.

"They're in here," said Thomas, hastily turning the key before his father realised that it had been left in the lock all night.

The sight which met their eyes was terrifying. Mr Nimble clutched his hanky to his face. Rats fled from the scene.

"No!" shouted Thomas, as he swung his lantern around the room searching for Lucy.

"What do you mean?" asked Mr Nimble. He couldn't make up his mind if he was shaking from the cold, or from the fear of seeing all these dead souls.

"There are some missing," replied Thomas. "The apothecary has gone and so has Lucy, and so have," he held up one hand, "five others, they've all gone."

Mr Nimble was not stupid. He looked hard at Thomas. "Did you leave the door unlocked? Answer me truthfully, Thomas. Did you forget to lock the doors?"

Thomas flinched, expecting a blow to fall on his head at any moment. He nodded.

Mr Nimble lowered his lantern, he was too tired to hit Thomas.

"You're sure she was dead?"

Again Thomas nodded.

"Then we've had body snatchers," replied Mr Nimble flatly. "Come on, Thomas, let's return to the house. We must talk about this, perhaps if she has died the Master will forgive us." He sighed as they locked the door behind them and slowly trudged back to the house.

Thomas was bewildered. How could they be pleased that body snatchers had taken her little body. Where had they taken her? It was the first time his father had mentioned the Master in such tones to him.

"Who is the Master?" he asked, as they entered the house.

"Sir Daniel Haggleton," replied Mr Nimble. He closed the door behind them.

"He owns this house, Thomas. He alleges that he bought it when the previous owners died, but there's something odd about it. I think he's hiding a dreadful secret from us. He put us here but, last year, we were told that we could only stay if we accepted the apothecary and his daughter."

"I don't understand," said Thomas.

"Neither do I," answered his father. "Sir Daniel is a very powerful man, Thomas. He's a magistrate and," Mr Nimble looked about him as if the walls were listening, "not too worried who he transports, or sends to the gallows. We must always be very careful when dealing with him."

Thomas nodded, though what it all meant, he was none too sure.

7

When Lucy awoke it was already dark, she had slept throughout the whole day. She could hardly move, none of her joints seemed to want to work, she felt as if she had been frozen to the spot. For several minutes she couldn't remember why she was there, what had happened, or why her head ached so much. Gradually the mists in her mind began to unravel, and were swiftly overtaken by great gnawing pangs of hunger.

'This must be night time,' she thought. 'Though I have no idea what day it is. What shall I do, Father? Do you think I should try to move? Shall I go back? Where shall I go?'

She stood up and squealed as the cramp in her legs knotted up. Push down, keep moving, she remembered her father's advice to patients. Yes, she would keep moving, and so slowly and painfully she made her way along the narrow path. After nearly half an hour of this tortuous journey, the path sloped down gently and came out onto a wider roadway, a green lane, forgotten by some but still used by farmers, wagoners, and drovers. There in front of her was a stone marker, the full moon shone down onto the lettering.

'*Twenty miles to London*' it read, an arrow conveniently pointing out the correct direction.

Lucy sighed. She had begun to imagine that she would walk back to London and find their old home, she was sure that friends and neighbours from the past would help her, but now, reading the stone, feeling the griping pains in her stomach, her courage almost failed her. But Lucy was not a girl to give in to fear that easily.

"I shall need to take lots of rests," she said to herself. "But most of all, I need to find some food."

Even as she said this she knew that it was virtually impossible to find food in the hedgerows at this time of the year. Slowly she became aware of the noise of a cart travelling towards her, and she felt instinctively that she must hide, she had no intention of being taken back to the workhouse. She would rather die than be a captive there again. Quickly she hid in the deep ditch which ran alongside the road, it was full of icy water.

A wagon slowly trundled its way past her. The horse pulling it was in no hurry and neither was the driver. He sat hunched up at the front, swathed in rugs, blankets and coats, he looked like a giant bear sitting there. The full moon bathed everything in an eerie glow so that Lucy would not have been surprised if this had proved to be true, that he really was a bear. His open wagon was full of pots, pans, barrels and tubs which he was taking to market. The previous day he had decided to make an early start so as to get the best pitch, he had plenty of time to get there, there was no need to hurry. From the back of his wagon the dangling pans clanked together to the steady rhythm of the wheels, only to be broken when it hit a pot hole. Then the wagoner would let out a guttural curse as if expecting the horse to spot these and guide his cargo around such hazards.

Lucy waited until the wagon was out of sight and then began her journey again. It was much harder scrambling out of the ditch than she had imagined. Her feet were now wet and almost numb with the cold where she had crouched in the icy ditch water. With a supreme effort she struggled up the slippery sides and out onto the road. She would walk as far as possible by this moonlight, and then she would hide during the day, but she desperately needed food and warmth.

She tried so hard to push herself forward, to keep her body moving but the road was beginning to sway and seemed to her to meander one way and then the other like a feckless river. Her head was throbbing and, although she was icy cold, her forehead was hot, damp and wet, she knew she was beginning to develop a fever. It was then that she saw what looked like a body lying in the middle of the road. Had the wagoner fallen from his wagon? Was the poor horse dragging the wagon to market on its own? Worse still had the wagoner been attacked and was lying dead upon the ground? Carefully she approached the dark heap. Once there, she fell onto her knees and wept with joy and relief. The dark heap was a coat which the wagoner had flung so carelessly over the tailpiece of his wagon. He had kept it there to wear at the market. As she struggled to put it on she felt inside one of the pockets and there found an apple, a piece of cheese and a hunk of dry bread – the wagoner's lunch.

"Oh thank you, thank you," she whispered, as if the wagoner had deliberately left it there for her to find.

The coat was so large that it wrapped right around her which meant that she could now use the shawl, which Samuel had left her, as a headscarf and cover her pulsating gash.

'Yes, I'll easily make London with such a feast,' she thought. The need now was to find somewhere to rest and hide before the new day broke. Already the sun was beginning to make its presence known, small birds were beginning to flit in and out of the hedgerows, and a cockerel could be heard flexing its vocal chords in a distant farmyard.

'I must have walked miles,' she thought in her growing delirium. 'Miles and miles.'

Eagerly she made her way forward to where there was another stone marker expecting the distance to be halved, but the number etched on it caused her to sway and to burst into tears.

'*Nineteen miles to London*' it read, an arrow conveniently pointing out the direction once more.

"Oh, Father," she sobbed. "What can I do? I'll never reach it. It's too far."

She stumbled to the side of the road and lay down under a hedge. She made no effort at hiding herself, she was too ill and too tired, she was beaten, and it was better that she die there amongst the creatures than back in that dreadful workhouse.

And there she lay for the whole day, not a single person passed her, not a single wagon or cart, until just before midnight.

If Lucy had been conscious she would have felt the hoof beats as the rider slowly approached. Dressed entirely in black, the rider was deftly guiding his horse from one side of the road to the other, although the horse was such a magnificent black beast it could probably have carried out such manoeuvres on its own. They were obviously searching for something or someone. Between them they made little or no sound as though experienced in such things. When the rider saw the small black bundle that Lucy had become he hastily dismounted and went to her. Very gently he lifted her up and carried her to his horse.

"So I've found you at last, and none too soon, I think," he whispered.

At the sound of his voice Lucy opened a bleary eye and promptly fainted. Her rescuer was wearing a mask. He was a highwayman.

8

Sir Daniel Haggleton leant back in his chair and regarded this wretched creature before him. He wasn't yet a Lord, but he rather enjoyed the way this grovelling excuse for a man kept calling him 'Your Lordship, Sire'. It was only a matter of time before his distant elderly cousin died and then he would inherit the title, so it rather pleased him to hear himself being called 'Your Lordship'. The man was afraid of him and that suited him too, the more people who feared him the better he liked it.

"So explain to me again, Mr Nimble," he said in soft viper like tones. "How did you come to lose the apothecary?"

Horatio Nimble wrung his hands together. He was sure that his knees were knocking, he couldn't stop shaking, he was desperately tired and wanted to sit down but this was not to be allowed. He had deliberately been kept waiting and standing for nearly an hour in front of Sir Daniel's desk. He was so pleased that he hadn't brought Thomas with him, the lad would never have been able to put up with this and would probably have been sent to an asylum. Hadn't His Lordship been listening? Why did he have to go through it all again? But he did as he was asked, knowing that he was in dangerous territory.

"Amos, the apothecary, was a wonderful man, Your Lordship, Sire. It was indeed an excellent idea of yours that we should admit him to the House. He brought with him new ways and amazing medical knowledge that helped our residents to better health and more useful employment, just as you foresaw, Your Lordship, Sire."

Sir Haggleton nodded his head at the tall man dressed in black standing behind Mr Nimble.

"Get on with it," he grunted as he hit him around the head.

Mr Nimble nearly fell over from the blow.

"Unfortunately," he said, wincing from the pain in his head. "Unfortunately he was unable to save himself, and I regret to say that he died of the cholera which swept the House."

"And the girl?" whispered Sir Haggleton, leaning forwards in his chair as if ready to strike.

"The girl?" Mr Nimble tried to sound as if she was of no consequence, but he knew now that her whereabouts was of vital importance as to whether or not he escaped with his life from this evil house.

Sir Haggleton gave a nod and Mr Nimble felt the blow again, only this time it seemed much harder.

Mr Nimble was thinking fast. Having had to stand in this room for almost an hour waiting for his Lordship he had had plenty of time to gaze at the life-sized portrait on the wall. It was of a beautiful woman dressed in blue silk. A charming family scene, she was reading to her two children, a small boy and a young girl. It was the painting of the girl which had caused Mr Nimble to gasp when he first saw it. Without doubt it was the likeness of Lucy.

"I regret to say, Your Lordship, Sire, that she died too," he said quietly.

"You lie!" shouted Sir Haggleton, springing up from his chair and leaning across the desk. The spit from his venom reached Mr Nimble's face but he dare not wipe it away.

"Calm down, Father, calm down."

Mr Nimble turned in surprise to see a young man enter the room. He was dressed in the latest fashion and wore an impeccably powdered wig. In his right hand he had a pair of dice which he nonchalantly tossed up and down. The young man walked round to the other side of the desk and placed a hand protectively on his father's shoulder. It was William, Sir Daniel Haggleton's only son. Mr Nimble grunted from another blow around his head.

"Oh, Morgan," sighed William. "Why must you always be so rough? I'm sure this gentleman will give us all the information we need, whatever it is, without you pummelling the life out of him. What is it you want to know, Father?"

Sir Haggleton took a deep breath. "You don't understand, William, and I don't wish you to concern yourself about it."

William just smiled and patted his father's shoulder. "Tell me, and then perhaps I can begin to understand," he said.

"It is about the apothecary and his daughter, Sire," said Mr Nimble boldly, hoping that this young man's intervention might save him from another blow around his head. "They're both dead."

William laughed, it wasn't a pleasant sound. "So what have they to do with us? If they're dead then that's good, surely?" He looked down at his father.

His father spat on the floor. "I need to see their bodies," he said gruffly.

"They're in the lime pit with all the others," said Mr Nimble hastily. "No one will see them in there. They'll be unrecognizable very shortly."

William immediately clutched a lace handkerchief to his mouth as if fending off any bad infections which might have travelled with the unfortunate man.

Another blow rained down upon Mr Nimble's head. Morgan was enjoying himself.

"Lies again!" shouted Sir Haggleton. "When will you tell the truth? I have been told that their bodies, amongst others, were missing from your makeshift vault. So where are they now?"

Mr Nimble had no idea how Sir Haggleton knew this, he must have spies within the House. He now knew he had no choice but to tell about the body snatchers.

"Body snatchers came in the night and took them," muttered Mr Nimble.

"Took them where?" shouted Sir Haggleton.

Suddenly Mr Nimble had had enough. He had answered all the questions, he had endured standing in this room being cross-questioned by this evil man, he had been beaten and shouted at, he had had enough.

"I don't know," he shouted at the top of his voice. "If I did, I'd have sent the lot there. It would have saved Thomas having to dig a pit on such hard and frosty ground."

For a moment there was silence, a long and unending silence which grew heavier by the minute, it was suddenly broken by a slow hand-clapping from William.

"Oh well done, little tadpole, well done," he broke into laughter. "You should see your face, Morgan, you really should. Let him be, Father. He's told you all he knows. These two creatures, whoever they are, are no longer. So what do we care? They are dead. They cannot bother you any more, whatever it was they bothered you about, they cannot..."

"Oh be quiet, William," growled his father, he was quietly seething with rage. He looked hard at Mr Nimble. "And will you swear that the apothecary and his daughter are both dead? Will you swear to this, Mr Nimble?"

"Yes, your Lordship, Sire," replied Mr Nimble.

"Very well then," Sir Haggleton took a deep intake of breath. "You may go. Morgan will see you out. Go back to the House and carry on as best as you are able."

"Thank you, your Lordship, Sire," replied Mr Nimble giving a low bow. He couldn't believe his good fortune. He had half expected to be thrown there and then straight into prison. His bow almost caused him to topple over.

This caused the young man to go into peals of laughter. Neither he nor Mr Nimble saw the silent message which passed from Sir Haggleton to Morgan.

9

Lucy felt as if she was climbing out of a deep pit. The more she tried to reach the top, the harder it seemed to become. Voices were floating above her head, all around her. Who were they? Where did they come from?

'Go away,' she thought. 'Go away and let me be. I'm tired I just want to sleep. Please leave me alone.'

But the voices wouldn't go, they were coming closer and closer. Someone was pulling at her clothes.

'Kill me if you must,' she thought. 'I'm too tired to bother, just do it.'

She fell back into the pit and all was blackness.

How long was she there? She had no idea, it could have been ten minutes, ten hours, even ten days, but gradually she began to regain consciousness. She was surprised to find that she was not in a pit but lying in a bed, a comfortable bed, with clean sheets. A woman was sitting on a chair at the bottom of the bed quietly knitting. A plump woman, wearing a mob cap over her brown curly hair, she was humming to herself. Lucy went to move but found she couldn't, there was a heavy weight on the bed. She looked down at it, and found to her astonishment a little girl, fast asleep by her side. It was Alice!

Lucy's movement caused the woman to look up from her knitting and for a moment their eyes met. The woman's face broke into a big smile.

"Ah, Lucy," she whispered. "You've come back to us. Well done, my little one, that was quite a battle."

Lucy tried to speak but couldn't, her throat was too dry and when she tried to swallow she realised that it was incredibly sore.

"Shh," said the woman. Laying down her knitting she picked up a cloth and walked around to the side of Lucy's bed. Once there she dipped it into a bowl and gently wiped Lucy's lips with the mixture, it was warm and sweet like honey. At this point Alice woke up and was about to fling herself upon Lucy in sheer delight but fortunately the woman stopped her.

"Now, now, Alice dear," she said gently. "You must let Lucy rest. She's been very ill and she needs to regain her strength. There'll be plenty of time for hugs later."

"Oh, Lucy," said Alice, almost in tears. "I knew you'd get better. I knew Nelly would make you better, but you took so long, I was so worried about you. This is the best place in the world, Lucy. You'll be safe now."

Lucy smiled and tried to stroke Alice's head but she couldn't lift her arm. Tiredness swept over her and she fell asleep but this time it was peaceful, the kind of sleep which heals and makes one well again.

*   *   *   *

It was the sound of birdsong which eventually woke her, it was such a long time since she had heard such sounds that for a moment she couldn't make out where it was coming from. The woman, who Alice had called Nelly, was still sitting at the bottom of her bed but her head was slumped forward and she was obviously dozing. Lucy took the opportunity to look around. She was in a strange room. It was long and entirely made of wood, even the ceiling was wooden; all the windows, and there were many, were small and covered with shutters. A soft yellow glow came from candles which had been placed carefully near her own bed. It was then that she realised hers was only one amongst many. Several other beds lined the room and all seemed to be occupied. Alice was sleeping soundly in the bed next to hers.

Nelly woke with a start, suddenly aware that Lucy was awake.

"Now, little one," she said gently. "Would you like something to drink?"

Lucy nodded and Nelly left, to return very shortly with a mug of warm sweet milk. It tasted wonderful.

"Don't drink it too quickly," whispered Nelly. "You must take things very slowly at first, you've been very ill, Lucy."

"How do you know my name?" asked Lucy, after she had taken a few sips.

Nelly smiled. "Well, from Alice, of course. As soon as she saw it was you, she made certain that everyone knew your name, and how kind you and your father were to her and to others like her in that dreadful place."

"But how did I get here? All I can remember is that terrible masked face coming closer and closer to me." Lucy shuddered at the memory.

Nelly shook her head. "I've told him before that he mustn't frighten you young people, but he never listens." She paused as she encouraged Lucy to drink a little more milk. "That was Noah. The children call him Mr Noah. He's a highwayman, I don't know where he comes from, but I do know that he is kindness itself. He's always rescuing folk who've been mistreated or wrongly arrested. He brings them all here and then, when they are well, he makes certain that they find new families or homes where they will be well cared for. The children call this Noah's Ark."

"Are we on a ship?" asked Lucy in amazement. She had not felt any swaying from the waves.

"We are and we aren't," replied Nelly mysteriously. "You get some more sleep and I'll explain it all later. The others are beginning to wake up and they'll all be wanting their breakfasts, you mark my words. Oh no, here comes trouble." This last remark was directed at the bundle which had occupied Alice's bed. It suddenly sprang into action and a very happy Alice clambered onto Lucy's bed.

"Are you feeling better, Lucy? Will you be getting up today?"

Nelly waggled her finger under Alice's nose. "Now don't bother Lucy, there's a good girl. She needs her rest. She'll be up and about very soon, don't you worry."

Alice gave Lucy a big kiss, and then went skipping off to join the other girls who were beginning to make their way to the wash room before going upstairs for breakfast.

Lucy lay back on her pillow and sighed. It all seemed like a dream, too good to be true. Suddenly she burst into floods of tears as she remembered all that she had lost – her father, the sound of his voice, the comfort of his presence. She would never see him again.

"Come along, little one," whispered Nelly. She sat on the bed beside Lucy and gave her a big hug. "You have a good cry. It'll do you good."

They were alone, surrounded only by the shadows from the glowing candles. Lucy leant against Nelly's shoulder and sobbed.

10

Days drifted into weeks, and the more Lucy learnt about Noah's Ark, the more she was amazed by the incredible work of her benefactor, and of the two ladies who ran the Ark.

It appeared that several years ago a very rich, but eccentric, merchant had visited Chatham dockyards in Kent, and Buckler's Hard in Hampshire. Here he had been impressed by the speed and expertise of the men building the ships for the nation. He was particularly taken by the work on a new ship of the line which, he was told, would be named HMS *Victory*. Being a man with great inherited wealth but little common sense, he had immediately invested much of his money in the building of a great ship of his own. Despite the remonstrations of his relations and friends, he had employed some unscrupulous men to begin this work on his estate which bordered the River Thames. There was plenty of room, they assured him, to build his vessel in the creek which led directly into the main river. They failed to mention the impossibility of launching it, nor the inadequate depth or width of the river at this point. The hull and the internal decks were duly completed as were the rectangular portholes for the guns. The money flowed like water from the merchant to the shipbuilders and it was at this point that, at last, he began to realise he was fast approaching a deep whirlpool of debt. Matters came to a head when he discovered that he had also invested money in a worthless mining deal in the Far East. He was facing ruin and the debtors' prison.

His luck turned when he met the highwayman, Noah, who quickly saw the potential of this hulk which if left would have slowly rotted away. Noah paid off all the debts of the merchant in exchange for the half-finished ship, a ship that would never sail but which would become an ideal home for all his rescued children, children who had been destined for the gallows or transportation. Nelly Mere, herself sentenced to slavery in the colonies, became their cook, their foster mother, and cared for them as if they were her own. Then came Polly Sneed, a widow whose husband had been unjustly accused of helping to murder a young musician. It didn't matter that Polly swore that her husband was at home with her at the time of this dreadful deed, the magistrate refused to believe her and he was hung the very next day. Noah found Polly wandering the streets one night, intent upon killing herself. He took her to Nelly who cared for her until she was fit and well again. Then he persuaded the two women to look after his Ark and the children whom he rescued from the gallows or slavery. Polly was a clever woman and undertook to educate the little ones, as well as helping to find them suitable work or good homes in other parts of the country. These two women ran the Ark, cared for the children on a daily basis, comforted them during their nightmares, and wiped away their tears when they cried for their lost parents.

As Lucy's health improved she began to help in the school house for this was where the final design of the ship mirrored pictures she had seen of the real Noah's Ark. Instead of masts rising from the main deck, there was a longhouse made of logs. At one end Nelly cooked their meals and organised the washing, she felt that cooking the meals on the top deck was less of a fire risk, the other end was used as a school. The two lower decks were where the children slept – girls on the upper deck, boys below.

Alice followed Lucy everywhere, as far as she was concerned Lucy was her big sister. There were fifteen children on the Ark and, as Polly pointed out, it would soon be time for some of them to move on, it was hard work feeding so many and keeping them warmly clothed. Fortunately a nearby farmer was glad of their help and the two women had worked out a good pattern for each day to the mutual benefit of all. The children worked in shifts on his land, scaring birds, picking stones, collecting eggs and even learning to milk cows. In return they would earn eggs, corn, sometimes the odd rabbit, milk or perhaps, on special days, a chicken. Such a special day was Christmas which, despite all that had happened in her life, Lucy declared to be one of the happiest she had ever had. The highwayman visited the Ark on Christmas morning and this was the first time that Lucy had seen him since her arrival. He still wore his mask but none of the children were afraid of him.

"Uncle Noah!" the little ones shrieked. Even the older ones gave a big grin when they saw him. He brought sweets and fruit, and new clothes for all, he joined in their games and ate their Christmas meal with them. Later, whilst several were trying to peel hot chestnuts, he took Lucy to one side and asked her how she was feeling, and if she was happy in the Ark.

"I am, sir," she replied shyly. "And I haven't yet thanked you properly for saving my life, for surely I would have died if you hadn't found me that night."

He smiled. "Surely you would have," he said, gently mocking her formal politeness. "But it is Samuel you must thank, for if he hadn't told me about you, I don't think I could have found you in time."

Lucy looked bewildered. "Who is Samuel?" she asked.

Noah paused. "He was one of the two men who came to rob the crypt that night. He realised that you were still alive and he told me everything. I just hoped that you had followed the path which he had indicated. Then I met a wagoner who was cursing and swearing because he had lost his coat with his lunch in one of the pockets, so I knew you couldn't be far away, and sure enough I found you, just in time I think."

"The poor wagoner," murmured Lucy, but then gave a little giggle.

"That's better," said Noah. "You look much better when you smile."

"Do you never take off your mask?" asked Lucy timidly.

"Never," he replied firmly. "What you don't know cannot harm you. Now young lady, I think your little shadow wants to play blind man's bluff with you, so you had better go."

Alice was hopping up and down looking towards Lucy.

Lucy went to join her but not before she had turned to the highwayman once more.

"Thank you," she said and touched his hand. "Thank you so much."

He held her hand for a moment and then suddenly bent down, and gently kissed it.

11

Life on the Ark brought with it a whole new vocabulary for Lucy. Despite the fact that their ship would never sail anywhere, the children were encouraged to learn the appropriate nautical terms wherever possible. She learnt that the keel was the base of the ship. The Ark's keel was so firmly embedded in the mud of the tributary that, despite the slight rise of the waters with the tide, there was no prospect of it ever floating or launching itself into the main river. Left became port, and right, starboard, and the windows were always referred to as portholes. The children worked, and had their meals, on the upper deck beneath the log cabin, but their sleeping quarters were below deck. The girls had the first deck and the boys the lower deck. They didn't go through doors but through hatchways, and when Alfie first asked her to 'come up the companion', she didn't know what he was talking about, until she realised that he meant the ladder.

Alfie was the oldest of the boys, sandy-haired and a good bit taller than Lucy. She had first taken particular notice of him one March morning when she heard raised voices coming from the pathway on the port side. Looking through the porthole she saw that Alfie was arguing with the highwayman. Noah placed his hands on Alfie's shoulders as if trying to calm him but it was no use, Alfie shrugged him off and strode up the gangplank onto the Ark. The highwayman turned away, gave a sharp whistle and through the nearby trees came the most beautiful black horse that Lucy had ever seen. With one bound Noah leapt onto its back and rode away.

Lucy went to find Alfie and found him back on deck and furiously kicking one of the leather buckets which they always kept handy in case of fire, fortunately there was no water in it. She hesitated, it was obvious he was in a black mood.

"What do you want, Miss Goody?" he asked bitterly. "You can't do anything wrong, can you?"

"Do you want to talk?" she asked quietly.

"Why should I want to talk to you?" he retorted, and gave the bucket such a kick that it sailed past the outer door of the log cabin and down onto the grass below. A little squeal told them that it had found a target. They both laughed.

"What's the matter?" she ventured.

With a sigh Alfie sat down on the floor, he hugged his knees and for a moment rocked back and forth whilst he stared at her. Lucy began to feel a little uncomfortable.

"How old are you?" he asked.

Surprised by his question Lucy nevertheless answered, "Thirteen. My birthday was last October 21st."

He nodded as if that was a good answer. "I'm thirteen too," he said. "But I was born in March. March 17th, I'm seven months older than you. I'll be fourteen soon."

"Is that important?"

"It is to me," he replied. "It means that I'm the oldest one on the Ark, apart from Nelly and Polly, that is. It's time I left. Do you know how long I've been here?"

Lucy shook her head.

"I've been here nearly a whole year. A whole year." He looked at her, she wasn't quite sure whether or not he expected some sort of a response, but he carried on, "I need to get away. I can't stand it here any longer being cooped up with all these little ones. I want to go to sea. My father and grandfather were both seamen. I can't stand being on this worthless hulk, I want to be on a proper ship."

"Is that what you were arguing about with Noah this morning?"

He nodded.

"Why doesn't Noah want you to leave?" she asked.

"I was caught for stealing," he sighed. "I was hungry, so I took this loaf of bread. I'd tried to get work but no one would have me and I was getting desperate. I couldn't help it. I was collared, sent before the beak, y'know, the magistrate, and sentenced to transportation the same day. No one asked me why I took the loaf, no one tried to defend me, it was all over before I knew what was happening. The beak said if I ever came back he would see to it that I never walked the streets again."

"So how did you get away?" asked Lucy in horror.

"It was the highwayman, of course," he replied. "He held up the coach and took me and the others off. We were all brought here. The others have been found good homes but no one wants me," he paused. "I'm too old y'see."

For a moment they sat in silence.

"Noah reckons that the beak and his mob are still on the lookout for me. He says that I must wait a bit longer before it will be safe for me to move about near the docks. But I can't wait. I'm going to leave very soon."

"But if Noah says…" began Lucy.

"But if Noah says," mocked Alfie. "How would he know?"

"You must have done something else, Alfie, to annoy the magistrate so much," persisted Lucy. "What makes Noah think that he's still after you?"

Alfie sighed but then, to Lucy's surprise, he started to grin. "Well," he replied with the air of someone about to tell a good story. "I managed to kick the brute of a man who captured me, and then…" He paused. "When I was sentenced I broke away from the guard and bit the beak on his hand. He hollered and I just laughed."

"Oh, Alfie," said Lucy, shaking her head. "You only made matters worse."

"That's what Noah says," replied Alfie, making a face. "But that magistrate, well, he's a wicked man, Lucy, he really is. Folk say that he sends some prisoners to his estates abroad to work as slaves, and if he's in a bad mood he'll have you hanged, and no one seems to want to stop him. They're all scared of him."

"Except Noah," said Lucy firmly.

"If he caught Noah then he'd have him hanged for certain. Highwaymen always get done in and Noah wouldn't have a chance. The beak hates him and says that he'll be pleading to be hanged before he finishes with him."

"Has this magistrate a name?" asked Lucy fearfully.

"Oh yes," replied Alfie, with some venom in his voice. "It's Sir Daniel Haggleton."

12

Lucy was filled with an overwhelming sense of sadness and fear after her talk with Alfie. All night she had tossed and turned thinking of his words. He was going to leave, of that she was certain, but should she tell Polly or Nelly, she couldn't be sure. The next day she escorted a group of the younger children along the towpath to the farmer's fields where their morning's work would be stone picking. She had to keep her wits about her because, despite all the warnings, some of the little ones often walked too close to the riverbank, so she had no time to talk to Alfie all day. It was not until the evening, after supper, that she had time to speak to him.

"Please don't go, Alfie," she whispered, as they helped to clear away the dishes from the table. "Stay here where it's safe, we need you here."

"You don't need me," he replied scornfully. "I have to get away, Lucy. Can't you see that? I'm not a prisoner. I need my freedom. I'm nearly fourteen."

Lucy wouldn't admit it, but yes she could see his point. She, herself, had no desire to remain on the Ark for ever, but she trusted in Noah's good judgement as to when it would be safe for her to leave. Not that she had any reason to imagine anyone would be searching for her, as they obviously were for Alfie.

Alice couldn't understand Lucy's quiet mood that night.

"Are you cross with me, Lucy?" she asked timidly, as they were getting ready for bed.

"No of course not, little one," replied Lucy, kissing the top of her head. "I've just been thinking hard all day, that's all."

"Then you shouldn't do it," replied Alice solemnly. "Thinking makes you look very sad and that's not nice."

Lucy laughed and gave Alice a big hug. Sometimes Alice's comments made her feel much older than her thirteen years.

It came as no surprise when the next morning Alfie was reported missing.

The two women were beside themselves with worry and immediately Polly Sneed set off to find Noah. So that was how the following day Lucy found herself face-to-face with the masked man, who was none too pleased with her.

"If you knew he was leaving that night, Lucy, why didn't you tell someone? Why didn't you let Nelly or Polly know?" he asked.

"I didn't know when it would happen," she replied. "I guessed it might be soon, but not that soon."

"If only you had said something," he sounded frustrated.

"Did you say anything to the two ladies?" she asked defiantly. She certainly wasn't going to accept the blame for Alfie's disappearance. "You were arguing with him the other morning. I saw you. Did you warn the ladies?"

"No, I didn't," he answered shaking his head. "You're quite right, of course, I should have realised, it was wrong of me."

"But where will he have gone?" she asked fearfully. "And is it true, is that horrible man still looking for him? What will he do if he catches Alfie again?"

The highwayman gave a rueful smile. "Undoubtedly he will be on the lookout for Alfie, he is not a man to forgive lightly. He has many others working for him, and they are just as unpleasant as he is, if not, he would as easily be rid of them too."

"What can we do?"

Once again Noah smiled. He took hold of Lucy's hand. "We? You will do nothing, dear Lucy. You will stay here and help Mrs Sneed and Mrs Mere in their daily tasks of looking after all these children. In the meantime I will ask around and see where this impatient young man has got to. If only he could have waited a little longer, but it is as much my fault as anyone's. You're right, of course, I should have seen this coming." He stood up. "Now I must be away. Stay alert, Lucy, watch over the other children safely, and report at once to the ladies if you see any strangers in the area. Do you understand? I feel dangerous times are coming to us all."

Lucy nodded, she felt shivers of fear run up and down her spine. What had Alfie said? 'The highwayman would be begging to be hanged once Sir Haggleton had found him.'

"Please be careful," she said, clutching at his sleeve. "They will be looking for you too."

He looked down at her and hesitated. The moment was over, he suddenly turned on his heels and left.

13

Alfie tried to stand up but once again a heavy blow to the back of his neck forced him down onto his knees. Morgan grinned. This was the kind of work he excelled at. He hadn't been able to knock someone about like this since that ridiculous workhouse overseer, Mr Nimble, had annoyed his Master. On that day he had sent the poor creature back to his workhouse unable to stand or barely remember his own name. Undoubtedly several of Mr Nimble's bones had been broken, and today Morgan would have the opportunity to break a few more bones – just a few more minutes and he'd start on the boy's legs.

A gruff voice interrupted his thoughts. "'e says you're to bring 'im up."

"Have I got time to…?" began Morgan.

"No," came the short reply. "'e's in a black mood, Morgan. I wouldn't risk it." The man gave a cough and spat on the ground. He waved his lantern in the direction of Alfie. "Gawd! What have you done to 'is face? Can 'e still talk?"

"He can talk alright," grunted Morgan. "But he won't, that's his problem. Come on, give me a hand to drag him upstairs."

At first Alfie had thought that he was already in prison, but as the day wore on he began to realise that he was in the cellars below the kitchen of a large house. Sir Haggleton had turned them into his own personal jail. The two men carried him up the stairs into the main part of the house and into the Master's study. The sun streamed in through the giant French windows, and the light caused him to place his hands

51

over his eyes. A chair had been placed in front of Sir Haggleton's desk, but Alfie was made to stand.

He looked about him. His left eye was virtually closed so this was not easy. His nose was bleeding, he guessed it had been broken, and one of his teeth was definitely a lot looser than it should have been. It was then that he saw the same portrait that had so astounded Mr Nimble. He gazed at it in amazement. All this time Sir Haggleton had said nothing, he just watched like a bird of prey about to make a swoop. Morgan grinned maliciously, any moment now and he would receive the signal to deliver more blows to the boy's body. So the next move of Sir Haggleton came as a complete surprise to him.

Suddenly his Lordship placed his hands together like a supplicant at prayer, and said in the softest of tones, "Let the boy sit down, Morgan. Let him rest for a while."

Alfie couldn't believe it, but he couldn't take his eyes off the portrait either.

"Give the boy a drink of cider, Morgan," said Sir Haggleton carefully, gazing at the portrait as though he and Alfie were viewing at an art gallery together. "Very beautiful isn't she? That is a portrait of my wife and our two children. I also had a wonderful little granddaughter, but she was stolen from me when quite young. I have looked everywhere for her, I'd give my entire fortune to have her back here safe with me." He gave a quiet sob. "She must be about thirteen years old by now. It's hopeless, hopeless."

"No it's not," mumbled Alfie. It was difficult for him to speak after the beating he had received from Morgan. "It's not diffi…diffi…hard."

"Have you seen her then?" Sir Haggleton leant forward across his desk. It wasn't a big movement but just enough to make Alfie hesitate. It was at that moment when the door burst open and in walked William like a conceited popinjay.

"I say, Father, have you…" He stopped obviously perplexed by the scene before him. As far as he could make out a dirty urchin was sitting on one of his father's chairs and sipping cider with him, albeit that the urchin's hand was shaking so much that the cider was slopping over the edge of the goblet and on to the floor.

Sir Haggleton raised his hand signalling William to be quiet.

"Tell me, Alfred, such a good English name if I may say so." His voice became even softer, more seductive. "Tell me, have you seen my dear little granddaughter?"

He produced a handkerchief from his sleeve and dabbed his eyes.

'Careful,' thought Morgan. 'Don't overdo it.'

Alfie took another sip of cider. He'd had no food for two days and the cider quickly went to his head. All he could see was that this man, who had been so ready a few moments ago to have him hanged, was a grandfather grieving for his grandchild. His only experience of grandparents had been his own, who had cared for him and fed him when he had lost his parents. Perhaps Sir Haggleton had a kindly side after all.

Sir Haggleton leant back in his chair, he knew he had his prey well and truly hooked, now he just had to reel him in.

"Tell me, Alfred," he said gently. "What is it that you desire most of all?"

"Oh really, Father," interrupted an impatient William. "What does it matter what he wants, let's get rid of him, throw him out, he smells, throw him back to the gutter where he belongs." He made to move towards Alfie but Morgan barred his way.

"Patience, William," said Sir Haggleton firmly. "Young Alfred is about to tell me his life's ambitions and, who knows, I might be able to help him."

"Help him!" screamed William in disbelief. "Help him! What an absolutely obnoxious idea."

He made such a face and looked so nonplussed that if it hadn't been such a serious situation Alfie might have laughed, but then he couldn't smile anyway because of his beaten face.

"Alfred?" coaxed Sir Haggleton.

"If I was free," whispered Alfie. "I'd like a boat like me father's. One what I could go fishin' in. That's what I want."

"Tell me what I want to know, Alfie, and it's yours," replied Sir Haggleton coolly. "I can be no fairer than that."

The room became deathly quiet. Alfie thought of Lucy. He was in no doubt that she was this man's long-lost granddaughter. The likeness to the portrait of her mother was incredible. Yes, she should live here amongst all this splendour, have the chance of nice clothes, good food and a loving grandfather, she shouldn't be trapped in a worthless boat stuck in a muddy creek of the Thames. That boat wasn't going anywhere and neither was Lucy if she stayed there. She'd probably end up in another workhouse or even worse.

William was pacing up and down, occasionally giving a chair a kick. Suddenly he said, "It's not fair. Why should he get his heart's desire? What about mine?"

Even his father looked at him in amazement. "What do you need, William," he asked, "apart from some more money? I take it that's why you're here. How much this time?"

William just shrugged his shoulders and deftly caught the bag of coins which Sir Haggleton produced from a drawer and threw at him.

"I'll take you to her," whispered Alfie.

Sir Haggleton could hardly believe his ears. "Again."

"I'll take you to her, as long as you promise no harm will come to her, and you keep your promise to me about a boat," he answered.

"Done," replied Sir Haggleton quickly. He turned to his manservant. "Morgan, make the necessary arrangements."

"Oh really. It's just not fair!" shouted William in frustration, and promptly left the room.

Morgan began to lead Alfie across to the side door which led back to his prison.

"Morgan," called Sir Haggleton.

"Sir?"

"And I mean *all* the arrangements, Morgan. You do understand me don't you?"

"Of course, sir," replied Morgan, gripping Alfie's arm even tighter. "The young gentleman will get his boat as soon as we bring your granddaughter back here. I understand perfectly, sir."

Sir Haggleton gave a great sigh of satisfaction. It had been a lot easier than he had imagined. "I knew you would understand, Morgan," he said quietly.

14

Lucy woke with a start, someone was shaking her and whispering her name. It was Nelly Mere.

She signalled to Lucy to remain silent. "Get dressed and wake the others. We must leave here at once. Men are gathering down below on the port side. We'll have to leave by the starboard escape door. Keep everyone quiet and as calm as possible."

With that she left Lucy and went to help Polly deal with the other children. There had always been escape plans, and exits had been arranged on both sides of the Ark but no one had ever believed that they would be needed. The starboard route led along the towpath to the farm, and a child had already been despatched to the farmer. He would know what to do, and transport would be ready for them once they arrived there.

As Lucy was helping one of the little ones to dress so she heard a voice shout.

"It's no use. We can't scale these walls. They've pulled up all their gangplanks and ropes. We should have brought ladders."

"We don't need to do any climbing," came the reply. "They'll come out to us. Light the fire!"

"No!" shouted someone, and Lucy paused to peer out of a porthole to see Alfie vainly hitting at the legs of a man on horseback. It was futile, the man just laughed at him.

"You said you weren't going to hurt anyone!" shouted Alfie. "You said you were going to help Lucy."

"Oh, shut up," growled the man, and promptly kicked Alfie in the head. He fell to the ground, unconscious. "Take this idiot back to Sir Haggleton."

Another man immediately came forward, and Alfie was thrown across a horse and taken away.

The younger children began to sense that they were in grave danger despite Lucy assuring them that they were off on an exciting night journey. Several were silently crying and nearly all of them were white-faced and anxious.

"Come on," she said, trying to sound as normal as possible. "We must leave as quickly and quietly as possible. Come along everyone."

Several of the younger boys came climbing up the ladders to the girls' deck, they were coughing badly.

"There's lots of smoke, Lucy," said one of the little ones. "The Ark's on fire."

"Make your way to the bow all of you," said Lucy firmly. "Come away from the stern end. Go on, I'll follow on behind, quickly now. The escape door will be open on the starboard side. Nelly and Polly will be there for you."

She began steering them along the deck towards the exit. By this time the smoke was really thick and the ominous sound of crackling flames could be heard. The groans and cries of the Ark filled the air as it was slowly and relentlessly devoured by the fire. At the end of the deck she met Polly who was encouraging the children to climb down the ladders to safety, where Nelly, with the help of two of the older children, was leading them towards the towpath. None of the men were aware of this as the Ark obscured their view of this side of the bank. The last child was just leaving when Lucy heard that terrible scream again. It brought back all the memories of the dreadful evening at the workhouse when the children had been taken away to make room for the new inmates.

"Alice!" she shouted, and turned to go back.

"You mustn't, you can't," said Polly, grabbing her wrist. "You must come, Lucy, you will have to leave her."

"I can't leave her," shouted Lucy, tearing herself away. "I failed her last time, I have to go. You go with the others, we'll catch you up." She ran back the way she had come, all the time calling the child's name.

Picking up a shawl, which was lying on the floor, she wrapped it around her head and moved into the thick smoke. It was hard to see and even harder to breathe, the flames were a mixed blessing as they drove away layers of smoke. As she reached their sleeping area she saw Alice huddled in a corner, her favourite rag doll clutched in her hands, she looked terrified. Flames were eagerly licking the surrounding walls, it was only a matter of time before she was engulfed.

Lucy rushed towards her and gathered her up. "I thought you left with the others," she said, holding the child close to her.

"I came back for Ellie," sobbed Alice, clutching at her doll. "I came back for Ellie."

"Come on," said Lucy, holding Alice's hand tightly. "We must run, Alice, before the flames catch us." She placed the shawl over Alice's head, and started to guide her to the exit. The old tarred planks of the Ark began to fall into the fire and were hungrily devoured. The heat was tremendous as the fire growled and roared its way towards the two girls. It was as if the flames were taunting her, laughing at her feebleness, she could almost imagine they were calling her name.

When they reached the exit, the sudden rush of cold air took her by surprise.

"Run, Alice, run!" she gasped, trying to catch her breath. "I'll follow as quickly as I can. Go on run, don't look back!"

Alice did as she was told and sped off to the farm. When she was out of sight a voice suddenly said, "But you won't be going anywhere, my lovely."

Before Lucy could move, a sack was placed over her head and she was picked up and thrown over the shoulder of a man.

"I've got her, Morgan," shouted her captor. "You were right, they was all escapin' out of the other side of the boat. Shall we go after the others?"

"There's no need," replied a harsh deep voice, which Lucy assumed must belong to this Morgan. "We've got what we came for. We can go back."

"Let me go!" she shouted from the sack. You have no right to keep me in here. Let me go!"

"Rights," replied Morgan, his stinking breath reaching through the fibres of her prison. "You'll soon find out who's got rights, my dear." With that he punched at her head and Lucy was silenced.

15

When Lucy awoke she was filled with an all-consuming fear. She had been buried alive, she was sure of it, it was so dark, the earth beneath her body smelt old and decayed, she lay there panting and trembling. A scrabbling sound nearby made her think of rats. She let out a terrified scream.

The harsh sound of a bolt being drawn, and the creaking of a reluctant door slowly opening, made her realise that her first fears were unfounded. Heavy footsteps sounded as the yellow glow of a lantern swung towards her. She was in a prison.

"So yer awake at last," said a voice like gravel.

The lantern swayed to reveal an old cracked face almost hidden within a bush of wild grey hair. He turned to go.

"Don't go!" shouted Lucy. "Don't leave me. Where am I? What is this place?"

He stopped. "I 'ave to let Morgan know that yer awake. If yer lonely, talk to yer friend there, in the corner… that is if 'e can still talk." He began cackling with laughter like a demented seagull.

"Then please leave the lantern," pleaded Lucy. "Just a little glow. I promise to keep quiet if you leave it."

The old man shrugged his shoulders. "Makes no difference to me," he said, and placed it on the ground just beyond the bars. It cast a pale glow across the floor. Lucy stretched her hands out but found it impossible to reach the lantern, she turned to look at whoever it was sharing this dreadful place with her.

The bundle of rags in the corner moved and moaned. Even in such poor light, Lucy could see that whoever it was had been badly beaten. Carefully she moved towards the sounds. It was Alfie.

"Oh, Alfie," she whispered. "What have they done to you?"

"I'm so sorry, Lucy," he spoke softly, each word seemed to cause him pain. "I really thought that I would be helping you. I knew he was bad, I knew he could hang me, but I believed him when he said that you were his missing granddaughter. I was a fool. I even believed him when he said he would get me a boat of my own. I thought I was helping." He clutched at his side and groaned.

"I don't understand," she replied. "I have no living grandfathers. All my grandparents died before I was born. Even my parents are both dead. I don't know what you mean."

Before Alfie could answer, the door to their prison opened once more and in stepped the large figure of Morgan. Two men followed him with more lanterns.

"Ah," he said, looking down at them both. "I see we are now awake. I'm afraid, my dear," he added in a mocking tone, "we cannot allow you to sleep any longer. My goodness it will soon be time for some lunch, and it would never do for you to miss that now, would it?"

He signalled to the old man to unlock the cell door, and immediately the other man came in and grabbed Alfie who groaned as he was dragged from the cell.

"Now," said Morgan, looking down at her. "Do I have to carry you, or will you walk, madam?"

Lucy stood up and, despite feeling giddy, walked stiffly to the door and out into a corridor. There were several steps to climb, and Lucy began to realise that the prison had been made from the cellars beneath a house. As they climbed higher so they passed other corridors, which, from the smells, she thought must lead to the kitchens. Eventually they arrived at the ground floor. There were no servants about, they had had strict instructions to remain in their

61

quarters. No one saw this strange group of Morgan, his two henchmen dragging Alfie, and Lucy go into Sir Daniel Haggleton's library.

Sir Daniel was sitting behind his desk, a poorly dressed man in a long black coat stood before him. He turned as the group entered the room, his face registering disbelief when he saw Lucy.

Lucy was by no means cowed. "What right have you to keep us here?" she demanded, as they were marched towards the desk. "And what have you done to my friend, Alfie?"

It was clear now that they were in the daylight that Alfie was in a bad way. For a brief moment the man in the long coat took charge. He directed the two henchmen to get a chair and ordered them to carefully place Alfie on it. He felt Alfie's pulse and inspected his wounds. All this time Sir Daniel watched him as a cat might watch its prey.

"This boy needs medical attention urgently," exclaimed the man.

"Yes, well he won't be getting it here, will he, Doctor? He has a boat to catch shortly," came the reply. "We have much more urgent business to attend to here and now."

At this point Lucy looked to her left, to the wall which bordered the long French windows. There was the portrait of the beautiful woman and her two children. Lucy thought that the girl could easily have been her own sister, but why was it here? What had Alfie said about a grandfather? She looked back at this repulsive man sitting behind his desk.

"Who are you?" she asked.

"More to the point," he snarled. "Who are you?"

He turned to the doctor. "Did you not promise Morgan on that night many years ago, that you would take full responsibility and dispose of it?"

The doctor looked at him with disgust. "If you are referring to the little baby born here on the twenty-first of October, then the answer is yes."

"And so Morgan, in good faith, left that task to you," came the reply.

"Sir, it was your daughter's only child, a little girl. I thought that in time you might…"

"Did not I say, at the time," shouted Sir Daniel, "that I had no daughter! Did I not say that?"

"But…" began the doctor.

"Silence!" Everyone froze. It was Lucy who broke the silence.

"Please," she said quietly. "Will someone please tell me. Who is that girl in the portrait?"

No one spoke until the doctor finally said, "It is a painting of your mother when she was about the same age as you are now."

16

Lucy held the lantern as high as she could so that the doctor might see more easily. Her mind was in a whirl. All her short life she had believed that Amos was her father, a much loved father. Her mother, Amos's wife, had died when Lucy was quite small. All this Lucy had been told and had no reason to doubt it, and now, here was this strange doctor telling her that she had been born here, in this dreadful house, and that her true mother had died giving birth to her. It was all too much to comprehend.

"Hold the lantern a little higher, please," said the doctor. He could sense her confusion. A great argument had ensued upstairs after his explanation of Lucy's birth. Sir Daniel had turned purple with rage when the doctor had given names to the people in the large portrait. 'The man is definitely heading for a heart attack, and the sooner the better,' thought the doctor angrily.

They had been bundled unceremoniously down to the makeshift prison in the cellars of this large house. He had managed to persuade the elderly retainer to leave them the lantern. After all, as he had explained, what sort of price would they fetch for Sir Daniel if they arrived at the ship in such a bad condition. Alfie definitely needed some medical attention. Their fate had been decided in the library under that beautiful portrait – they were to be taken to one of Sir Daniel's ships, a slave trader, and sold in the colonies. Lucy's mother and grandmother would have been torn apart with anguish if they could have seen into the future at the moment when they had sat so happily for the artist. Why Sir Daniel should be so full of hatred, the doctor could not understand.

"Your petticoat has proven to be most useful, Lucy," he said gently. "I've nearly finished, Alfie."

"When we get out of this, Lucy," grunted Alfie. "I promise I will buy you a new one. Aahh."

"Try not to move too much," said the doctor. "You have two or perhaps three broken ribs. I have bound them up as well as I can, but I'm afraid Lucy's petticoat was never intended to act as a bandage. Your nose is also broken, but it will heal in a week or so, as will all the bruises, but there is some internal damage which I'm afraid I am not able to assess at this moment. You are a very strong lad to have withstood that animal, for Morgan is no more than that. He seems more than willing to do his master's bidding."

"I'm so sorry, Lucy," said Alfie, as he gingerly pulled down his shirt and tucked it into his trousers. "I believed him when he told me about you. He was almost in tears. He told me that his daughter had died a few days after the baby was born. He said that she had had the best of medical care but it had proved no use."

The doctor gave a loud snort of anger.

Alfie continued. "He told me how, when only a few weeks old the baby had been kidnapped by gypsies, and how he had had men searching everywhere for you. He had never given up hope. I thought it must be you, you are so like that portrait, and when he told me that you would inherit so much of what he has, and that you would live in luxury for the rest of your life. I believed him. I was a fool."

"Yes, you were a fool," replied Lucy, with some force. "You were a fool to leave the Ark, Alfie, to ignore Noah, but you were not a fool to believe that man, I think he could lie about anything. No matter what he says, I cannot believe he is my grandfather."

"He's nothing like I remember my grandfather," said Alfie. "Mine was a good man, and he looked after my mother and me after my father died. No he's nothing like mine. Aahh!" He grimaced as he tried to move to a more comfortable position.

"I have told you not to move too much, Alfie. Lucy's petticoat is not a miracle worker!" The doctor frowned, and taking the lantern from Lucy he placed it on a ledge in the corner of their cell.

"Lucy," he said looking down at her. "I came here on a very foggy and cold night. It was the twenty-first of October, 1785, the day you were born. Your mother was very ill. She had married a musician, I believe a young violinist. Her husband had died, how or why I do not know. Your grandfather never forgave her. Consequently she had fallen upon really bad times, and when she tried to return to this house your grandfather sent her away. However, the cook smuggled her back in and kept her below stairs, and that night you were born."

"How do you know all this?" asked Lucy.

"The cook told me, and later the poor woman lost her position here but I was able to find her another placement with one of my friends. Your grandfather refused to see you and instructed Morgan to dispose of you."

Lucy gave a gasp and Alfie moved forward to hold her hand.

"It seems that even Morgan has his limits. Killing a newborn baby was one of them. The cook and I persuaded Morgan that we would be able to do the job. As I explained, I was a doctor and was used to this sort of thing. I took you straight away to Amos the Apothecary. I knew that he and his wife had recently lost a little baby and I knew them to be kind and loving people. I think that over the years, Sir Daniel began to suspect that you were still living and that is why your new family fell upon hard times. I think he must have traced you and decided to make your life very difficult. He wouldn't harm you directly, but he would make certain that your circumstances became so harsh that your survival would be precarious."

"Well, he's succeeded then, hasn't he?" sobbed Lucy. "We're all going to be sold as slaves."

"That little boy in the painting…" began Alfie.

"That is William Haggleton, the younger brother of Margaret, Lucy's mother. He was about ten years younger than his sister when she died," replied the doctor.

"Oh, then he's useless," said Alfie in disgust. "I think I've met him. All he was worried about was getting some more money to go gambling."

"That would be right, Alfie," said the doctor. "William has a terrible reputation for drinking and gambling. He moves in some very dubious circles, and his father doesn't seem to care, in fact he rather encourages it. It is common gossip that Sir Daniel seems to prefer Morgan's company to that of his own son."

"So now we are to be sold as slaves," said Lucy, fighting back the tears.

"We must try to keep together when they come to move us," said the doctor, not answering her question directly.

They fell into an uneasy silence. Alfie's mind was full of pain, Lucy's was in a turmoil, and the doctor was desperately trying to think of a plan of escape. They had no idea of the time but Lucy watched fearfully as the candle burnt lower, as it came towards the end of its short life, the door to the stairs opened. It was the old man again, but he had brought a younger man with him.

"Now I dunn want no trouble," said the old man. "But I got to tie you all up an' get you ready for the journey."

The young man stood tall and did his best to look menacing. The doctor saw this and decided to take advantage of it.

"Before you begin," he said quietly, "may I ask one or two favours of you?"

"May I arsk," repeated the old man, trying to mock the doctor's tone. "Cors you may arsk, but I don't suppose it will do much good."

The doctor smiled. "The young lady is exhausted, she won't cause you any trouble of this I am sure. Would you tie her hands in front of her and not use a gag." He had noted the dirty cloths in the young man's hands.

The two men looked at one another. They nodded.

"Then there's young, Alfie here," continued the doctor. "He has several broken ribs and can barely breathe through his nose because it's broken. If Sir Daniel is to get a good price for him at the slave market, he must be reasonably fit." He watched their faces. "Think how pleased Sir Daniel will be, if not only do you get rid of us, but you also get a good price for us at the slave market."

Lucy shuddered and gave a little sob.

"What do you want then?" asked the old man.

"Tie his hands in front, his ribs will not take the strain of them being behind, and give him the lightest of gags so that he can still breathe, and I will give you this." He pulled out a silver coin from his pocket.

The two men stared at it in disbelief.

"I thought you searched 'im when you brought 'im down 'ere," said the old man.

"I did, pa," replied the young man. "I'm sure I did."

"What's to stop us takin' your money and not doin' as you arsk?" said the old man, slyly.

"Because," replied the doctor calmly. "You both look like a pair of honest men really, who just have to do these things to make a living."

"You're right there, sir, we ain't got no choice, just as you say," said the old man, taking the coin being offered to him. "We'll do as you arsk, and thank you kindly," he said biting the coin just in case. "But we'll 'ave to truss you up good an' proper, I'm afraid."

The doctor nodded. If he could get some consideration for Lucy and Alfie then he was quite happy. He reasoned that he would be pushing his luck too far if he tried for any more concessions.

The men were true to their word. Lucy did not have to suffer a gag, though the men made certain that the ropes binding her hands were very tight. Alfie found it difficult to breathe despite having a slightly looser gag, but the doctor paid hard for his bartering. His gag was so tight that he looked as if he might be sick, and his arms were harshly pulled back behind him. They were made to walk along a twisting passage to the back of the cellar, the roof was so low that even Lucy had to bend her head. At the end of this they were pushed through a door which led up some short steps to a courtyard at the back of the house. No one was about and Lucy heard the nearby clock strike midnight. A black coach was waiting in the yard for them. There was no crest or coat of arms on its side. Two horses were pawing at the cobbles, impatient to be on their journey. The two men lifted Lucy into the coach and once there they tied up her feet; they had to lift Alfie inside, it was obvious he was in great pain, beads of sweat were rolling down his face. The doctor was then pushed in, and he and Alfie also had their feet tied, which, Lucy knew, was going to make it very hard for them to keep their balance once the coach was underway. The blinds had been pulled down which would not help.

"Enjoy your journey," cackled the old man, as he closed the carriage door.

"Get orff!" he shouted to the coach driver.

A crack of the whip, the clatter of horses' hoofs upon the cobbles, Lucy realised this could be her final journey in England.

17

Immediately, as the coach lurched forward, the three prisoners became aware of their problems. They had each been bundled into a corner of the coach but this did not prevent them from being thrown about by each jolt and dip of the carriage. Unable to use their hands there was no way in which to brace themselves from the battering. With her hands tied in front of her Lucy stood and toppled across to the other side of the carriage. Once there she went to the aid of Alfie and helped him to pull down his gag.

"Help the doctor," whispered Alfie hoarsely. "Look, his gag is choking him."

Beads of sweat were already travelling down the doctor's forehead, he was finding it hard to breathe; not only had the men bound his face with a cloth, but they had also first pushed a filthy rag into his mouth. By the time Lucy had removed his gag, her own hands were turning maroon from the pressure of the ropes which bound them.

"Inside my left lapel there's a secret pocket," said the doctor, gasping for air. "Be careful. I keep a long knife in there, it's a scalpel, I carry it for emergencies. If you can pull that out we can soon cut through our bonds, but be very careful, it's very sharp."

Lucy did as she was asked. It was hard with her hands tied so tightly together, the constant movement of the coach made the blade slip from her grasp several times, but eventually she managed it. She had to pass it to Alfie as she was only able to pull it out by the tip if its blade. Immediately he began by cutting through her ropes. How her fingers ached and throbbed as the circulation began to return but she couldn't stop to worry about that, it was important to cut Alfie free, she could see the sweat running down his face as he tried to control the pain from his broken ribs. They cut through the ropes around their legs, both of them managed to nick their own fingers with the sharp blade.

"You must be careful," warned the doctor, as they began to free him.

The triumph they felt at being free soon evaporated when they realised that they were still in the coach and had no idea where they going. The doctor pulled up one of the blinds, they were now in the countryside outside the city walls. But where?

"Do you know where Sir Daniel anchors his ships?" asked Alfie, gently stretching his back before sinking back in the coach.

The doctor shook his head. "We are, I think, well past Greenwich and I am wondering if we may be going to Gravesend or even the Medway. I think Sir Daniel would not want his slave ships to be too close to the city, but I may be wrong. On the other hand I have no idea where we are, so we may even be travelling towards Southampton or Bristol."

It was on the tip of Alfie's tongue to say 'that's not much use', when Lucy interrupted. "We still have to get out of this coach if we are going to escape being slaves. Alfie cannot jump from the coach whilst it's travelling, and I don't think I can either, so somehow we must make a plan."

The doctor and Alfie smiled. "Practical as always, Lucy," said Alfie kindly.

They fell into a deep silence. The coachman was urging the horses forward, he had no wish to be driving a coach through the night. It was dangerous, both from the state of the roads, and also the robbers or criminals they might encounter. It had only been the promise of a substantial reward that had enticed him on such a journey and, of course, his bodyguard riding beside him. The roads were pitted with potholes and he felt sorry for his passengers, but Sir Daniel had said they were enemies of the people, spies from France, so he put all thoughts of pity behind him. Mind you, they hadn't looked so bad when he had caught a glimpse of them – an older man, a young lad, obviously in some pain, and a young girl who looked as though she had been crying.

It was pitch-black outside, but for the occasional light from a cottage they might have been travelling in hell. Well, he thought, heaven would definitely have to help them all if they met a highwayman or his mob.

Inside the coach the three were trying to make plans for their escape.

"When we have our first stop, which must come very soon," said Alfie. "We must all rush out from the coach. We'll use both sides. The doctor and I will go out together, Lucy, then you can go from the other side. They'll be so busy trying to catch us they'll not see you."

"Very funny," said Lucy dryly. "And how far do you think you'll get, Alfie, with your broken nose, broken ribs and kicked legs?"

"It won't do," said the doctor. "We'll have to think of something else."

The coach gave a shudder and a jolt, there was a grating noise and the ominous sound of a wheel splitting and everything tipped to one side. Alfie grunted as Lucy fell against him. The driver swore and there was a short shotgun blast, followed by a pistol shot and a commanding voice shouted, "Stop, if you value your lives!"

A lantern swayed towards them and the door was pulled open. Alfie prepared to punch the entrant and the doctor drew his knife.

"Well, I must say, this is a fine way to greet your rescuer," said a voice they knew so well. It was Noah.

"Oh, Noah," cried Lucy, and leapt into his arms.

"Careful," replied the highwayman. "Now out you get, all of you, as quickly as possible, we don't have much time."

The coach was surrounded by several men on horseback all with lanterns. The driver and his bodyguard had already been pulled from their seats and were standing with their hands held high. The front right wheel of the coach had fallen into a deep hole which it seemed had been concealed under twigs, it had been a well-laid trap.

"Who are you?" asked the doctor, still clutching his knife. "We are but poor travellers, we do not carry money for villains such as yourselves."

The highwayman gave a low mocking bow. "We are here to rescue you, sir, unless, that is, you would prefer to meet the slaver which is lying in the Medway waiting your arrival?"

"This is our friend," explained Lucy. "He won't harm us, Doctor."

Alfie had remained silent. "I don't deserve to be rescued," he muttered.

"I agree," answered Noah cheerfully. "But we'll talk about that later, much later. First you must get away from here."

All this time Noah's men had been unharnessing the coach horses, quietly soothing them and calming them down.

"The three of you will travel with my men," said Noah. He helped Lucy and the doctor to each mount up behind one of the riders. Then he turned to Alfie. "Come on, Alfie, surely you can get up behind the rider without any help?" He grabbed hold of Alfie's arm, and the boy yelled out in pain.

"He has broken ribs, and other injuries, courtesy of a fiend called Morgan," called the doctor. "He has been in great pain throughout the whole journey."

Noah paused. "I'm sorry, Alfie," he said quietly. "I had no idea you'd been so badly hurt." With that he carefully helped Alfie up onto the horse. A quick mutter to one of the riders and all three set off. Noah turned to his three remaining men. "Now we'll sort out these two," he said harshly.

"Take your trousers off," he commanded. Then he ordered his men to blindfold and gag the two who were now visibly shaking. They then tied their hands behind their backs, and their legs together, as though they were in a three-legged race. After that they faced them the way they had come, and sent them off on their way. The two men were so grateful that they had not lost their lives to these desperate highwaymen, that they didn't seem to mind about their own discomfort.

Noah and his men then pushed the coach off the road onto the slight incline of the hill, one push and it gathered speed, but then lurched to the side where the wheel had been damaged and crashed.

"Now we must scatter," said Noah. "Off you go, we'll meet up again at the usual rendezvous."

The men nodded and rode off in different directions. Noah watched them go and then set off to follow Lucy and the others.

18

The journey for Lucy and the others was a nightmare of mixed emotions. The doctor was bewildered as to who these men were, but comforted by the realisation that Lucy appeared to trust their leader, Noah, and relieved that they were no longer destined for the jaws of a slave ship. He was, however, concerned for Alfie who he knew must be suffering great pain clinging to the back of his rider. As for Lucy, her mind was in a turmoil. Who was that terrible man who so easily had condemned them all to possible slavery? She could not believe that he could be her grandfather. Why did he hate her so much? She was the daughter of an apothecary, Amos had been her wonderful and caring father, there was no way that she could be related to that evil man. Although she liked the doctor she felt that he must be mistaken, he had muddled her up with someone else, of that she was sure.

They were travelling across north Kent, keeping to the quiet paths and lanes. These last days of March brought with them cold and icy nights, the moments before dawn were often the coldest and tonight was no exception. It was still dark and the stars were particularly bright and shimmering in the frosty air, Lucy shivered, her hands were beginning to go numb with the cold when suddenly the leading horse stopped, and the rider signalled everyone to dismount.

"We will stop here for a moment," he said, his voice sounded muffled from inside his hood. "The horses need a rest, as, I think, does our young friend there."

Lucy turned to see Alfie slumped against his rider. The others rushed to his aid and the doctor directed them to rest Alfie against a nearby tree.

All three of their rescuers wore hoods, sacks with slits for eyes and mouth, unlike Noah, she thought, who always wore a black mask which covered only the front of his face. She shivered and one of the men brought her a cloak to wrap around her shoulders. Whilst she and the doctor tried to make Alfie comfortable, one member of their group tended to the horses.

"Stop fussing," said Alfie, fiercely to the doctor. "I'll be alright. We mustn't stop, we must get away from here. He mustn't catch us again. He mustn't catch Lucy."

"A great deal of 'mustn'ts', Alfie," said the doctor, kindly. "But you are not in a fit state to travel much further."

The leader approached them.

"We need to journey another ten miles," he said gently. "By then the sun will begin to rise, and we must be in hiding before that happens. There is an abandoned shepherd's hut which we can use for shelter during the day, but at nightfall we must ride hard to our destination, only then will you be safe."

"Where are you taking us?" asked the doctor.

"There is no need for you to know that," replied the leader. He turned his head towards Alfie. "Do you think you can manage another short ride tonight?"

"Of course," replied Alfie gruffly. He scrambled to his feet and swayed against Lucy.

The doctor sounded cross, "Your heroics may be the death of you, Alfie," he grumbled. "Your condition is not to be taken lightly."

"Good lad," said their leader, ignoring the doctor's glare. "Now you ride with me and sit in front. I can hold you better that way, we'll be in no danger of losing you from the back end of a horse!"

Alfie grinned, despite his pain, as two of the men carefully helped him onto the largest of the three horses.

"Right everyone, follow me. We must be as swift and silent as possible. Once through this wood we shall be onto more open land, we have approximately four miles in the open. I want to be through that before sunrise. Let's go!"

The woods seemed to go on for ever. At any moment Lucy expected the sun to rise behind them, and Sir Daniel and his men would come rushing out from the trees to recapture them, but, just as the stars began to fade, they burst out onto downland, and immediately the riders urged their horses into a gallop. The rising sun began to bathe the sky in delicate shades of pastel blue and yellow. They thundered across the open fields, scattering early feeding rabbits. The only other noise came from the jingle of harnesses and the heavy panting of horses and riders. How these magnificent animals kept up the pace Lucy couldn't imagine, but they did, and very soon their destination, a shepherd's hut, became visible in the distance. Lucy felt as if all the air in her lungs was being battered, and she clung to her rider fearful that in these last desperate moments she might fall.

At last they reached the hut. Immediately the men dismounted and carried Alfie inside, Lucy jumped down and went to help him, the doctor followed. The riders left them in peace, their horses needed tending to. It was some time before they returned, and by then, the doctor had checked Alfie, rebound his ribs and, with Lucy's help, had managed to prop him up on the one small bed of rags which was in the corner of the hut.

"I think we can trust you now," said the leader, as they entered. "So we intend to remove these hoods, but before we do, you must all swear an oath that you will never reveal our identity. Will you do that?"

The three nodded.

"It was so hot in this," complained the smallest one, shaking her long dark hair over her shoulders.

"You're a woman," exclaimed Lucy in amazement.

"I hope so!" she laughed.

"This is my sister," said the tall well-built young man who was obviously their leader. "She's an excellent horsewoman, and I couldn't have left her out of this venture even if I had wanted to!"

The third member of the party was also young, not quite as big as their leader but nevertheless he looked very strong.

"You need not know our names," said the leader. "It is sufficient you know that we are friends of Noah, and will always help him in his fight against the injustice which is meted out by Sir Daniel. We often use this hut which has been derelict for some time, so there should be a small store of food and wine somewhere in a cupboard, though I cannot vouch for its freshness."

"Let's see what we can find, Lucy," said his sister.

In a small cupboard at the back of the hut they found some wine, a few apples, some bread which was not too stale, and some cheese.

"It's a real feast," laughed the young man, as they put it on the table. "But I have some better bread in my saddle bag. I placed it there yesterday morning when I learnt of our impending journey."

"And I have some fresh wine!" laughed their leader. "What more could we want."

"Well," said the doctor, stamping his feet and blowing on his hands. "We could do with a little more heat."

"That, I'm afraid, is something we cannot have. Smoke rising from this shepherd's hut would be dangerous. It has been abandoned for so long, the owner might become suspicious."

"Who is the owner?" asked Lucy.

"Sir Daniel," replied the leader.

The shocked look on Lucy's face made their rescuers burst into laughter.

"Don't worry, Lucy," said the young man gently. "He never comes to visit his flock or his farms. I doubt if he's been in the area for many years. He leaves all that sort of thing to his shepherds and farmers. "

"He owns a great deal of land then?" said Lucy.

The leader nodded. "He's a very powerful man and very dangerous. Now let's eat and then we must get some sleep, for tonight we have a long journey."

Lucy could tell that their three rescuers were doing their best to lighten the atmosphere but how, she kept thinking, were they ever going to be rid of such an evil man. The doctor was not a young man, and Alfie was definitely not well, in fact she could see that the doctor was so concerned for Alfie's well-being that he was asking him if he knew of any relations still alive. Alfie knew why the questions were being asked and just kept giving silly answers.

In response to the question as to the name of his father he answered, "The King of Hastings!" much to the annoyance of the doctor.

As for Lucy, well, her mind was in a complete muddle. It appeared to her that everyone was here because of her mistaken identity. They were all risking their lives because of that evil madman. It wasn't right. She would have to think of a way to make life safe again, not only for herself but also for these kind friends whom she had suddenly acquired.

19

"And where might you be going?"

Lucy gasped as the young woman tightened her grip around Lucy's wrist.

"How did you know?" she spluttered. "I thought everyone was asleep. I need some fresh air, there's no need for you to come outside with me."

"You're very bad at telling lies, Lucy," replied the woman. "There's enough fresh air inside that hut without you having to come outside. It's not very weatherproof. You must come back in. It's only mid-afternoon, but when the dark comes we must start the last part of our journey."

"But it's not fair," said Lucy, almost in tears. "Why should you all risk your lives to save me from that dreadful man? I cannot believe that he is my grandfather, no grandfather could be as cruel as him. It's a mistaken identity, I'm no relation to him, and when I go back to talk to him, I'm sure he will see sense and stop pursuing us."

"You know that's nonsense, Lucy. You'll never get a fair hearing from that man." The young woman gently led her back inside the hut, all the men were still asleep. "Hard though it may seem, we are not all doing this just for you. Sir Daniel is a cruel and evil man, he has enslaved many young people, both in this country and in the colonies. We're determined to stop him and we believe you are the key to his downfall. Not only did he refuse to help your mother, Margaret, no don't shake your head, but there are also rumours concerning the death of your grandmother, who was a very rich woman before she married him. So you see, Lucy, in a strange way we need you just as much as you need us. Now, quietly go and lie down and have a little more rest before we start the rest of our journey."

One of the men started snoring loudly, it was the doctor. For a moment Lucy hesitated, but then she turned and gave the young woman a big hug.

"Thank you," she whispered and curled up on her bed of straw on the floor.

"Well done," muttered the leader to his sister. "I've been watching, I thought she'd make a run for it. You seem to have calmed her down."

"I hope so," sighed his sister.

"Get some sleep now," replied her brother. "I'll stand watch until we're ready to go."

She needed no second telling, in seconds his sister was asleep.

*   *   *   *

As the sun began to set, so the six travellers prepared to begin the last part of their journey. The doctor was particularly worried about Alfie. He knew that despite Alfie's outward bravado, the boy was in great pain. He was extremely worried in case one of his broken ribs should pierce his lungs. A journey on horseback was not going to help the healing process. Their leader, however, did everything he could to make Alfie comfortable, and made sure that he supported him in the saddle as much as possible. Gathering everything up they made their way across the fields and into the forest, from there they travelled along small rivers to find crossings and safe fords. As the stars began to emerge so Lucy could only marvel that their leader was so certain of the way. She had no idea where they were going, she had very little idea where they had come from. She was lost somewhere in the south of England, it might well have been the south of anywhere as far as she was concerned. When Lucy was sure that they could go no further, the leader signalled that they should turn left and so they began a steady climb down a slope towards a drover's road. After about a mile, still travelling west, they came upon a crossroad, and there on a corner stood an inn, a coaching inn called 'The Merry Fiddler'.

The dawn of a new day was beginning to break.

The leader reined in his horse. "We must be as quiet as possible," he said. "Follow me, we'll ride round to the side entrance and into the courtyard. There will probably be other travellers there. The landlady and her husband are expecting us, so do exactly what she says, but don't draw attention to yourselves."

Lucy felt tingles of anxious fear run over her. What if Sir Daniel was there? What if that horrible man, Morgan, was there? What if…?

"Shh," said the young woman, as if she could hear Lucy's thoughts.

They clattered into the cobbled courtyard. It was full of activity. A coach was being prepared for the long journey to Southampton, and another one for an even longer journey down to the West Country. Apart from a quick glance, no one was bothered by this wraggle-taggle group of travellers, they had too much work of their own.

A large buxom middle-aged woman came bounding across to them, her arms wide open.

"Cousin George," she boomed. "How wonderful to see you, and all your family too. Come in, come in, you must be so tired."

'So much for our quiet entrance,' thought Lucy.

"Bring your horses to the end stable," she said. "The stable boy will see to them for you."

They all rode towards the last stable block. In the growing light Lucy could see that the courtyard was bordered by the back of the inn, three sets of stables and sleeping quarters for the grooms and coachmen. The last stable block was set a little apart from the others and they were able to ride in and so conceal Alfie from any prying eyes. It would not be easy to lower him from the horse without attracting too much attention. All this time the innkeeper's wife and the young man kept watch.

"Come through this way," signalled the innkeeper's wife, when all had been completed. They were led through a side door into a small garden which lay behind the stables. There in front of them was a farmer's cottage. In silence they followed the woman into a warm kitchen with a blazing log fire.

"Sit down all of you," she said gently. "You must be exhausted."

Their leader laughed. "Well, Moll," he said. "I've never been called Cousin George before."

"I hope you didn't mind, m'lord," she answered. "I thought it best to pretend you were part of my family, then no questions would be asked when I brought you round here."

"Very sensible," he replied. "But then, dear Moll, you always did have brains as well," he paused, "as everything else."

Moll blushed and laughed heartily. "And you was always a naughty boy!" she answered.

20

Moll soon had them all settled. It quickly became apparent that she was the driving force behind The Merry Fiddler. From organising the meals for the many travellers, to sorting out who would sleep in which room, and who should pay and when, she was the one to whom everyone turned for help. Quietly, in the background, her husband, Nathaniel, cared for the horses, making sure that they were attended to by the grooms and the coachmen before they drank themselves silly with ale. His thick black beard was beginning to show flecks of grey, and under his bushy black eyebrows twinkled the clearest blue eyes Lucy had ever seen. He was a big man, but his rough weather-beaten hands could calm any horse no matter how skittish or wilful they might seem.

Carefully they helped Alfie into a small side room where a bed had been made ready for him. Whilst the doctor attended to him, the others returned to the kitchen where Moll gave each one of them a large bowl of hot gruel. As she said, late March mornings could still be very cold and they all looked as though they could do with some warmth. Nobody argued, they all felt too tired.

"Now," she said, looking at their leader. "You must all try to get some rest. A coach has been ordered for you at noon to take you back to London. You'll be able to snatch a few hours' sleep. Lucy, Alfie and the doctor are to remain here with me."

"Has Noah been here and organised this?" asked the young woman.

Moll nodded. "He came by yesterday. He's not stopped since you rescued these three. You're to return before you're missed, and he'll be coming back here to arrange the rest of the journey for Lucy and her friends. He says there's to be another shipment in nine days' time, and he needs you to help him prevent the sailing."

"Shipment?" asked Lucy. "What does that mean?"

"It means another ship load of poor souls to be sold into slavery," said their leader grimly.

"No more chattering now," said their landlady firmly. "I've made the beds for you. There will be fresh clothes for you when you wake. You men in that room over there and you, Doctor, sharing the room with Alfie." She turned to the young woman. "If you don't mind, your Ladyship, sharing with Lucy just for this morning, I'd be grateful."

The young woman smiled. "Of course I don't mind, Moll. Come on, Lucy, I shall fall asleep standing up soon."

Lucy was too tired to argue. She slept through the whole day and into the early hours of the next morning, it was a deep sleep, one of sheer exhaustion, so she didn't hear the young woman leave, nor the sound of the coach which took their rescuers back to London. When she finally woke, Moll was sitting on the edge of her bed with a mug of steaming apple juice and honey.

"This will soon put some colour in your cheeks," she said. "It's my own brew, and there's a little extra something in it to help."

Lucy sat up and carefully took the mug, Moll held on to it, she could see that Lucy was still a bit wobbly.

"You poor soul," said Moll gently. "You've had so much to understand just lately. I can see the bewilderment in your eyes." She stroked the girl's head as she spoke.

"Amos was my father," said Lucy, in between sips of the hot drink. "Sir What's'is name has it all wrong. My father was an apothecary."

Moll shook her head. "Your father, my love, was a wonderful violinist. He even played here once, but he was far too good for the likes of us. He was destined for greatness. He met your mother at a concert in London. They fell in love, but Sir Daniel forbade it. Well," she sighed, "it was like that old King Canute. He could no more stop their love than Canute, God rest his soul, could stop the tide. So they gets married secretly, but your father, he's murdered and your mother, she dies just after you're born. It's just as well that the doctor knew Amos and his wife, who had never been able to have children of their own, otherwise… well it don't bear thinking about."

"Why didn't my father, why didn't Amos, tell me all this when he was alive?" asked Lucy angrily.

"I think he most likely wanted to but the time was not quite right for him. I'm sure he would have in time. From what I hear he was a good man and you were well cared for," replied Moll, gently taking away the mug.

"How do you know all this?" asked Lucy. "It seems to me that so many people know more about me than I do myself."

Moll took a deep breath. "Those three brave young people who helped Noah to save you and your friends, well, I used to be the cook for their family. Sir George, Lady Helen and young Sir Henry. They're wonderful people and, like Noah, they're against slavery wherever it may be."

"So why did you leave them?" Lucy pushed back the bedclothes preparing to get up.

Moll smiled. "I met Nathaniel," she said simply. "He was with a travelling group of actors, we fell in love and so were married. Then after a few years we decided to settle down and raise a family. So here we are."

"Your husband was an actor?" said Lucy in amazement. She had met actors in London and she couldn't imagine Nathaniel as one.

Moll sensed her disbelief, she laughed. "You should see him on the stage," she said. "And though I say it myself, he's so handsome! We still run a small theatre company here at The Merry Fiddler. We call ourselves 'The Travelling Turnips'. You must come and see one of our plays."

This time it was Lucy who laughed, and it felt good.

"Now get yourself dressed," said Moll, delighted to see the young girl smiling, "and then we'll go and see how Alfie and that doctor of yours are getting along."

21

Mr Horatio Nimble was uncertain as to how he arrived home. He had very little recollection of the events following his interview with Sir Daniel. He remembered leaving London and the feeling of relief when he had left those cursed streets behind him, but then he had been set upon. He knew it was Morgan and a few of his so-called friends, but he would never be able to prove it. Why they had decided to beat him near to death was beyond him. Didn't Sir Daniel realise that Mr Nimble would never have betrayed the secret of the apothecary's daughter? But now, after all this… he was uncertain. Instead of making him more cowed, it had made him more determined to, one day, have his revenge.

'That is,' he thought ruefully, 'if I live that long.'

They had thrown him back into his cart which was somewhat of a blessing as he felt certain that one of his legs had been broken. Though beaten about the head and in great pain, he had just enough energy to tell the horse to go home before he became unconscious.

She was a marvellous mare, she needed no second telling and slowly but surely she plodded her way home. Mr Nimble just slipped into a state of semi-consciousness, oblivious to any passers-by who, either averted their gaze, or decided that he must be a drunkard who'd been involved in some kind of fight. It was nothing to do with them. Mr Nimble slowly became unaware of the passing of time, and so when he eventually reached the workhouse he was more dead than alive. He had no knowledge of his wife's hysterical reaction when she first saw him, no knowledge of Thomas's gentle care as he was lifted from the cart and carried like a baby to his room. There he lay for two whole days fully clothed whilst Mrs Nimble tried to find a doctor who would come to attend his wounds, but no one would come. The fear of Sir Daniel was greater than their compassion. Thomas didn't know how to deal with his father's injuries. He guessed that the right leg was badly damaged, he could see that one eye was completely full of blood and that his lips were split, and he feared that there must be other injuries that he couldn't see, but where and how to start he had no idea.

Eliza Nimble looked down at her husband's body. He hadn't been moved since the fateful morning of his return. "Oh, Horatio," she moaned. "Whatever shall we do?"

She tried to bathe his wounds, but all she seemed to do was to create more pain for him.

That evening, when it became obvious that her husband was beginning to lose his battle, one of the women from the workhouse laundry came into their parlour. She looked frightened.

"Excuse me, Mrs Nimble, there's a very strange man at the door. He says he wants to talk to you, he says he can help, but he's very strange, missus, very strange," she said turning away and muttering to herself.

"Go and see, Thomas. Be careful, mind, in case it's one of Morgan's men," Mrs Nimble said fearfully.

Thomas left the room but in one hand he held a thick cudgel which he had taken to carrying ever since his father's return. Behind him crept a few of the children and old men, curious to see this strange visitor. On opening the door he was surprised to see a small man dressed in a long silk robe tied up at the waist. It was a Chinaman. His black hair was tied in a pigtail, and over his top lip he sported a marvellous drooping moustache.

"Ah," he said bowing low. "Good evening, young sir. I have been sent to you by Noah, my name is Fu Yong Song. I am here to heal your father."

Now Thomas had no knowledge of Noah and his thoughts turned immediately to the little knowledge that he had of the Bible. He knew that Noah was in the Old Testament but that there was no way that that Noah could have sent anyone unless…

"Are you an angel?" he asked, after all the little man was dressed strangely.

Fu Yong smiled, and when he smiled his whole face seemed to light up.

"No, no, young man. I am no angel. Please let me come in. Noah has told me that your father is in need of my skills."

Fu Yong took a step over the threshold and made to make his way past Thomas. Immediately Thomas raised his cudgel as if to hit the Chinaman. What happened next had everyone gasping in amazement. Thomas seemed to leap into the air and land on his back, and the cudgel ended up in the Chinaman's hand.

"Please do not be silly. I wish to help. Please take me to your father." He held out his hand, helped Thomas to his feet and returned the cudgel to him.

Everyone parted as the two men made their way to Mr Nimble's bedroom. Mrs Nimble gave a short scream and nearly fainted when she saw her visitor.

He gave a low bow. "I am Fu Yong Song," he said, and walked straight to Mr Nimble. After a few minutes he turned to Mrs Nimble who was clutching Thomas as if she was about to collapse any moment.

"Most honourable lady," he said, as he bowed to her. "Please go and boil much water. It must be boiling, you understand. Go now," he added firmly.

Mrs Nimble gave him a very confused curtsey and rushed off into their parlour. In the meantime Fu Yong produced a sharp knife from his bag and began cutting away much of Mr Nimble's clothing. So much of it was caked hard with blood and dirt, it was not easy to remove. When Mrs Nimble returned her husband was lying on the bed in his underwear and his other clothes were in tatters on the floor. Thomas gathered them up and took them away. Fu Yong Song took the boiling kettle from Mrs Nimble. From his bag he produced bowls and placed a light sprinkling of tea leaves in each one. Over this he poured the boiling water, and carefully made himself a cup of tea. He offered one to Mrs Nimble.

"You drink," he said firmly. "It is good tea. It will calm you and clear your mind. Come drink." He showed her how to hold the small cup which had no handles, and then bowing low he handed it to her.

"Drink," he commanded again, and she did.

When she had finished he said, "Now you go, but send in your worthy son. He will be of great assistance to me."

All that day Thomas fetched wood for Fu Yong Song. Wood to keep the fire going and to prevent his father from freezing to death, wood to create splints for his father's leg which had been broken in two places, and, as Fu Yong Song said, wood to keep the kettle boiling so that they might drink the refreshing tea. As the day drifted into the night, so Thomas began to feel exhausted but the little man did not stop. It seemed to Thomas that the Chinaman spent a great deal of time with 'the laying on of the hands' which the vicar had once explained to them in a sermon many months ago. It was in the middle of the night when Thomas woke from one of his naps to find his father's body covered in long needles. He leapt up convinced that his father was being tortured. The Chinaman smiled.

"You must have more tea, Thomas, and calm yourself. I am a doctor of many years. This we call acupuncture, it is a time-honoured method from my great country which will help to heal your father, you must trust me, Thomas, just as Noah does."

As they drank tea together Fu Yong Song explained, "I have found many places where your father's body is in pain.

I could feel his pain rising through my hands. My needles will find that pain and release it, they will help to make his body whole again. He has much bruising and he is bleeding inside. He has been greatly hurt, he must rest now, but soon, if he wishes, we will see him healing. Now you must rest too, Thomas. You also need to heal. I will watch over your father. When he awakes he will need some tea!"

Thomas hesitated. "Who is this Noah that you talk about?" he asked.

Fu Yong Song gave a chuckle. "All in good time, Thomas, all in good time."

Thomas frowned. "You know that one day I think I will have to kill Sir Daniel for what he has done to my parents."

The Chinaman gave a great sigh. "Drink your tea," he said firmly. "Then sleep, it is the best cure."

22

Lucy was so happy. For the past few days she had slowly begun to accept that perhaps all these people were right, perhaps Sir Daniel was her grandfather, but nevertheless she vowed that she would always consider Amos to be her father. How the jigsaw of her life fitted together she was unsure, even if her real father should turn out to be a wandering musician, she would never give up Amos. He had cared for her, looked after her when she had been ill with measles and fevers, and he had taught her all that she knew. No, she would never give up Amos, but now Moll had shown her a new life, and this had lifted her spirits. She had begun to help around the cottage and even serve in the inn. Moll had been cunning and had given her new clothes from the vast store of costumes needed for the Travelling Turnip Company. She had given Lucy a black wig, and clever makeup had turned the young fair-haired girl into a dark beauty who was 'staying for a few days with her Aunty Moll'. When Lucy went to visit Alfie in his room, at first he didn't recognise her and asked her, rather curtly, what she thought she was doing coming in unannounced.

Moll was also clever to point out that, if they continued to call the doctor by his title then, sharp-eared customers would begin to put two and two together. Rumour had it that there was a price on their heads.

"Two young ruffians, a boy and a girl, plus a doctor in league with the devil, are wanted. The magistrate, Sir Daniel Haggleton, has said that they are a danger to the public as they are well known for dabbling in black magic. There's a large reward for their capture alive or dead," announced one of their customers one evening.

"So, Doctor, you must become my long-lost brother. Lucy and Alfie will call you Uncle Jack, in fact we will all call you Uncle Jack!" Moll decided.

Slowly Alfie began to recover from his terrible beating. At first the doctor attended him constantly, and Lucy, with her knowledge of herbs, was a great help. She discovered that Moll had a large collection of dried herbs, such as yarrow, witch hazel and arnica, which they were able to use. As Alfie progressed so Lucy began to spend more time helping Moll and Nathaniel around the inn. Until one day, Nathaniel asked her if she would like to play a small part in their forthcoming production. It was a non-speaking part, she was to play the part of a serving wench. She was so excited, she ran back to the cottage to tell Alfie and there to her delight she found Noah. He was sitting in the kitchen talking to Moll, who was looking very serious. Lucy flung her arms around the highwayman.

"It's been such a long time," she exclaimed. "Does Alfie know you are here? Where have you been? Why haven't you been able to come before? I've missed you so much!"

"Steady," Noah gave a short laugh. "One question at a time. Let me look at you, I hardly recognised you, Moll's done a good job on your disguise."

"I must get back to the inn and give Nathaniel your news," Moll said standing up and signalling Lucy to take her place. "And I'll send Uncle Jack to you, he's helping in the stables, one of the horses doesn't look too well. You must tell Lucy and the others what you have just told me."

She left quickly and Lucy saw her wipe away a tear.

"Why's she so sad?" she asked. "What has happened?"

"All in good time, Lucy," replied Noah. "Let's wait for your new Uncle Jack to arrive and then I can tell you. I think Alfie is going to join us too."

At that moment the door to the bedroom opened and in stepped a very wobbly Alfie leaning on a crutch made for him by Nathaniel.

"I've been practising, while you've been rehearsing," he said to Lucy. "I wanted to surprise you."

"That's wonderful, Alfie," she said, clapping her hands together in delight. "But you'd best sit down quickly before you fall."

Alfie gratefully grabbed a chair and sank down on it. "I didn't know I was so weak," he said sounding out of breath, at which point in came the doctor wiping his hands on an old cloth. He looked surprised to see Noah.

"You look almost human without your wig on," teased Noah.

"And will we ever see if you are human?" retorted the doctor. "What sort of man has to wear a mask all the time?"

For the first time Lucy gave Noah's mask a close scrutiny. It was a clever disguise, there was no doubting that, the only parts of his face visible were the tip of his nose, part of his mouth and chin, and his eyes, a deep blue that seemed to bore right through you. A small scar was visible under one side of his mask. Even his hands were concealed inside black leather gloves. She pushed any bad thoughts from her mind.

"He's a highwayman," replied Lucy quickly. "But a very kind highwayman who has saved all our lives, including yours Uncle Jack, and you should be grateful for it."

"I apologise," replied the doctor, smiling at Lucy. "I gather from Moll that the news you are going to give us is not good."

Noah nodded. "I had hoped that you might all stay here for some time but I'm afraid events have taken place which make it too dangerous for you to remain. Therefore you must leave in two days' time and travel further west."

"Leave?" Lucy couldn't conceal her disappointment.

"What's happened?" asked Alfie.

"Sir Daniel Haggleton's cousin has died. This means that Sir Daniel now has the title of Lord Haggleton, a peer of the realm. He has acquired an enormous estate which entitles him to mobilise his own militia, in effect his own small army," he added, seeing Lucy's puzzled face. "This inn is now on the borders of his territory, and I've heard that he intends to send his men scouring the area. He's obsessed with the thought that all three of you are still alive and in hiding. This new extended estate brings with it a Rotten Borough which he intends to fill with one of his cronies. There's even talk of Morgan becoming the M.P. We're moving into very dangerous times."

"So where are you sending us?" asked the doctor.

"There's a safe haven waiting for you down in the West Country. I don't want to say more at this time in case..." he paused.

"In case one of us gets captured and is tortured," finished Alfie quietly.

Lucy shuddered.

"It won't come to that," replied Noah firmly. "Now, I've had a long talk with Moll and she'll get you ready to leave in two or three days' time. She'll give you a map and make certain that you've enough victuals for the journey. She's also got the name of the next inn where you may safely stop for a night. I will meet up with you later. I must return to London."

He pushed back his chair and stood up.

"I will take care of them, I promise," said the doctor, as he warmly shook the highwayman's hand.

"I know you will, Uncle Jack," replied Noah with a smile.

He looked at Alfie and gently placed his hand on the boy's shoulder.

"This is all my fault." Alfie looked close to tears. "If I had stayed at the Ark as you said, then none of this would have happened. I am so sorry."

"You mustn't think like that, Alfie," said Noah. "Lord Haggleton would never have given up searching for Lucy. He was bound to find her sooner or later. In fact, in some ways, it is good that it has happened now, before his inheritance and before he has the chance to become too powerful."

He turned to Lucy who flung her arms around him. Her hug took him by surprise but he quickly regained his composure and held her close for a while.

"There, there, child," he said gently stroking her hair. "It will all turn out right, you'll see." He turned her face towards him and carefully wiped away her tears. "One day we'll be rid of that evil man, mark my words."

23

The applause was tremendous. How the customers loved the pert young maid who said nothing, but conveyed so much with a look and a wiggle of her hips.

"More! More!" they shouted.

"Come down here, my pretty! We'll bring a flush to yer cheeks!" they yelled.

Lucy didn't want to leave the stage, but Nathaniel quickly ushered her away and out into the cool air of the courtyard.

"Well done, Lucy," he said. "You did really well. I wish you could stay, but now we must get you back to the cottage before you cause a riot!"

The last few days had been more hectic than he could ever remember. First his dear Moll had broken down and sobbed at the thought of losing her 'new family'. It had brought back all those feelings of anguish when her own three little ones had died of smallpox many years ago. Foolishly she had allowed herself to regard Lucy and Alfie as the children she might have had. She knew it was silly but she hadn't been able to stop herself. Then she had set about designing their disguises for their journey, and had made sure that trustworthy messengers alerted safe inns and homes along the westward route, so much had to be accomplished in three days. Nathaniel kept his promise and gave Lucy a small walk-on part in his latest short play which they had just performed. She was a natural, and if she had stayed he would have definitely kept her in the company. Still, he reasoned, her acting skills might well come in useful on their journey west. He wondered if she realised, if any of them realised, just how dangerous it could be.

They made their way quickly across the courtyard, past the stables and through the narrow passageway which led to the cottage. Nathaniel was very aware of the new coachmen who had just arrived and were bedding down their horses. He gave them a curt nod knowing that Lord Haggleton's spies could be anywhere. Lucy wanted to tell Moll all about her stage debut, but when they burst into the kitchen she found her engrossed in a conversation with a very grey and frail looking parson.

"Come in, my child," he croaked. "Come in, don't be shy." He beckoned her to sit by his side at the table.

It was only when she came closer that she realised that he was in fact the doctor. The disguise which Moll had given him, had aged him by about twenty years.

"Oh, Doctor, Uncle Jack, I mean… Oh dear… Who do I mean?" she spluttered as Moll burst into laughter.

"I think he can still be your Uncle Jack," said Moll. "He is returning you to your mother in Penzance. You have been staying with him in London helping him administer to the sick and needy."

"Have I?" Lucy sounded so amazed that all the others burst into laughter once more.

Suddenly the door to one of the bedrooms opened and in walked a tall, dark, young woman who seemed to have great difficulty in managing her dress.

"I don't know how you girls manage with all this rubbish around your legs," said a voice which sounded suspiciously like Alfie.

"Alfie," exclaimed Lucy. "Is that really you? You look like a proper girl, you look great!"

"I don't feel great," grumbled Alfie. "I feel really stupid and silly, and I hate this dress," he added, grabbing hold of Nathaniel to prevent himself from tripping over the hem once more.

Moll looked at him carefully. "Now, young man," she said cupping his chin in her hands. "You are beginning to grow a beard and that will never do. I think you had better wear a small veil."

"A veil!" Alfie looked horrified.

"Well, in the circumstances I think it would be wise. Let's see, you've been helping your Uncle Jack in the East End and sadly you've caught an illness of the skin, a scurvy or—"

"Smallpox," interrupted Uncle Jack. "There's always some of it about and it's very contagious, yes, I think, you will have had a small dose of smallpox."

"Oh, thank you very much," replied Alfie, with some sarcasm. "That's all I need. I get beaten up, nearly die, and then I get smallpox. Wonderful!"

"But it is only pretend, Alfie," said Lucy giving him a gentle smile. "You haven't really been ill, you're just wearing the veil to hide your face because… because… you don't look like a girl."

Alfie just stared at her and then gave a broad grin. "Well, thank goodness for that," he said, and slumped down heavily on a chair.

"But you will have to remember to behave in a more feminine manner," said Nathaniel firmly. "Moll and Lucy will have to give you some quick lessons in how to walk and move. At the moment you move like one of my carthorses and that will never do."

"You must also remember," said the doctor, "that you are not completely healed, young man. You must take things carefully."

"It's late now," said Moll, looking at their anxious faces. "We'll start first thing in the morning. Now off to bed all of you."

Even the doctor obeyed her, grateful to put his head on a pillow and to forget the persistent worries that were haunting him.

24

It took a little longer than anticipated to have everything ready. Nathaniel was meticulous in his planning. He made certain that they had enough food, blankets and spare clothing for their long journey to the west. Even now they had no idea of their final destination. Moll had sent riders to set up all the safe houses along North Hampshire and down into Dorset. They would keep away from the more usual coach routes but that could mean that they might come across various gangs or cut-throats, also in hiding from the law. It could prove a dangerous journey and so Nathaniel provided them each with a pistol. Lucy protested that she would never know how to fire it, but Alfie promised to teach her on the way.

On the morning of their departure, Moll bravely hid her tears. "I'm sure we'll meet again," she murmured, as she clasped Lucy to her.

"When we're safe, I'll somehow send a message to you," whispered Lucy, not sure when Moll would release her.

Nathaniel had provided them with a small covered wagon pulled by one sturdy carthorse, a shire. She was a docile animal and, according to Nathaniel, would walk the length of the country if treated right.

Uncle Jack sat at the front in the driver's seat. He gave an air of supreme confidence even if his stomach was feeling like jelly.

"Another good actor," said Nathaniel, giving him a big grin as they shook hands warmly. "I shall miss your doctor's expertise with the horses. Good luck and God speed."

"Thank you," replied Uncle Jack. "I shall miss this place and both you and Moll."

It would be true to say that whilst they had been staying at The Merry Fiddler he and Nathaniel had struck up a fine friendship.

And so in the early hours of a beautiful spring morning the three fugitives began their journey to the West Country.

At first everything seemed to be going well, in fact, as Lucy remarked, it was as if they were going on a country ride to a picnic, but by lunch time Alfie was complaining.

"I really don't see the need for me to keep this wig on all the time," he muttered as Lucy began to pack away the remains of their first lunch. "It's hot, it itches and I'm sure it's full of fleas." He lifted it up slightly and began scratching his scalp.

"It doesn't have fleas," returned Lucy crossly. "And your wearing of it could be the difference between all three of us being caught again or escaping to the west. So please stop moaning and keep it on."

She stomped back to the wagon just as Uncle Jack was settling the horse back between the shafts.

"A problem?" he said, looking at her flushed face.

"Nothing I can't cope with thank you," she replied stiffly. Then looking past his shoulder she saw a movement on the path. A small cart was coming their way, Uncle Jack followed her gaze.

He turned back and whispered, "It looks like a travelling tinker, you can hear his pots and pans jingling about. Get Alfie into the cart quickly, but you carry on packing things away as normally as possible, and tell Alfie to keep quiet," he added.

Alfie was already making his way to the back of their cart and adjusting his wig as well as he could. He needn't have worried, the tinker wasn't interested in him, but was happy to pass a few words with Uncle Jack about the weather, especially this cold spring, and the constant threat of a French invasion. He even let it be known that he didn't believe the latest 'prophets' who were to be found in various towns.

"They're a mad lot," he said, as he accepted the mug of ale which Lucy offered him. "They say that the end of 1799, by the grace of God, and begging your pardon, sir," he touched his forelock to Uncle Jack who had temporarily forgotten that he was disguised as a parson, "will be the end of everything, it will be the end of the world."

He began to make his way round to the back of their wagon. His eyes were darting everywhere, nothing was missed. Lucy sensed this, and in her haste to block his path, she dropped the tin plates they had been using. The tinker thought she was reacting to his information about the end of the world.

"Now, now, my dear," he said, gently helping her to pick up the plates. "There's no need for you to worry your pretty little head about such nonsense. Those doom merchants are mad, quite mad. I'm sure your father will tell you so." He glanced back at Uncle Jack who noted that there had been a deliberate emphasis on the word 'father'.

Uncle Jack came forward. "No, no dear man," he said, in a tone he thought befitting a clergyman. "This young lady is not my daughter, she is my niece. We are returning from London where we have been working in the East End, caring for the sick and suffering."

"You're taking a very strange path to wherever you may be going, if you don't mind my saying so," said the tinker. "Why aren't you taking the stage? Or using the main route? I imagine, by your direction, you're travelling further west. This is a very quiet route, you could very well be set upon by robbers, or highwaymen, folk up to no good."

At this point there was an awkward silence, only to be broken by a sudden moan from the back of their cart.

A quaking voice was heard. "Help me, sister dear. I fear the fever is coming back to me. Oh help me. Uncle come and pray for me."

The tinker stepped back. His face turned pale. "Who or what was that?" he asked.

Lucy dropped him a deep curtsey. "It is my sister, sir," she sounded near to tears. "She has caught smallpox. We've come this way to keep her from others. She worked so hard with the poor, we are trying to take her home before… before… Oh, Uncle, whatever will poor Ma'ma do?" She broke down and sobbed.

Another moan from the cart and the tinker leapt into action. He moved swiftly back to his own cart and began to lead his reluctant little horse past them and on eastwards.

"I'm sorry for your troubles," he called as he left. "But I must be on my way. Pots and pans to mend y'know." He was quickly gone.

When he was out of sight Uncle Jack gave Lucy a big hug. "Well done, my dear, well done," he said. "But I think to be on the safe side we had best move off as quickly as possible."

"And what about me?" asked Alfie, as he scrambled out from the back of the cart. "Y'see, Lucy. You're not the only one who can act! Wasn't that a wonderful groan from a dying sister." He did it again.

"It was very fine," replied Lucy smiling. "But it was a good job he didn't want to see you."

Alfie frowned. "I don't know what you mean," he said.

"Not many young ladies grow their hair down just one side of their face," said Uncle Jack. "And, without your veil, you look remarkably like a healthy young man dressed up in girls' apparel."

"Girls' what?" asked a bewildered Alfie.

"Girls' clothes," explained Lucy, trying to control her urge to laugh. "Back into the wagon, dear sister, and I'll tidy up your hair once again."

Within five minutes they had left the area and not a trace of their presence remained.

25

They had now travelled for several days. At each safe house they were cared for by the landlords or the owners, everyone seemed to know of their predicament and the cruelty of Lord Haggleton. Each safe house gave them directions for the next.

As one landlord remarked, "The less we know, the safer it will be for all of us."

"Why does he hate me so, Uncle Jack?" asked Lucy one evening. She had got into the habit of calling the doctor, Uncle Jack, at all times. Alfie had followed suit, and the doctor seemed to like it.

"Because you remind him of your mother," he answered. "What he did to your mother was very cruel, Lucy."

"Yes, but why hasn't he been as cruel to William? After all William is his son. If he can be so horrible to his daughter, why not his son? Why does he put up with him?" asked Alfie.

"Poor William," said Uncle Jack with a sigh. "He doesn't seem to realise that his father is allowing him, in fact encouraging him, to drink himself to death. He urges him to visit gambling houses, to mix with undesirables and to live the life of a rake. The poor boy doesn't seem to understand."

"But why?" asked Lucy, "is he killing him with kindness? My father, Amos, used to say that people could do that, though I don't really understand how."

Uncle Jack smiled, but then said something which sent a cold shiver down Lucy's back. "It's rumoured that when William gets further into debt and is unable to control his drinking, then Lord Haggleton will have him declared unfit to live in the normal world, unfit to inherit his vast fortune. He will have him declared insane and confined in a mad house."

"That's horrible," murmured Lucy.

"So who will inherit everything?" asked Alfie looking at Lucy.

"It will be Morgan," replied Uncle Jack.

"Morgan!" Alfie almost screamed the word in horror. "He's a monster. All he cares about is hurting others. You must be wrong. I mean, who told you that it would be Morgan?"

"No one," answered Uncle Jack simply. "But Morgan has lived in that house ever since he was a little child. He came with the family when they moved there from the country. Some even say that he's Daniel Haggleton's son by another woman. No one really knows, but you're right in saying that he's a monster. There are very few men who can match Lord Haggleton's lust for power by any means, and Morgan is one of them."

Alfie stifled a yawn. This was interesting and he wanted to ask more, but it had been a long day and he was growing tired of wearing girls' clothing.

"It's time we all had some sleep," announced Lucy, taking on a very maternal tone. "We'll have another long journey tomorrow no doubt and we can ask all these questions on the way."

"You're quite right, ma'am," said Uncle Jack with a teasing bow. "To bed it is."

This particular landlord had put them all in the same room with two beds. He was a bit short on rooms at the moment and as he explained to Uncle Jack, the two young girls could sleep together and their uncle could have the other bed. As it was, Lucy had one bed, Uncle Jack the other, whilst Alfie preferred to sleep on the floor.

The last three days had taken them through beautiful countryside, but it had proved hard, they had had to find fords to cross the fast flowing rivers, such as the Itchen and Test with their clear clean waters, and the mighty Avon with its many tributaries. They had the rolling hills of Cranbourne Chase behind them, and now, following instructions, they were moving deep into Dorset.

They set out the next morning refreshed with a bowl of gruel and carrying their precious bundle of bread, cheese and ale.

"Well," remarked Uncle Jack, as they negotiated yet another difficult bend. "He may not have been very talkative but our landlord has certainly packed us a feast for our lunch. Have you looked inside our bundle, Lucy?"

"It does seem large," said Lucy, and proceeded to open it whilst the wagon swayed its way down the side of the steep hill.

She gave a gasp of horror as the contents spilt out onto the wagon floor. Their 'loaf ' was no more than a rotten cabbage, the so-called cheese, wormy carrots, and as for the flagon of ale.

"Don't drink it!" she shouted, as Alfie raised it to his lips to test it. "It's probably poisoned or bad water from who knows where."

Alfie hurled it from the wagon as Uncle Jack reined in the horse. For a moment they sat in silence, all that could be heard were the alarm calls of nearby nesting larks and the buzz of insects.

"If he has given us such victuals," said Uncle Jack slowly. "Then…"

"It's likely that this route is not good," finished Alfie.

"The point is though," continued Uncle Jack. "Is it going to prove bad for the wagon or bad for us? In other words is he sending us into a trap?"

"Then we'd better make for those trees," said Lucy. "Out here in the open is not very sensible."

"How did such a wise head end up on such young shoulders?" asked Uncle Jack, gently teasing her. "We'll turn

107

off this route at the next fork, and try to find a way through that wood."

It was only about a quarter of a mile to where the trail divided and to their delight the left fork led down towards the wooded area. No one spoke, they had all realised that they had been betrayed. For what reason they had no idea. The landlord might just have wanted to make some extra money, or it might be their worst fear, he was in the pay of Lord Haggleton.

They made it to the wood and found that the track was wide enough to take their cart. Once there they paused.

"Have we any food or drink, Lucy?" asked Uncle Jack turning to look at her.

"I've saved three small pieces of cheese from the other day, and an apple," she replied.

"A veritable feast," he said, far too cheerfully.

Alfie and Lucy were not fooled at all. They knew they were in danger, they could either starve to death or hand themselves in and be captured by Lord Haggleton's men.

"We might find a friendly farmhouse," said Lucy. "Just because the last landlord has deceived us, it doesn't mean he's sent a message to Lord Haggleton about us."

"That's true," replied Uncle Jack. "There is, however, one other minor problem."

"Let me guess," said Alfie, angrily snatching off his wig and throwing it onto the wagon floor. "We don't know where we are or where we're going. We're lost."

Uncle Jack nodded. "Foolishly I haven't questioned any of the routes I've been given. I trusted that the innkeepers chosen by Moll would all be honest and would just send us to the next port of call. Not for once did I think one might betray us. All I know is that Noah intended us to travel far into the West Country, into Cornwall."

"You weren't to know," said Lucy gently. "We've all trusted too many people. We'll just keep travelling further west and I'm sure Noah will come to find us."

"Cornwall is a dangerous place," said Alfie. "My Pa was a sailor. He said that smugglers and wreckers live there. It's a bad coast to travel on a stormy night."

"Well, we're not going to be travelling at night along the coast, my young friend, so there is no need for you to concern yourself about that." Uncle Jack patted Alfie's head. "No, Lucy has the best idea. We must just keep heading west and hope that Noah will find us, somehow."

All day they followed the trail through the woods. It was late in the afternoon when they came across a broken signpost. On one arm it said 'SEA 30' and on another it said '280 NDON', the rest had been worn away or broken.

"I think it means London," said Uncle Jack, getting down from the wagon and struggling to prop up the post.

Alfie jumped down to help him and promptly fell over the hem of his dress and rolled into the ditch.

"Get back, Alfie," said Uncle Jack, stifling his laughter. "You're a girl, remember."

"Who's going to see me out here," grumbled Alfie, wiping his hands on his skirt.

"You never know," replied Uncle Jack. "We can't take any chances yet."

Lucy tidied up her 'sister' and they took the direction towards the coast. After nearly an hour travelling through the wood, the path suddenly ended. They had reached a junction. The new road before them travelled from east to west, and so they turned right into the setting sun, and there, just a few yards in front of them, stood a soldier, a sergeant, his men were sprawled on the grassy bank behind him.

26

"Keep very still and stay back in the shadows, Alfie," whispered Uncle Jack. "Don't utter a word."

Slowly they made their way towards the soldiers, Uncle Jack trying his hardest to look unconcerned and perhaps a little pleased to see the soldiers. For their part the soldiers sprawled on the bank didn't even bother to look up, but the sergeant was very different. Though unshaven and in a decidedly scruffy uniform that had seen better days, he nevertheless knew his duty. He was to stop any travellers on the road, especially those travelling west, to question them thoroughly, to expect some resistance and, if necessary, to squash it by the use of force. He liked that last bit 'the use of force', he was familiar with that term. He had been in many campaigns abroad, he was a good sergeant and looked after his men well, but he hated this waiting game and the fact that he and his men had been recruited to help some lord capture some absconders from justice. Why if every absconder was put in prison then there'd be no army left.

He looked at the clergyman approaching and noted that he seemed to be talking to someone behind him in the wagon.

"Good afternoon, sir," he said politely, as the horse obligingly pulled up. "Now what might you be doin' out as the sun is on 'er way down?" He held onto the horse's bridle and tried to peer past Uncle Jack and into the dark corners of the wagon.

"Good afternoon, my son," replied Uncle Jack, trying to sound as if he was about to deliver a sermon. "What a pleasant day it has been. I am making my way to my sister's home."

"And where might that be?" asked the sergeant, still holding tightly to the reins. "And who are your companions?"

"Ah," Uncle Jack hesitated. His mind was racing through places which he knew existed in the West Country. "She lives the other side of Plymouth, we still have a long way to go."

"Indeed you have, sir. So I ask once more, who is with you, sir?" asked the sergeant, politely but firmly.

"With me?"

"Yes, with you," he answered. "You said 'we still have a long way to go'. Who is 'we'?"

At this point Lucy popped her head out of the wagon and enquired innocently, "Why have we stopped, Uncle? Is there something the matter?"

The sound of her voice had an instant effect upon all the soldiers on the bank. They sat up and looked in her direction. The sergeant gave a great cough, clicked his heels together and gave her a nod.

"Good afternoon, Miss," he said, and turned to Uncle Jack. "May I ask why it is you've chosen to use such a deserted route with this young lady, sir? It would have been much more sensible to have travelled on a more major route."

One or two of the soldiers had stood up and were making their way around to the back of the wagon. Lucy knew that if they saw Alfie then there would be no hope for them.

"Tell them, Uncle Jack," she suddenly said, as if to break into tears at any moment. "You must tell them about poor dear Minerva and the smallpox and why we couldn't use the coach like the others. Tell them, Uncle." She began to sob.

"Smallpox?" The sergeant stepped back and signalled his men to do the same. "What d' you mean, smallpox?"

Uncle Jack looked suitably flustered. "We have been working in the East End of our great city of London. It has

111

been most wonderful to humbly undertake the work of the Lord, to minister to those that suffer and to—"

"Get on with it, sir," interrupted the sergeant. "What about the smallpox?"

"My two nieces came with me, but sadly Matilda caught smallpox and…"

"I thought you said 'er name was Minerva?" said the sergeant frowning. "I think I 'ad better 'ave a look in the back of this wagon just to make sure who you've been an' got in there."

He moved around the wagon and was just about to lift up the canvas flap when a shot rang out. The horse was startled and jolted the wagon so that Lucy rolled back towards the tailboard. There she had a good view of who had fired the shot. An officer was riding towards them at breakneck speed, the sergeant cursed as he swung round to salute him.

Although smartly dressed in a splendid uniform, the officer had obviously been in some battles. He wore a large patch over his left eye, whilst the right side of his face was hideously scarred.

"Get your men up on their feet, sergeant," he shouted. "Quickly man! We're in danger of being invaded! Leave these vagabonds, they're not worth it. Your country needs you, NOW!"

"But I've reason to believe sir…" began the sergeant. He didn't get any further.

"Are you questioning me, sergeant?" bellowed the officer.

"No, sir."

"Then obey your orders," came the brusque reply. The officer turned in his saddle. He briefly shook Uncle Jack's hand before saying, "Take your wagon and get out of here, sir. I should stop at the next dwelling if I were you, so that you may give your horse a good rest before nightfall." With that he turned to the sergeant who had mustered all his men together. Standing in his stirrups he addressed them as though they were the last fighting force left in England.

"Listen up, men," he said. "A French fleet has been spotted approaching Lyme Bay. The small garrison there is not strong enough to repel them if they attempt a landing, as surely they must do. You must hasten there with all speed. You will be England's finest in this hour of need. A light to shine through her darkest hour. At the double, men, follow your sergeant to Lyme and to history!"

"Where will you be going, sir?" asked the sergeant, as he watched the wagon disappear into the distance. It could have proved a useful mode of transport in this 'darkest hour'.

"I have to ride to Exeter to bring up more reinforcements and to alert the navy," replied the officer. "See to it, sergeant. They are depending on you at Lyme."

"Yes sir," replied the sergeant. "Quick march men. You heard the officer. On the double now to Lyme!"

The soldiers turned smartly and set off at a trot. The officer turned his horse, and looked towards the three travellers, he seemed satisfied that the little wagon was now almost out of sight, he gave his horse a gentle prod, and galloped off in the opposite direction.

27

Fu Yong Song surveyed the gardens before him.

"You have done well, Thomas," he said approvingly. "You have planted intelligently. Your parents must be very proud of you."

Thomas merely nodded. His parents had never said a word of praise about his work in the gardens. He had grown vegetables for the House for as long as he could remember. No one had ever said thank you, they just took it and cooked it. There were plenty of complaints if the carrots had wireworm or if the potatoes were rotten, but never a word of praise. He looked down at the little Chinaman who barely reached his shoulder. What an amazing man he was. Over the past few weeks he had steadily turned Mr Nimble from a feverish and battered wreck of a man, who everyone thought must die, into a patient making a positive recovery, and capable of holding a lucid conversation.

It was, however, the change in his mother which Thomas thought was quite miraculous. He could now see why his father had married her. The taut sharp lines in her face were gradually receding, she even sang – well, hummed – around the House whilst going about her work. The residents remarked how much kinder she was to them, she was happy when her husband called her Eliza and could be heard to refer to him as Horatio.

Thomas had asked Mr Fu, as he called him, what had caused this change.

Mr Fu just smiled and said, "I have taught your mother how to relax, how to take the energy which flows through her body, through all our bodies, and turn it into positive actions and not to drive it inwards, so that it builds and builds into a tension so strong that it will eventually snap." He gave a chuckle. "I have also taught her how to make an inestimable cup of tea. For this I have given her much praise. You will observe, Thomas, that in life, if people are praised for their worth and for their efforts, much more can be achieved."

Thomas thought this a good idea because now here was Mr Fu praising his work in the garden and Thomas was feeling like a seven foot giant.

"This place," said Mr Fu waving his arms about, "is wonderful and promises so much. We will harness its energy, Thomas, and produce an abundance of food to sustain all our lives. You will make it succeed, Thomas. We will have food from the earth, chickens for their eggs, sheep for their wool, and cows for their milk. I will teach the others how to care for these creatures. It will be a happy place."

Thomas shook his head. "We can't do all that, Mr Fu," he said kindly. "We have to get these people ready to leave soon. They will go to new homes, to new jobs, to a better life. The men will come for them and then later other poor souls will take their place and we start all over again."

Fu Yong Song gave a small snort. Slowly he began tracing random patterns in the dust with his foot, all the time he was making strange humming sounds. It was as if Thomas and the rest of the world did not exist. After a few moments he looked up and smiled.

"We will do these things, Thomas, and then, my young friend, we will also prepare to fight. Come, we will tell your parents to make ready for war. Noah would want this, of this I am sure."

Mr and Mrs Nimble looked at the Chinaman in astonishment.

"Are you insane?" asked Mr Nimble. He had been propped up in an armchair, his broken leg still supported on a comfortable stool, sipping a cup of the delicious tea which Mrs Nimble had made him.

Admittedly the Chinaman had introduced many good practices to the House, some of them not unlike the methods Amos the Apothecary had tried to encourage. The inmates had benefitted enormously from his ideas on cleanliness and had even enjoyed his strange methods of exercise. Everyone seemed much happier and more content. Now here he was saying that they should go to war!

"Are you insane?" he repeated, mopping his brow. "Have you any idea what would happen to us if we tried to fight off Morgan and his men? Have you ever met him? Have you never heard of Lord Haggleton?"

Fu Yong Song sat cross-legged on the floor. He gave a great sigh and spoke slowly. "I have met this Morgan, and I have met people such as Lord Haggleton, and I say to you, Horatio Nimble, that such people are evil, and there comes a time when you must stand up to them, and I believe such a time for you is very near. Noah would want this."

"There you go again," spluttered Mr Nimble. "You keep quoting Noah. You do realise, don't you, that Noah is in the Bible and died many years ago. He is not going to help us."

Fu Yong Song gave a small smile.

"But why should we have to do anything, Mr Fu?" asked Mrs Nimble quietly. "What difference does it make to us where these people go? As far as I know they just go off to better lives, isn't that right Horatio?"

Mr Nimble didn't answer.

"I will tell you a story," said Fu Yong Song. "Perhaps it will help you to understand why men, such as Morgan and Lord Haggleton must not be allowed to thrive."

The room became very quiet.

"Many years ago I studied to become a doctor. I learnt many good things from many wise men. Then I met a beautiful young girl, she was more beautiful than the petals from the most exquisite cherry tree. She had the most wonderful singing voice and her knowledge of the arts, of music and of painting was unsurpassed by any of her contemporaries. We fell in love and were married and went to live in a small village north of Shanghai. People came from the surrounding districts to be treated by me and to hear the beautiful music which my beloved could produce. We were so happy, eventually we had three wonderful sons. Today they would have been about the same age as your gracious son, Thomas."

Thomas felt his face redden with embarrassment.

"My sons were nine, seven and five years of age when the riders came in from the north. They attacked the village, they beat me to the ground and tied me to a stake, then they tortured and killed my beautiful wife in front of me. They then fired arrows into my body and left me for dead. All the elderly villagers were killed, all the young ones, including my sons, were taken into slavery. I do not know how long I hung there on that stake, but eventually a group of monks came and cut me down, they nursed me back to life, and gave a proper burial to all those poor souls, including my beloved, who had been tortured and killed. I went with the monks and I learnt much whilst I was with them. A year later a great warrior visited the monastery, and he laughed when I said that I was going to avenge my wife's murder and rescue my sons. This made me very angry, but he carefully explained to me that I was not ready for such an undertaking. He said that if I would act as his squire he would help me to track down the bandits and he would also teach me the skills of the warrior. This I agreed to."

"You poor man," whispered Mrs Nimble dabbing her eyes.

Fu Yong Song bowed his head and for a while the room became silent once more. Thomas began to think that perhaps the little man had nodded off to sleep so he gave a small cough. Fu Yong Song smiled and continued.

"For several months we followed the trail of these bandits. Sadly we came across many bodies of my former friends and relatives from the village. They had been left to

117

decay by the roadside. Many could only be recognised from their clothing." He paused. "And this was how I recognised my youngest son. It took us many days to bury them, and all this time I practised my martial skills under the watchful eye of my warrior."

"Oh how dreadful," sobbed Mrs Nimble.

"I shall stop," said Fu Yong Song abruptly. "I should have realised that my story would touch such a tender heart as yourself."

"No, no," replied Mr Nimble. "Please continue, we wish to know how you met Morgan," he paused, "that is, if you do not find it too distressing for yourself."

Fu Yong Song looked at Mrs Nimble. She nodded her head in agreement. "Please continue, Mr Fu, if you will."

"Eventually we reached the coast. You must realise that China is a vast country and three years had passed since the death of my beloved. My remaining two sons would now be ten and eight years of age. Such joy I found in the little fishing village which we first encountered. My middle son had been found wandering along the seashore. Apparently the bandits had struck a deal with some pirates, and several villagers, including my remaining two sons, had been taken away in their ships to work as slaves. They had thrown my little one overboard as they were leaving harbour believing he would drown, they considered him worthless. Somehow he survived and managed to reach the shore where a kind fisherman and his wife had taken him in and were bringing him up as if he was their own child. I could see that he was in safe hands, it was with a great sadness that I left him there. I could not take him with me on such a hazardous journey because, you see, I was determined to rescue my eldest son. What I have said all happened more than ten years ago. My eldest son will be grown up now, but I shall still recognise him, a father does not forget his sons."

"So how did you meet with Morgan?" asked Mr Nimble.

"I discovered that Morgan was one of the ringleaders of these pirates. He traded in people. I saw him bring young people from this country and sell them as slaves into many countries, and always in exchange for wealth and goods. I then discovered that Morgan worked for a Lord Haggleton. In order to find this out I had to sign on to one of his ships. I have travelled to Africa, to the West Indies, the New World and to many parts of Europe but nowhere have I found anyone as evil as those two men. They are dangerous and they are murderers."

"And Noah?" queried Thomas, who had been silent all this time. "Where does he fit into all your journeys?"

Fu Yong Song smiled. "I met the man known as Noah the night I decided to jump ship. We had docked near the place you call Gravesend. I saw an opportunity to escape but they saw me and began to fire. A highwayman suddenly arrived, and signalled me to climb up behind him on his magnificent horse. We rode like the wind, away from the docks and into the woods. They had no hope of catching us. Later I learnt that his name was Noah, and his main aim was to destroy the terrible trade of slavery which Daniel Haggleton and Morgan had set up between them. He then told me of your troubles and I have agreed to help, and in return, he has agreed to help me find out what has happened to my remaining son. We have made a bargain to help one another."

"And are you saying that some of the residents here are being shipped abroad to slavery?" asked Mr Nimble, huffing and puffing to sit more upright in his chair.

"Yes," replied Fu Yong Song simply.

"Oh, Horatio," said Mrs Nimble in horror. "This is dreadful. We cannot let this happen anymore. I thought they were going to the factories of the North, to good homes where they would learn to serve their country. How could I have been so stupid."

"You are quite right, my dear. We have both been stupid," replied her husband. "Mr Fu, we will do as you say. We will fight, yes, we will fight these monsters."

"Tell us what to do, Mr Fu," said Thomas. "Are we going to march to London?"

Fu Yong Song smiled. "No, brave Thomas," he replied. "We are not going to march anywhere. First of all we will ask your delightful mother to make us a delicious tea!"

28

For some time they sat in silence. The only sounds came from the jingle of the horse's harness and the constant rhythmic squeak of the wagon wheels. Uncle Jack stared straight ahead, his eyes never wavering from the road. Alfie sat sullen in the corner of the wagon, he had already pulled off his wig and thrown it to the far end. Lucy was sitting very still but her mind was in a feverish race. They had been very close to disaster. What if the sergeant had peered into the wagon? What if they had seen Alfie or dragged him out into the light? What if they had dragged her out of the wagon? What if...?

"It was a good job that the officer came along when he did," said Uncle Jack as if reading her thoughts. "They were nothing but a bunch of mercenaries. Ah, I think we will stop here for a moment."

He guided the horse a little way off the road and onto a flat grassy space at the edge of a copse.

"Don't look so worried, Lucy dear," he said kindly. "I would never let anything bad happen to you, you must know that."

"Me neither," mumbled Alfie, struggling out of his dress and forgetting he only had on his underpants.

Despite her fears Lucy couldn't help laughing at him. When Alfie realised his predicament, he promptly leapt from the wagon skilfully grabbing his own clothes on the way. He reappeared quite quickly but his shirt was on the wrong way round.

"At least you've managed to have your trousers on the right way," said Uncle Jack with a grin. He began to unroll a piece of paper which he had been clutching ever since they had left the soldiers.

"Where did you get that?" asked Alfie.

"The officer passed it to me when he was telling us to move on. He shook my hand, which I thought was a little unnecessary. I think the sergeant might have suspected something too but didn't dare ask. Aha, just as I thought." He gave a smile. "It's a message from Noah. I thought I recognised that horse, it was one of the creatures I checked over in Moll's stables. A fine animal."

"Do you mean that that officer was really Noah?" asked Lucy, in amazement.

"I believe so," replied Uncle Jack. "He has written us a message."

"What does it say?" asked Alfie, jumping up beside him on the wagoner's seat.

"Wait," came the reply. "Be patient."

Uncle Jack gave a short cough and read:

Dear Friends,

You have made very good progress despite taking a wrong path and losing your way! You will need to keep the setting sun before you. Miranda will need frequent rests as the terrain is hard and full of rolling hills and deep valleys. Beware of robbers and bandits, LH has many such friends who will be on the lookout for you. You must avoid Exeter and make your way west between the two great moors. There are several rivers to cross but I hope to be with you before you reach the Tamar. Once across that river you will be safe. Remember to care for Miranda, she is your life line!

N

"Who on earth is Miranda?" asked Alfie.

Uncle Jack looked at him and smiled. "Why our horse, of course," he replied. "I thought you knew that, Alfie."

"That explains why he, I mean she, has never taken any notice of me when I've called her Nelson," he said in a solemn tone.

This caused Lucy to begin giggling until they were all laughing.

"That feels better," said Uncle Jack, looking at his two young companions. "We could all do with a little light relief, laughter is good for our souls."

"Be my guest," replied Alfie, with mock seriousness. "I'm pleased my stupidity has caused you some humour."

"But Noah is quite right," said Lucy. "Without Miranda we would never make such a journey safely."

"Even with her, it is going to be hard," replied Uncle Jack. "We have little idea where we are, we have no maps and I have very little knowledge of the county of Devon."

"We do have a map," said Lucy. "Look at the other side of Noah's letter. Those aren't odd lines or drawings, I think he has given us a map."

"You're right, Lucy," exclaimed Uncle Jack. "Crude I admit, but nevertheless it is a map. Look, there are the two moors, Exmoor and Dartmoor, marked clearly, and there is Exeter and Plymouth, and back here is Lyme, where we have just been."

They fell silent, for although the map gave them a sense of direction and some security, it also brought with it the realisation that they still had a very long and dangerous journey before them.

"There seem to be a large number of rivers before us," said Alfie.

The sun was beginning to drop fast, it would soon be dark.

"We must move on," said Uncle Jack, folding up the map carefully. "I'm afraid we must ask Miranda for one more effort today, so that we may find a place of safety for the night."

123

He gave a click on the reins and Miranda slowly moved them back onto the road and once more towards the west.

Despite the map, any confidence which the travellers might have felt was wiped away, literally, the next day. The night had brought in a high wind and with it torrential rain. Roads, which were already no more than country lanes, became awash with mud and rubble. The trees bowed to the wind but that didn't stop its relentless onslaught. The noise through the trees was horrendous, and Uncle Jack had to shout his orders to the others.

"Lucy, you must guide the horse using the reins – Alfie, you come with me. We'll hold the horse's head and help her along the path!"

It was hard work getting the horse harnessed up to the wagon, and even harder moving the wagon out of the corner of the field where they had stayed the night. If only the wind would lessen, but it was coming up from the west and driving the rain like icy shards straight into their faces. Their road was fast becoming an angry river, and it wasn't long before the three travellers plus Miranda were soaked through to the skin.

"This is hopeless," shouted Alfie, as he slipped once more in the mud. "We should stop and shelter until this passes. Noah said we should take care of Miranda, we'll kill her if we carry on in this."

"You're right," shouted back Uncle Jack. He pointed to a narrow path on the right. "This way, Lucy," he called. "It looks as though it might lead to higher ground."

Slowly Lucy guided Miranda round and they made their way into the shelter of the trees.

"Look!" shouted Alfie.

There in front of them were the remnants of a barn. It had lost one side and the roof looked as if it might collapse at any moment. Carefully they steered the horse and wagon into the more substantial part of the barn.

"Well," said Uncle Jack, taking stock of their surroundings. "This will have to serve as our lodgings for tonight."

Together they unhitched the horse and set about making themselves comfortable. Even though the barn was nothing more than an abandoned shack, it still gave them some protection from the driving rain, but the noise of the wind through the trees persisted.

"I think we're in for a very wet and cold time," he said, after they had finished rubbing down the horse.

"No we're not," replied Alfie cheerfully, as if trying to rally his troops. "We can make up beds with some of this straw." He pointed to a semi-rotting pile which had been left in a corner.

"And I've found a feast," announced Lucy, much to their surprise. "Look!"

She held up a bunch of carrots which had seen much better days. "I'm sure I can make something of these, and if one of you can light up a fire, then we can have some carrot stew. It will warm us up if nothing else."

"What would I do without you," said Uncle Jack, looking at them both in admiration.

"Well," replied Lucy gravely. "If it wasn't for me neither of you would be in this mess. You might all be sitting at home in front of a warm fire."

"I wouldn't have missed all this for anything," said Alfie, grinning at her.

"And neither would I," added Uncle Jack, and gave her a big hug.

29

Lord Haggleton was angry. By rights he should have been a very happy man. After all he had the title for which he had so long craved, and with the title came considerable land, a seat in the House of Lords, more wealth, and best of all even greater power. He sat at his desk, the tension in his hands as he pushed his fingers together seemed to permeate throughout the whole room. He was surrounded by idiots. Even Morgan had not been able to carry out his instructions properly, and as for William, words failed him. There was the boy, he could not bring himself to think of him as a man, lolling back in a chair, picking at his teeth and then polishing his fingers on his coat, a beautiful coat which probably cost as much as the price of a cottage.

"Tell me again slowly, Morgan. How did those three revolting persons escape the clutches of our two well-armed and experienced men. Remind me, they were a thin, unfit doctor, a boy with several broken bones, and a slim girl of about twelve years. Am I not right?" the sarcasm in his voice slid across the floor to where Morgan was standing.

William looked up, if he was expecting Morgan to look worried or scared then he was disappointed. Morgan stood tall and showed no fear. He was probably the only man in that whole household who never betrayed any emotion which might be construed as a weakness.

"As I explained earlier, m'lord," he replied firmly and in a steady tone. "The coach was ambushed by several men, their leader being the man they call Noah. The coachmen stood no chance."

"You did not think to escort the coach yourself then?" asked Lord Haggleton.

126

"No, m'lord. I did not. You said, yourself, the two men were well armed and should, in normal circumstances, have been able to transport the three prisoners to their destination."

William couldn't but help admire Morgan's calmness. He looked at Lord Haggleton who was obviously seething beneath his cold exterior. A long tense silence ensued which William found unbearable.

"I wager that if you had been there, Morgan, you'd have given this Moses chap a bloody nose, or challenged him to a sword fight, or something equivalent," he spluttered.

"His name is Noah, sir," said Morgan with a smirk. "And yes, I would have defeated him, I'm sure of it." Everyone knew that, not only was Morgan a remarkable and strong pugilist, but also a skilful master swordsman. In fact he had been given the task of training William in these skills, but with little success.

"What a pity you didn't bother to go with them then," said Lord Haggleton sarcastically. "The two coachmen, I presume, have received their punishment."

"They have, m'lord," replied Morgan. "They are now working in one of your coalmines in Nottingham. Their families have been sent with them."

"I say, Morgan," said William in admiration. "You do come up with some brilliant punishments."

"I'm afraid I cannot take the credit for that, sir," said Morgan. "It was his Lordship's idea."

"Stop your babbling, William," growled Lord Haggleton. "We've work to do. Now, Morgan, where do you think the three of 'em are at this moment?"

"My spies tell me that they have been making their way westward," replied Morgan. "They may be trying to settle in Dorset."

Before Lord Haggleton could answer, William rose from his seat, took an apple from the desk and turned to face Morgan.

"You have spies, Morgan?" he asked. "Now that's very impressive, very impressive indeed. Did you know he had spies, sir?" He addressed this last remark to Lord Haggleton.

"Of course I know, you idiot," replied his Lordship angrily. "I pay for them!"

"Oh," said William, obviously deflated by this last remark. He sat back in his chair and took a large bite from his apple which he proceeded to eat noisily.

"Are your spies reliable, Morgan?" asked his Lordship.

"Very," came the curt reply.

Another silence descended on the group, the only sound was the scrunching of William's teeth upon the apple. It was beginning to irritate Lord Haggleton.

"I don't think you need worry anymore," said Morgan, stretching his back. He was tired of standing still for so long. "I think you can forget them."

Lord Haggleton slammed his fist down on the desk, which caused William to drop his apple. "I'll decide when I can forget them, Morgan, not you!" he shouted.

Morgan didn't answer.

"And what about the Nimbles?" Lord Haggleton took some long deep breaths. "What about those two incompetents? How could they have let Amos die and that slip of a girl escape? Did Mr Nimble get my message, do you think?"

"Oh yes, your Lordship," replied Morgan. He smiled as he remembered how Mr Nimble had whimpered with pain. "He received your message, I delivered it personally, myself. I'm sure Mrs Nimble is now well aware of it too."

"Thank you, Morgan." Lord Haggleton gave a satisfied sigh. "I know I can always rely upon you. We'll leave them alone for a while, perhaps let them think over what has happened. I'm not a harsh man, but keep a watch around those Dorset borders, won't you. I want to know the moment our absconders try to move back to London, you understand?"

128

Morgan gave a short bow and left the room.

William watched him leave and spat out an apple pip in his direction.

"Why do we keep Morgan?" he asked. "I could do the sort of work that he does for you. You wouldn't have to pay me."

"Morgan has been with me for many years," replied Lord Haggleton. "We have an arrangement. He knows where his bed lies, I would trust him with my life." He paused and looked long and hard at William. "And I would strongly advise, William, that you do the same. Morgan is not the sort of man you would want as an enemy."

William tossed his apple core into a corner of the room and pouted.

30

It couldn't be said that it had been a pleasant night but at least the three friends had kept fairly dry. Lucy was not at all happy about the mice which ran freely about the floor, but when she saw the rats she decided it was time to sleep inside the wagon. It wasn't long before she was joined by Uncle Jack and Alfie.

"I'm not worried about the rats," muttered Alfie. "Just a bit cold out there, that's all."

Lucy smiled and dropped back to sleep. She wasn't sorry to have their company and warmth in the wagon.

The morning brought with it the reminder that they were very hungry and Uncle Jack realised that the lack of food and nourishment would soon be a source of danger for them all.

"I've decided to go into the next village and see if I can barter some of my skills for food," he announced, as they began to prepare to leave.

Lucy looked at him in horror. "You mustn't do that," she said. "Supposing someone recognises you? Or there could be spies about. No it's too dangerous. You mustn't go."

Alfie looked at her in surprise. "What an outburst," he said laughing. "You sound just like Moll, mind you, I have to agree. It could be dangerous, Uncle Jack, you never know who could be about."

"Look," he replied. "We're miles from London, we don't really know where we are, possibly in the County of Devonshire, we're not using the main route, so our journey is taking us far longer than the usual three days by coach from the Great City to Cornwall. We are fast running out of edible food and we are getting weaker by the day. Also, if you haven't noticed, our main source of transport is getting weaker too. Poor Miranda won't last much longer if we cannot find more nourishment for her, let alone ourselves." He gave a great sigh. "We cannot go on like this for much longer."

There was a long silence.

Finally Alfie spoke. "You're right, of course, but perhaps we could think of another way, one that won't put you in such danger."

"You said that it only takes three days by coach to Cornwall," said Lucy.

"That's correct," replied Uncle Jack. "You see," he added gently, "it's all very well Moll and Noah saying we must keep off the main route but down here, in the valleys, we've had to push this cart through fords and mud, and along roads barely wide enough for our needs. We've been lucky that we haven't broken a wheel or an axle. The last part through Dorset was particularly bad, and we must not fool ourselves. People will have seen us. They must be wondering why three, such as us, are pushing ourselves through such terrain when, not too far away, the stagecoach is travelling by with comparative ease."

"I think," said Lucy. "You mean that we should endeavour to find the coach route and use that."

"Yes."

"Then let's do it," said Alfie. "At least we may be able to travel a little faster and it will be easier for Miranda. You never know, we may come across a friendly coaching inn. I'm sure I could earn us some food."

"And I could work in their kitchens," said Lucy.

"And I'll offer my services for their stables and for their customers," added Uncle Jack.

They all looked at one another and began to laugh.

"So we have a plan," said Alfie happily.

"There's only one problem," said Lucy.

"What's that?"

"Which way is the road?"

The silence returned, then Uncle Jack said firmly, "We must travel upwards, out of this valley. It must be drier on the high ground, so that's where we will head."

So they began their journey, pushing and pulling Miranda and the wagon along the muddy track until they reached a fork in the road.

"Upwards and onwards!" exclaimed Uncle Jack, with new-found enthusiasm.

But they were not to reach their destination. Just after midday, when the sun was at its hottest, a young man burst through a hedge in front of them. He had obviously been running and was in a great state of agitation. He grabbed hold of Miranda's bridle so that they were unable to move forwards.

"Stop! You must stop!" he shouted. "You must come at once. My wife is dying, please, come now before it's too late."

31

Later when Lucy looked back, she thought this sudden appearance of the young man marked the beginning of some of the happiest weeks of her life.

Miranda seemed to sense his anxiety and broke into a steady trot despite the rise in the track, for this road was no more than a wagon's width. As they turned the corner they could see it was leading them to a farmhouse. Such a house as Lucy had never before seen.

Crowned by a thatched roof, it seemed to have been constructed of every conceivable piece of building material. Bricks of all sizes, timber, stone and flint, even an occasional piece of broken pottery, it looked as if it should be in a fairy tale. She had no time to gaze at it before the young man, who had been running alongside Miranda and urging the horse to quicken its pace, ran back to her and pulled at her arm.

"Come quickly," he said. "You're a young woman, you must help my wife."

"Calm down," replied Uncle Jack, his years of training as a doctor soon summed up the situation. "Take me to your wife, I will help, Lucy may assist me."

"No, no," the young man was already pulling Lucy towards the open front door. "She doesn't need a man of the cloth, no, not a minister, no not yet."

"Uncle Jack is a doctor," said Alfie. He jumped down from the wagon and pushed the young man away from Lucy. "Do as he says and calm down. You're not doing anyone any good by behaving like a mad man."

By this time they had reached the threshold and it quickly became apparent as to what had happened.

Lying on the floor, sprawled on her back was a heavily pregnant young woman. She was lying in a pool of milk, the upturned churn was by her side and she was laughing.

"Oh dear, Hannibal," she said between giggles and gasps. "Why did you rush off like that? And who are all these strangers you've brought back with you? I don't need a clergyman, I need Mrs Oaks from the village, my time has come, you silly man." She grasped at her side and let out a loud, "Oooh!"

"Madam," said Uncle Jack firmly. "You cannot carry on a conversation like this whilst lying prostrate on the floor. I am a doctor and, with the help of my assistant," he looked at Lucy, "we will endeavour to raise you up and get you to a dry place." There was a box bed in the corner of the room.

"But how can you help me, sir?" she said between gasps. "What can you know of bringing a baby into this world?"

Lucy had already thrown her bonnet and her shawl onto the kitchen table which dominated the room. "Uncle Jack was a doctor before he became a minister," she said, as she helped the young woman onto the bed.

"I would have you know, madam, that I was well known in London as one of the few doctors who could safely deliver a woman of her child. In all my years of practice I lost but one woman, and I don't intend to lose you," added Uncle Jack with some authority.

Lucy signalled to Alfie, who quickly understood her meaning.

"I think we should leave them to their work," he said to Hannibal, who was shaking with fear for his wife. "Perhaps you could show me where we might stable our horse, she's had a long day and needs to rest. Don't worry, your wife is in good hands."

With that he gently turned the young man around and headed him outside.

"Stoke up the fire, Lucy, and make sure there is plenty of hot water, then we must wash our hands thoroughly before we help this young lady out of her clothes," said Uncle Jack.

"Take off my clothes!" exclaimed the woman in horror. "I b'aint taking my clothes off in front of any strange man."

"What is your name?" asked Uncle Jack gently, trying hard not to smile.

"I'm Agnes," she said meekly. "Agnes Liddelcombe, and married to the kindest man you might ever meet. I'm a good woman, I b'aint…"

"Mrs Liddelcombe, Agnes, my dear, you cannot have your baby dressed in clothes that have been soaked in cow's milk and mud from your barn. Now please be sensible and allow Lucy to help you out of your things, so that I may safely deliver your child," he said firmly.

With another twinge coming Mrs Liddelcombe decided it was time to do as requested and very soon Lucy had a pile of muddy and sodden clothes which, for the time being, she tucked under the kitchen table out of the way.

"How did you come to fall over, Mrs Liddelcombe?" she asked, as she gently sponged the woman's face.

"Call me Agnes, my dear." Agnes smiled, despite her discomfort. "I was just bringing in a small churn of milk to start making some butter when I slipped on the flag and went arse-over-head, if you'll forgive the expression, Lucy."

"Flag?" Lucy looked puzzled.

"Why them there flagstones what my husband, Lord bless his soul, did place on our floor with his own hands. We have a proper floor, not mud like some poor folk around here." She grasped at her side again and gave a little moan. "I think this one's in a hurry," she added, "as my dear mother would say, and she should know, she's had plenty."

"You come from a large family then," said Lucy.

"Bless you child, that I do, and I've helped deliver some of my own brothers and sisters. Why my dear mother has

135

had fourteen children and not lost one. I'm the eldest, you see, A for Agnes and… oohh! I think she's coming."

Uncle Jack laughed. "In all my years of delivering babies, Mrs Liddelcombe, I have never yet met anyone like you. You're quite right, now a small push and here we are!"

There was a tiny murmur followed quickly by a lusty cry, as Uncle Jack soundly smacked the bottom of a small, sturdy looking baby.

"You have a beautiful baby daughter, Mrs Liddelcombe," he said with tears of joy in his eyes. "Well done."

Lucy burst into tears, she remembered the young mother in the workhouse who had died giving birth to a very sickly baby. It had happened on the same dreadful day that Amos had died.

"Come, come now, child," said Agnes gently, misunderstanding this sudden outburst. "I'm still here, nothing bad has happened, and look I have a beautiful little girl. I knew it was goin' to be a girl. Go and tell Hannibal of our good news. Please fetch him here."

Lucy ran from the room, glad to be out in the cool evening air. Hannibal needed no second bidding to be by his wife's side. Uncle Jack made sure that all was well and then, he too, stepped outside to join his two friends, pleased to know that he had enabled another new life to enter the world safely.

32

It soon became apparent that Agnes and Hannibal could do with their help around the farm, and so they stayed.

'Perhaps,' thought Lucy, 'this is what Noah meant. We have travelled west and found a sort of Paradise.'

She ventured this idea to Uncle Jack, but he just laughed and shook his head.

"A lovely thought, Lucy, but I don't think so," he said. "We'll help this young couple but we cannot, no must not, stay too long."

But they did.

Lucy busied herself helping around the house, and she surprised Agnes when she showed that she could milk their two cows with some expertise. Her time at the Ark had been very educational. She also surprised Agnes by her interest in local herbs and their uses.

"My father was an apothecary," she explained. She still thought of Amos as her true father.

Uncle Jack revived his medical skills and used them for the animals. Apart from the two cows, Hannibal kept a horse called Jupiter, a sow, a dozen sheep for their wool, chickens, geese and ducks. It was a great deal of work for one man, as he also maintained a vegetable garden. It soon became known in the surrounding cottages that Uncle Jack was a man of great medical knowledge, and folk began to turn up with their own ailments rather than those of their animals. The three friends realised that such attention could be dangerous.

Alfie kept busy stone picking. He was quite convinced that the stones grew overnight. He also helped Hannibal in the vegetable garden, which he really enjoyed.

Lucy thought the evenings were the best, when they would gather around the fireside, talk over the day's work, and plan for the next. It was during these times that they learnt of Hannibal's past and how he and Agnes came to be together.

"I come from a family of solicitors," he announced one evening. "My father thought that I would naturally follow into the family business – Liddelcombe, Liddelcombe and Sons. I am the youngest of four sons and one daughter, but I've never been interested in the law, I've always had a deep longing to work on the land and to have my own farm. I studied a great deal from books and visited the markets whenever I could. I think I take after my mother's side of the family."

"That's where we met," said Agnes. "I was bringing in some of our lambs to be sold at the market and there he was, we just fell in love!" She gave a little giggle.

"Agnes's father owns Trenar Farm, it covers a thousand acres or more," continued Hannibal. "My father bought a small amount of land from him, and the first thing I had to do was to build this house to make into our home. When I did that then they allowed us to marry."

"Then my father gave us a few chickens and a pig to get started," said Agnes.

At this point the baby began to cry and Agnes went to comfort it.

There was a quiet pause in the conversation and Uncle Jack realised that this was the moment when their host was gently encouraging them to reveal a little more about their own history.

Alfie sensed this too.

"I come from Hastings," he said, taking a large gulp from his tankard of ale. "My Pa owned a fishing boat, and he'd come back each day with a boat full of fish which we'd sell to local people and to gentry folk from London, or so my

Ma told me. I don't remember very much about him 'cos he drowned at sea when I was about five."

"I always thought that you came from London," said Lucy.

"Well, I do now," replied Alfie. "You see, after my Pa died, my Ma took me to live with her parents, my Granny and Granfer. Granfer Toby had a barge on the Thames and Granny Toby, well she took in washing from the big houses. We were doing fine until..." He stopped and took another gulp.

There was a long silence.

"Perhaps it's time that we should all be going to bed," said Uncle Jack gently.

"A good idea," agreed Hannibal, thinking that Uncle Jack was closing the proceedings because he could see that Alfie was upset.

Lucy, however, guessed that it was more likely he was concerned that Alfie might reveal too much about their past.

"Sorry," Alfie grinned and looked deep into his tankard. "I didn't mean to sound so miserable. Don't go to bed too early just because of me."

"It's not just that," said Uncle Jack kindly. "We all have a great deal to do tomorrow. Up at sunrise, and it gets earlier every day at this time of the year."

"It certainly does," said Hannibal. "A bit of a mixed blessing really. We can talk some more tomorrow. I'll just make sure everything is locked down securely."

"I'll come with you," said Uncle Jack, giving a groan as he rose from his chair. "It's at times like this when I realise that I'm getting older!"

When they had left the room Lucy turned to Alfie. "I didn't realise that you came from Hastings, Alfie, and that your father had drowned. I'm sorry."

"What for?" answered Alfie brusquely. "It wasn't your fault, there was nothing you could have done about it."

"That's not what I meant," began Lucy. "I just—"

"It's alright," interrupted Alfie. "Just don't go on." He paused and they sat in silence staring at the fire. After a while he turned to her. "Do you want to know why we believe my Pa drowned, how his boat sank?"

She nodded.

"My Pa was an honest fisherman. We had one boat and it was the best. He worked it with his two friends, and they'd done this since they were young lads. You see, my Pa had inherited the boat from his Pa, and it would have been mine if it hadn't been wrecked."

"How did that happen?" asked Lucy, eager to hear the end of the story before Hannibal and Uncle Jack returned.

"A man came to visit us, I found out later that it was Morgan, he wanted us to join his smuggling group. Pa was to collect items dropped in the Channel near certain buoys, and to go out to meet French boats and exchange different goods, even to smuggle in the odd Frenchman."

"A spy?"asked Lucy in horror.

Alfie nodded.

"What did he do?" asked Lucy.

"Well, he refused, of course," replied Alfie. "He even reported Morgan to the authorities. Guess who was in charge?" He gave a short cynical laugh.

"You don't mean, Lord Haggleton?" she asked in anger.

Alfie nodded again. "It wasn't long after that, that Pa's boat was rammed when he was out fishing in the channel. They said it was a bad fog, and that the other boat couldn't see him because he didn't have his correct lights on. Pa and his two friends were thrown overboard by the force of the collision and disappeared. My mother told the authorities that my Pa was a good swimmer and so were his two friends, but they said that they had probably got caught up in the nets and so drowned."

"So that's when you went to live in London."

"Yes," replied Alfie. "My Granfer Toby owned a Thames barge. There weren't nothing he couldn't transport on that barge. I used to go with him and we'd take all sorts of things down to the bigger ships near Greenwich. It was fantastic. Then one day my Ma recognised Morgan near the quayside. Granny said that she ran up to him and started yelling at him, and saying that he'd killed my Pa. Later that day she was killed. They said she wasn't looking where she was going and so the coach couldn't stop in time."

Lucy looked at him in horror. "That's dreadful, Alfie. Did no one take Morgan to court? Did no one ask him to explain?"

"You're very innocent, Lucy," said Alfie. "Who could challenge him? He was, no is, the right-hand man of Lord Haggleton. Who can challenge him?"

Lucy shuddered. What chance did they have against this monster, this evil man?

"And your Granfer Toby? What happened to him?" she asked fearfully.

"Granfer died of a heart attack later that month," replied Alfie. "His barge caught fire whilst it was unloading some coal. They tried to save it but it was no use. The barge was his life and he knew that without it we had nothing. I stayed with Granny Toby and we took in the washing of the well-to-do and we were all right for quite some time because Granfer Toby had left us a small amount of money which he had saved. It wasn't long, though, before Granny could no longer manage the washing, the cold water ate into her hands, and at night I could hear her crying with the pain. She couldn't hold things and then, one night when I was about ten, she just took herself to bed and that was that. She never got up, she just died."

"Oh, Alfie that's dreadful," said Lucy, she was genuinely upset by his story. "Here you are trying to help me, and risking your own life, when you have had such a terrible time yourself. And you have had a terrible time because of people who are supposed to be my relations. It's awful."

141

"Morgan isn't one of your relations," replied Alfie. "And in any case, you can't help having your relations, no one can. I'm sorry to have troubled you with all this. It must be the warm fire and the ale, it's gone to my head."

They sat in silence for a few moments.

"Just remember, Alfie," said Lucy, as she rose to go to bed. "That you will always be my best friend. No matter what happens."

With that she kissed the top of his head and left the room, leaving Alfie by the fireside thinking of what might have been.

33

It came as quite a surprise to the three friends, when the next day Hannibal asked them if they would undertake a very special favour for him.

"You have been here for three weeks," he announced solemnly at breakfast.

"Oh my goodness," exclaimed Lucy, before she could stop herself. "Have we really? Oh dear, what will Noah say? We should have moved on, we should have…"

"Stop, Lucy," replied Uncle Jack quickly. "You mustn't get agitated. I'm sure that your Uncle Noah will understand, in fact I have sent him a letter so that he and my dear sister would not worry about us."

"Really?" Lucy looked at him in amazement.

Alfie gave a cough and said, "Perhaps, Lucy, it would be better to be quiet, and let Hannibal finish his sentence."

For his part, Hannibal merely smiled at Lucy's outburst and said, "Please don't misunderstand me. I don't know how we would have coped without your help during these last few weeks. My favour is this; would you consider staying a little longer so that I may visit my family in Bristol? Agnes cannot travel with the baby yet, and it would be a great relief to me to know that I could leave her here safely with you. I know I can trust you, and when I introduce you to the villagers who call here at our home, you must have noticed that I always introduce you as my friends. This is not said lightly, I cannot explain it, but from the moment of our first meeting I have considered you as such. There, I have said too much. I must let you talk together and make your own decision."

Uncle Jack looked at the others. They nodded.

Uncle Jack smiled. "I don't think we need to have any discussion," he replied. "The look on their faces tells me that Lucy and Alfie would be pleased to stay longer. I think the start of our journey was so hard, that the days here have been like a paradise for us. This stay has helped us as much as it has you and your good wife. But you have reminded us that, when you return, we must seriously begin thinking of moving on towards our destination. You do understand this, don't you?"

Hannibal stood up and warmly shook his hand. "You cannot know how much this means to me," he answered. "I must speak at length with my father concerning matters of finance which affect our ability to remain here. I am also hoping to visit Agnes's parents, who have promised that a sister and a brother will come to live with us. This will be to our mutual benefit. It will mean two less mouths for them to feed, and two willing helpers for us." He shook hands with Alfie too, and kissed the top of Lucy's head. "I'm sure your Uncle Noah won't mind," he said gently. "Especially if he's as pleasant as your Uncle Jack."

The next day he set off on Jupiter with strict instructions from Agnes to be careful, and to keep away from all cut-throats and robbers. Once he had left they quickly settled into a routine of housework, cooking, gardening and caring for the animals. It was during this time that the travelling shearer came to shear the twelve sheep, ten of which had had safe deliveries of lambs two weeks' earlier. Alfie and Uncle Jack spent a great deal of time watching and learning this skill.

It was also about this time that the pedlar arrived. Lucy spotted him first, shuffling around the front vegetable garden. Uncle Jack and Alfie were up on the high field with the shearer.

"I don't like the look of him," said Agnes, as she cradled the baby in her arms.

"I'll go and see what he wants," said Lucy boldly.

144

"Do be careful," replied Agnes. "Here, take this with you." She handed Lucy a large wooden rolling pin. "Just in case," she added with a worried look.

Lucy opened the door and strode purposefully out into the garden.

"What do you want?" she called, making certain that she kept the cabbage patch between herself and the man.

"Good afternoon, sweet one," he croaked. "I was wonderin' if I might interest the lady of the 'ouse in these ribbons, and all I want in return is a drink of cider or ale. Surely that ain't too much to give to an old soldier what 'as served 'is country in far-off lands?"

Lucy turned to look at Agnes who was standing in the doorway with the baby.

"We do not need your ribbons, sir," called Agnes. "But if you remain there, my friend will bring you a tankard of ale."

"You are very kind, dear lady," he replied, pulling at his hat as though saluting her.

Lucy returned to the kitchen and poured out a tankard.

"Be careful, Lucy," warned Agnes. "Keep your distance from him. I will watch carefully."

Lucy carried the tankard out and placed it amongst the cabbages. She glanced up at the pedlar. His clothes were caked in mud and very ragged. He looked as though he had been sleeping rough for some time, she felt sorry for him, she knew how hard it must be as she recalled the early days of their travelling. He gave her a toothless grin, there was a large patch over one eye, and his grey hair struck out in all directions from beneath his hat. He could easily have been a pirate, she gave a little shudder and stepped back.

"Thank you, my sweet one," he gurgled, as he slurped back the ale. "You will never know how much I needed that. Although your mistress says she does not want my ribbons, I will leave you some for your kindness."

He placed a bundle of colours on top of a cabbage and turned to leave.

145

"Farewell, sweet one," he cackled, as he left their garden. "Fare you well, perhaps we shall meet again one day. I am in your debt. Take care of the ribbons."

He left and could be heard muttering and chuckling to himself as he made his way along the lane.

Lucy picked up the bundle, there was something hard and crinkly amongst the ribbons. She began pulling them apart as she made her way back into the house.

"What is it?" asked Agnes. "I told him we didn't want any of his filthy ribbons. What has he given you?"

"The ribbons are really very clean and quite nice," replied Lucy, as she teased out a small package. "Oh!" she exclaimed, and hastily hid it from Agnes. She felt her cheeks burn red, she wasn't very good at lying. "It's just a stone, fancy putting a stone amongst such pretty ribbons."

Whether Agnes realised she was lying was hard to tell, the colours of the ribbons seemed to hold her attention. "These are beautiful," she said. "We should have given the poor man something for them. Perhaps I was too hasty. I will be able to use them to embroider little Annie's clothes. Won't I my lovely?" She gave the baby a kiss on the forehead.

She turned to Lucy. "Now you take a tankard of cider up to the men, I expect they could do with a drink by now. Off you go, I'll be alright, but don't be too long in case that pedlar comes back."

Lucy needed no second bidding and did as she was asked. The shearer had left and Alfie was mucking out the pig sty, whilst Uncle Jack was grooming Miranda.

"Look what I've got," she called, as she approached them.

"Wonderful!" answered Alfie, thinking she meant the cider.

"What's the meaning of this sudden generosity in the middle of the afternoon?" asked Uncle Jack, as he downed the first gulp. "We don't usually have such gifts at this time of the day."

146

"Agnes sent me, and I've also brought this!" she answered, waving the package in the air. She then explained the visit of the pedlar, and about the ribbons. "I recognised the handwriting on the package. It's the same as the soldier's letter near Lyme Regis. I think it's from Noah."

The writing on the outside said, *To My Friends.* Very carefully Uncle Jack unwrapped it. Inside was a map and a letter.

Dear Friends,

Why are you staying here so long? I have been searching for some time, and have at last tracked you down. You must continue your journey to the west where you will be safe, a map is enclosed for your use. LH's militia is but four days away. They have heard reports of a wonderful physician and his two companions on the borders of Devonshire! I wonder who they can be?! Be Careful. Leave as soon as possible.

N

"Did Agnes see this?" asked Uncle Jack.

Lucy felt her face burning again. "No," she replied. "I made up a silly lie that it was a stone. I'm sure she guessed it was something different, she gave me such a strange look."

"Oh, Lucy," said Uncle Jack, stroking the top of her head. "I think tonight we had better explain to Agnes some of our circumstances."

"I'll go back now," said Lucy. "I'll tell her I lied." With that she ran back to the house.

Agnes listened as Lucy began to apologise but then raised her hand and said, "Stop!" Lucy didn't know what to make of this sudden, firm and authoritative Agnes.

"I have thirteen younger brothers and sisters, Lucy," she said kindly. "Do you imagine that I stop loving them each time they tell me a little fib? Of course, there must be things you do not wish me to know, I understand that, just as there are things about me that I don't tell you. We must forget this silly moment and look forward to tomorrow when Hannibal

147

will return with news from his parents and from mine too."
With that she gave the younger girl a kiss and they set about
making some bread together before the baby woke up.

34

As it was, Agnes asked them to defer all their explanations until the next day when her beloved Hannibal would return. This also seemed sensible to Uncle Jack as it meant that he would only have to explain everything just the once.

Hannibal arrived to great excitement and noise the next afternoon. First the geese began honking his arrival, then the dog began barking, and Miranda set up such a whinny when she saw Jupiter that all agreed the whole county must know of his return.

His news was good. His parents were delighted with his progress on his farm, they intended to visit at the end of the month to see Agnes and their new granddaughter. On the other hand, Agnes's parents would be coming in a week's time, they would be bringing Cedric and Elizabeth with them who would stay and help with the farm. Agnes was delighted. Cedric was her second brother, Bartholomew being the eldest, and Elizabeth the fifth child of her mother's large family.

"Then we can leave you with a clear heart," said Uncle Jack that evening, "knowing that you will have your family around you, and reliable help on your farm."

"Leave us?" Hannibal looked puzzled. "There is no need for you to go. I have said that you may stay as long as you wish, and I meant it."

Agnes shook her head. "I think they have to leave, Hannibal. I believe they have had some bad news."

"Tell me," replied Hannibal. He left the table and returned with a large poster. "Tell me something that I don't already know and don't believe." He unrolled the poster and there was a drawing of the likeness of Uncle Jack, Lucy and Alfie. Underneath their faces it read.

FRENCH SPIES
WANTED DEAD OR ALIVE

"Now," he said. "Why would this Lord Haggleton put such a vicious statement out about three of the kindest people I have ever had the good fortune to know?"

"Where did you get that?" asked Alfie, his face had turned a deathly white.

"From my father," replied Hannibal. "If you remember I come from a family of solicitors. Apparently Lord Haggleton has had thousands of these posters printed and they have been sent across the country. The reward is said to run into hundreds of guineas. My father says that few of his friends are interested, most agree that Lord Haggleton is an evil, underhand person who should never have been given such powers, but no one is prepared to challenge him, they are too scared. So tell me what it's all about."

So they did. First Lucy told of her time with her father, the apothecary, and the Nimbles, of her escape and eventual arrival at the Ark with Noah. Then Alfie told his story, the death of his father, mother and grandparents. He said it was all his fault for running away from the Ark. Then Uncle Jack put it all in order and filled in the missing parts by which time it was well and truly dark outside, and little Annie had had her last feed of the night. Agnes put bowls of broth and some of the new bread on the table, all this talking and listening had made her feel hungry.

"So, if I have understood this properly," said Hannibal, tearing a chunk of bread from the loaf. "The militia could be here in three days' time."

The others nodded.

"Then sadly, you must be away as soon as possible," he said. "Agnes, we must help them get everything prepared tomorrow." He turned to Uncle Jack. "I will go through the map with you, Jack, so that you may plan your best route. This man, Noah, obviously means you to get to Cornwall, though I notice that the map he has given you ends just inside the boundary. Clever man, if it should fall into the wrong hands then no one can plot your final destination."

He gave a long hard stare at Lucy. "When you began your journey from The Merry Fiddler you said that Alfie had to dress as a girl, well, why not reverse it." He turned to his wife. "How would it be if, Agnes, you were to dress Lucy as a boy? Then Jack could have his 'two sons' with him and needn't dress as a man of the cloth anymore. What say you, everyone?"

They all thought it was a splendid idea, not least Lucy who had always secretly envied boys and their freedom of movement.

So it was all arranged and, despite her anxiety at the thought of the approaching militia, Lucy slept soundly that night.

35

It had been raining again in the night, the smell of wet grass drifted through the windows, and despite the approaching summer season, it was cold.

"It will be a hard walk," said Uncle Jack, looking at Lucy. "I hope you will not find it too tiring, Lucy."

Lucy glared at him over her porridge. "I'll have you know, Uncle Jack…" she began, but then seeing Alfie's grin and the smile on Uncle Jack's face, she realised that she was being teased.

"I'm sorry," he said. "I have no doubt you will cope as well as either of us but, seriously, this will be a harder journey without Miranda."

The three friends had decided to leave the horse with Hannibal and Agnes. Miranda had formed a firm attachment to Jupiter, and he with her, apart from which, she was an old horse, and they felt they would have more opportunity to travel in less conspicuous areas if they travelled on foot, even if it proved to be slower.

"Come on then, little brother," said Alfie, giving Lucy a resounding pat on the back. "We'd best be getting ready to leave, the sun's already up."

"Careful!" admonished Agnes. " I may have dressed Lucy as a young man but inside she's still a young lady, though I must say, my dear, you have turned out to be a remarkably handsome young man."

Lucy laughed. "Don't worry, Agnes. I will bide my time and have my own back on Alfie later."

"I'm sure you will, my dear," said Uncle Jack, standing up and giving a stretch. "But Alfie is right, we must move quickly. The militia must be but three days away now, possibly two, so we must keep ahead of them."

After several goodbyes, and a few tears between Agnes and Lucy, and many promises to return when the troubles had ended, they set off on their journey. They began the long climb along the edge of the field which bordered the farmhouse. This was a ten-acre field known as Ben's Hill. The track which Hannibal had shown them would keep them away from any main routes and lead them into forests where they might find shelter. Hannibal walked with them for a while to make sure they travelled in the right direction.

"What if some of the villagers talk?" asked Uncle Jack. "What if they say that you've had visitors? You and Agnes could be in danger."

"The folk around here are very discreet and loyal," replied Hannibal. "And even if someone talks, we can readily explain that the two young people were none other than Cedric and Elizabeth, my wife's brother and sister, the physician was but a passing traveller." He looked at their worried faces and smiled. "But it won't come to that. As soon as people realise that the militia comes from Lord Haggleton, no one will raise a finger to help them, you have nothing to fear." He paused and looked towards the horizon. A dark mass began to show in the distance. "There," he said, pointing. "That is Dartmoor. You must skirt that and make your way down towards Bodmin Moor, but do not venture on to either moor, try to keep between them. They can be very dangerous, mists can come down with a suddenness that can take your breath away and your life."

Seeing Lucy give a shudder he mistook her action and he rubbed his hands together. "You are right, Lucy it's very cold, in fact this has been one of the wettest and coldest springs that I can remember." He gave a short laugh. "Some are even saying that we're approaching the end of the world, we'll not get far into 1800."

153

"Do you believe them?" asked Alfie.

"Of course not," replied Hannibal. "I hope to see all of you in the not too distant future, so the world cannot end in 1800! Now leave, go safely and I must return to Agnes."

Once again they made their farewells, and Hannibal turned sharply to make his return.

"Come on," said Uncle Jack. "We must begin our journey once more."

The fog hung like a shroud in the valleys, and as the day wore on so the sun tried hard to burn it away but it was not to be, and by early evening a sharp drizzle began to soak the three friends.

"We'll shelter in that distant copse," said Uncle Jack, pointing to a group of trees. "I think it's about two miles away. Come on, we can easily make that before nightfall."

He sounded optimistic but inside he felt tired and exhausted. This first day of travelling had been much harder than he expected. Alfie and Lucy felt the same, but no one complained, they all knew it was important to put as much mileage as possible between themselves and the following militia.

"Do you really think that we are being followed?" asked Lucy later that evening.

"I don't think so," replied Uncle Jack. "But I think that it would be sensible not to have a fire tonight, just in case someone spots our smoke. Perhaps in two or three days' time we might manage one, but not before then."

"Well," said Alfie. "Let's hope that my shelters will keep us warm as well as dry."

Ever since they had stopped in the copse, Alfie had been busy making small structures from twigs, branches and bracken for them to sleep under.

"That is so clever, Alfie," said Lucy. "Thank you."

Alfie gave a big grin. "I will escort you to your castle, m'lady," he said bowing low. "Oh no, I forgot, you're a boy.

Then you can get in yourself!" With that he gave her a gentle push towards her sleeping quarters for the night.

36

"Are you telling me, Morgan, that these wretched people have employed a giant Chinaman to defend them?"

Morgan looked at the colours which were raging across Lord Haggleton's face. From red to crimson to a deep maroon, they thundered across his countenance. He decided, in the circumstances, that it would be wise to try to placate his Lordship.

"I am not certain as to his size, m'lord," he said quietly. "But there can be no doubt that he is a warrior of some skill."

"A warrior of some skill," mocked Lord Haggleton, mopping his brow with a lace handkerchief which he had taken to using since inheriting his title. "I sent four men to visit that house, they were to collect the next consignment. Are you telling me that this single Chinaman stopped all four of them?"

"I believe, m'lord, he has organised the residents into some sort of army, capable of defending themselves. When I have completed my duties in the west country, I will take great delight in dealing with him personally."

"So, Morgan, is there any *good* news?" asked his master forlornly.

At this point William came striding into the room eating yet another apple.

"Go away! Get out!" shouted Lord Haggleton. "Can't you see we're discussing business."

"Surprisingly, Father," replied William, looking scornfully at Morgan, "I could not see it was a business meeting until after I had opened the door, by which time it was too late, I was already in the room. You see, I have many gifts, but one of them is not being able to see through thick wooden doors."

Lord Haggleton smiled dangerously. "So what has brought about this sudden burst of vitriolic humour? Have you run out of money, yet again?"

"It is the small matter of my forthcoming marriage," replied William, launching himself into a nearby chair. "Perhaps Morgan had better leave whilst we discuss family matters, as this will be of no concern to him as it has nothing to do with business…" His tone was one of contempt for the man standing before him. Lord Haggleton's next words were, therefore, doubly annoying.

"I have no secrets from Morgan and neither should you, he is one of us," replied Lord Haggleton.

"You may not have secrets from Morgan," answered William angrily. "But it doesn't seem to stop you from having secrets from me. I learnt this morning that I am to marry the Duchess of Woolbeck. And who told me? Why the cook, of course! She offered me her congratulations, and I am sure went away giggling. When was I to be let into this little arrangement, I wonder?" He threw the remains of his apple at the wall. "Have you met her? She is at least twice my age. In fact you are better suited to marry her." This last remark was directed with full force at Lord Haggleton.

For his part, his Lordship just smiled.

"Well, William," he said. "This is perhaps the first time I have ever seen you so animated. You will marry her. She is a very wealthy lady, and, as you have so cleverly observed, she is a mature lady who may not be long for this world. You will be a very wealthy man in your own right, once you are married."

Morgan gave a short cough to conceal his obvious laughter. This made William even more angry and he rose from his chair to strike out at the servant, but Morgan was too quick for him and pushed him back down in his chair.

"Did you see that, Father," whimpered William, with a sudden change of mood. "He hit me."

"Morgan did not strike you, William," replied Lord Haggleton, with some impatience. "He merely pushed you back into your chair. Sometimes I wish you had more backbone like Morgan. It would do you good to go with him when he visits the western counties in search of the escaped prisoners. Yes, I think that is a good idea. You will travel with Morgan when he leaves in two days' time."

Morgan looked horrified at the thought of trailing William around with him, but he need not have worried. William looked absolutely petrified.

"You know I hate travelling too far by horseback," said William in horror. "All that bumping up and down makes me feel sick. And I find any form of violence repugnant, it was dreadful when you made Morgan teach me about fisticuffs, such a common way of fighting, not to mention those dreadful classes in sword fencing." He shuddered as he recalled the lessons.

"Perhaps, m'lord," said Morgan, "Sir William is annoyed because he already has his eye set upon another young lady."

Lord Haggleton leant across the desk and peered more closely at William.

"Is that correct, William?" he asked, in a mocking tone. "Have you for once actually made a decision, a choice, as to which young lady you might want to marry? It can easily be arranged, as long as she has money."

William began to bite his nails and just shook his head.

"So this outburst was just because your pride has been hurt, and you don't particularly like the look of the Duchess?"

William nodded, it seemed as though all his earlier bravado had suddenly left him.

Lord Haggleton gave a sigh of satisfaction. "I will make available another fifty guineas for your use at the gaming tables, and in the meantime you will become acquainted with the Duchess of Woolbeck and tell her of your undying love." He burst out laughing at William's sudden capitulation. "When you marry her you will be able to waste your own money in the gambling dens, and leave mine to me."

Morgan looked at William with contempt. "I am sure, Sir William, you will find her to be a woman of great kindness and warmth, in fact, enormous kindness and warmth," he said mockingly.

"Then you marry her!" shouted William. He rose, knocking his chair over as he did so. With a curse he left it lying on the floor and stomped from the room like a petulant child.

Morgan lifted the chair back to its position. "Do I really have to take him with me?" he asked.

Lord Haggleton smiled. "No, of course not. Even I can see that he would be a hindrance. The boy has no backbone, he is an utter waste to the human race, but the thought that he might have to go with you will keep him on his toes. In the meantime, Morgan, let us get down to business once again. So you say, you believe our prisoners to be somewhere below Lyme Regis?" He nodded for Morgan to sit in the chair vacated by William.

"I believe so, m'lord," replied Morgan. "I have taken the liberty of sending a detail of soldiers from your militia, with luck they will apprehend the prisoners quite quickly."

"And those who help them?"

"They will be punished severely, m'lord," replied Morgan.

Lord Haggleton gave a sigh of satisfaction.

37

Mr Nimble surveyed his 'army' with pride. They had all gathered in the Great Entrance Hall, so he was forced to stand on the staircase in order to speak to them. He imagined that this might be as a general felt when addressing his troops after a glorious victory. There they stood, a ragged band of old men, women and children, their faces looking up at him expectantly, but to Mr Nimble they were a triumphant band of fierce warriors, and he was their King Alfred who had led them to victory against the invading hordes. Dear Granny Murphy, how she had wielded her rolling pin, and little Peter Simpson had swung the saucepans at the men's knees with great vigour, but when the cry went up for the Chinaman, Mr Nimble quickly realised that the victory of the day was undoubtedly due to the leadership of Fu Yong Song, and he happily joined in the cheers.

Fu Yong Song bowed to the gathering and held up his hand for silence.

"Well done, my gentle warriors," he said smiling at them. "But this is only the beginning. They will come back in greater numbers, of this I am certain. We must continue to be vigilant, and to practise our skills, it can only be a matter of time before they return."

The people looked worried.

"We thought that would be an end of it," called out one man.

"If they come back with more men, how will we protect ourselves? We'll, no you, will never be able to defeat all of them," said another.

For even if Mr Nimble had been slow to realise it, the residents of the workhouse were only too well aware that without the little man's undoubted martial skills they wouldn't have stood a chance.

"We will all be transported."

"Or hung."

"Then," said Fu Yong Song, "we must make certain that we win!"

"That's what I likes to hear," said Granny Murphy, with such force that everyone laughed despite the seriousness of their situation.

"Now," said Fu Yong Song. "We must care for those who were wounded in our battle and repair any damage to the house. Thomas and I will examine the outside of the building to make certain that the four men who attacked us have indeed left, perhaps some of the younger men will come with us." Three men quickly stepped forward. "Mr Nimble, perhaps you, and your good lady wife, will help in the restoration of this most beautiful house."

"It will be my pleasure," replied Mr Nimble, as, with the help of Mrs Nimble, he hobbled down the steps. He had to admit, this new-found camaraderie made him feel good. Here were people who, like himself, had fallen upon bad times, he no longer viewed them as inmates to be shipped off to unknown destinations, they were human beings, they had feelings, worries, aspirations, and they had become his friends.

Once outside, Fu Yong Song directed the men to search the store houses, whilst he and Thomas made their way to the gardens and the various outbuildings.

None of Morgan's men had stayed, they had been overwhelmed by the speed of attack from the Chinaman, and the ferocity which followed from the residents who were fighting for their lives. They had fled as soon as they felt the full fury of the Chinaman's attack.

"Now, Thomas," said Fu Yong Song. He placed a hand on the young man's shoulder. "You are achieving so much in your garden." Thomas felt a surge of pride. "But," continued his mentor, "I think you can achieve even more. We must be self-reliant, Thomas, we must be able to feed ourselves and to withstand a siege if necessary. We need animals, one cow and a few chickens is not enough. We need a sow, some geese and some sheep on this land and—"

Thomas had to interrupt him. "Mr Fu, stop, you cannot go on saying these things. All these animals will cost money, we do not have such money and we will never be able to pay for their food or care."

Fu Yong Song smiled, he tapped the side of his nose with a finger. "Do not worry, my young friend," he said quietly. "I will get everything. Do not worry."

"But…" began Thomas. He never finished his sentence, Fu Yong Song had turned smartly, strode towards the house, and disappeared inside. A few moments later he returned with a few possessions in a bundle, which he carefully placed over his shoulder. He began to walk down the pathway.

"I will be but a few days, Thomas," he called as he left. "Look after your garden, make certain that everyone continues to practise their skills. I will return shortly with all that we need."

It was all so sudden that Thomas forgot to ask him where he was going, but no one doubted that he would return.

It was early on the fourth morning that there was such a kerfuffle and clatter in the yard, that everyone rushed outside thinking that Morgan had returned with his men. There they found the Chinaman looking very happy and riding a donkey surrounded by two cows, one flustered sow and several geese and sheep. With him were two men who were mopping their brows trying to keep the animals in some order. Everyone started laughing and talking at once, but the Chinaman said that frivolities could come later after the animals had been settled down, fed and watered.

162

Afterwards, when everyone was questioning him and trying to find out where the animals had come from, Fu Yong Song just gave one answer.

"My friend Noah is a very kind and generous man. There is nothing that he would not do to help those who are less fortunate."

Thomas could not help wondering who this Noah might be.

38

Four days of travelling on rough terrain and through heavy showers had begun to take a toll on Lucy, but not once did she complain. Alfie, too, was struggling. His beating from Morgan had been savage and had left him weaker than he cared to admit. He had enjoyed his work on Hannibal's farm but, unbeknown to him, Uncle Jack had kept a close eye on any physical work which he had undertaken. Nothing, however, could protect any of them from this vicious weather. They had been soaked through to the skin so many times that Lucy began to feel that this was normal, but the worst thing was that they could not have any warm food or drink. As Uncle Jack pointed out, a following militia would quickly spot their camp fire, even through these mists and driving rain.

They had stopped at the edge of a small wood. Alfie looked at the piece of stale bread which Lucy had offered him. He bit into it savagely.

"Perhaps, everyone is right," he growled. "The end of the world isn't so far away."

Despite their predicament Lucy gave a small giggle. "You look like an old wild man," she said. "I used to have a book with pictures in it, and you look like one of those."

"Thanks," muttered Alfie.

"This is ridiculous," said Uncle Jack suddenly.

"What do you mean?" asked Lucy.

"I mean," he said firmly, "that we must get ourselves some decent food. We can't live on stale bread and cheese for ever, we need warm food inside us. We need this person, Noah, to make an appearance so that we're not travelling vaguely to the west with no real idea where we are going. We need to take a risk, light a fire and cook some food."

"Wonderful," replied Alfie with a hint of sarcasm. "A great idea, Uncle Jack, but what do you suggest we cook? Cheese and stale bread? "

"I don't know," said Uncle Jack, in frustration. He picked up a nearby stone and threw it angrily at the base of a nearby tree. There was a small squeal, Alfie rushed to the spot, picked up a large stick and brought it down heavily. He turned to the others a look of triumph on his face. In one hand he held the weapon, in the other dangled a dead rabbit. The others looked at him in astonishment.

"Oh!" exclaimed Lucy, not sure whether to be sorry for the rabbit or pleased at the realisation that they could be eating meat that night. "Now, you really are the wild man."

"I don't believe it," said Uncle Jack and started laughing. Alfie let out a whoop of joy and began dancing around, so that Lucy, too, was caught up in the excitement of the moment.

After they had all calmed down, Uncle Jack said, "We must go further into this wood if we are to find a reasonably safe place to cook our feast. You must both know, however, that the smoke from our fire might be seen, so we must be alert and ready to leave quickly if need be. Do you understand?"

They both nodded.

"But," he added with a twinkle in his eye. "I think it's worth the risk, so let's make our way!"

By dusk they had found what they believed to be a fairly safe place, a small glade within the forest. Alfie collected the firewood, Uncle Jack skinned the rabbit, and Lucy made a spit with three small branches. Soon she had it slowly cooking over the fire. From her pouch she took a few dried herbs and sprinkled these over the meat. Alfie collected water from a nearby stream which they heated up in their can, so, as Lucy said, they might make a broth with any bits

165

left over, though secretly she didn't believe there would be anything left over.

As night fell and the glowing embers from the fire continued to warm them, they fell into a contented silence. The meal had been a real banquet, Lucy had eventually placed all the rabbit with the herbs into the pan of hot water, Uncle Jack had found a few parasol mushrooms, and even the stale bread had tasted good when dipped in the juices. The only problem had been that Uncle Jack had insisted on them eating slowly, as he said that it had been so long since they had had any meat, it needed to be consumed with less haste. This was agony for Alfie who wanted to gulp it down with no thought of savouring each bite.

"It's so good to be warm again," said Lucy. "It makes you look at things differently. Somehow when you get so cold and wet and—"

"Hungry," interrupted Alfie.

"Yes, and hungry," said Lucy with a smile. "It seems to stop you thinking properly. It's very strange."

"Not really," said Uncle Jack contentedly. For the first time since leaving Hannibal's farm, he had lit up his clay tobacco-pipe, he took a long draught and blew out the smoke. "We were running out of fuel to give us energy."

"Fuel?" Alfie looked at him. "We were eating a meal, not lumps of wood or coal."

"Food is our fuel, Alfie," replied Uncle Jack. "You see…"

"Quiet," whispered Lucy suddenly. "I can hear something, over there, behind those trees."

They could hear low voices, something or someone was coming through the undergrowth towards them.

"Pick up your things," muttered Uncle Jack. "Move away from the firelight into the darkness. Quietly now."

They moved slowly and cautiously and waited in the shadows hoping that whoever or whatever it was would pass

166

them by. If not they would have to talk their way out of trouble or make a run for it.

Lucy was certain that they could hear her heart beating, and Alfie was glad that he had taken Uncle Jack's advice and not rushed his meal. They waited.

The swishing of feet through grass came nearer, then stopped. All was silent, both groups were listening for one another. A tall upright man suddenly stepped into the clearing, his face obscured in the darkness, he turned to look behind him.

"I'm sure it's them," he whispered. "Come and see for yourself, they can't be far away."

From the bushes stepped the figure of a woman.

"Moll!" cried Lucy, and rushed towards her.

Oh, what a happy reunion it turned out to be, but Nathaniel, for it was he who had come with Moll, soon cut short all the hugs, back-slapping and shaking of hands with an urgent warning.

"If we can find you so easily, how much more quickly can the following militia. Douse your fire and come with us, we are not camped that far away. We can tell stories of our adventures back there."

They hastily killed the fire with earth, water was too precious to use, grabbed all their belongings and followed their friends. Lucy was so happy she wanted to cry. Several times Nathaniel signalled them to stop and listen, once it was a small family of deer moving through the trees, another time a badger, but thankfully they met no other humans. It was a good half hour before Nathaniel beckoned them to stop whilst he went forward into a small glade. Three travellers' caravans were arranged in a semi-circle, a camp fire blazed in the centre. There sitting on logs and warming themselves by the fire were two groups of people. An old man smoking a clay pipe was staring into the embers, he had one arm gently around a little girl who was leaning against him. On another log sat four, it was the stable boy and one of the young girls who used to serve in the inn, the two older people were their parents.

"It's all right," said Nathaniel, as he came into view. "It's me. Moll and I have found our 'lost souls'."

The family clustered round to greet Lucy and her friends. They all remembered her from their time at The Merry Fiddler. The old man stayed sitting with the little girl, his granddaughter, who was nearly asleep.

"Found them living a life of luxury and dining on roast rabbit," said Moll teasing.

"It is so good to see you," said Uncle Jack, with genuine feeling. "It's so good to be back again with friends."

Moll sensed his weariness. "Tonight," she said kindly. "You will all sleep in the shelter of our wagons. Tomorrow we will listen to one another's stories, but for now, we will all get some well-earned rest. Uncle Jack you can share the wagon with us, Alfie you go with Benjamin and Sara, and Lucy you sleep with Silas and his granddaughter, Charity. Kill the fire, Nathaniel. I'll take the first watch."

"No," replied Nathaniel firmly. "I'll take the first watch, Benjamin will take the second. Moll, you must make sure everyone is settled in the wagons with enough bedding and room."

"You're right, of course, Nathaniel," replied Moll smiling. If truth be known she was exhausted. The past few weeks had been very hard, settling folk into their quarters would be so much easier than staying awake on a long watch.

"Come along, Lucy, I'll introduce you to Silas and his dear little granddaughter, Charity, who's very sensible and is already asleep!"

Very soon a silence swept across the camp, just a few snores drifted out on the night air. Whilst the others slept, Nathaniel kept a careful watch on the shadows which surrounded them.

39

"It's been bad, Lucy, very bad," said Moll.

They had spent the next two days travelling westwards. Much to Lucy's annoyance, Nathaniel and Moll had insisted on putting a good distance between themselves and whoever might be following, before setting up camp once more. It seemed that Silas and his granddaughter had no objections and were pleased just to be with them. Lucy was dying to hear the whole story but all she could glean was that times had been very dangerous, and that they must keep their eyes peeled for spies. At last, on the third evening, they settled down before a good campfire, and so Moll began their story.

"A few days after you'd left, Nathaniel noticed a shifty looking rider arrive at the inn. He asked a lot of searching questions about a fair-haired girl and two male companions. Most of our regulars guessed that he might be up to no good. One even asked him if he worked for Lord Haggleton, and he just laughed, and said that there would be a substantial reward for those who could help capture the French spies."

"But we're not..." began Lucy.

"We know that," replied Moll, gently patting her hand. "Anyway the next day a tinker came by and he heard the rider asking questions and he was only too keen to tell about this odd group he had met on his travels, though he wasn't paid as handsomely as he expected. He was found the next day in a nearby ditch with his throat cut."

Nathaniel took up the story. "Folk began to suspect one another, saying that he'd been robbed for his reward money, but Moll and I were certain that it was the rider who took back his money. That night Noah turned up, told us to pack up our belongings, and to get away as fast as possible. He said at the very least, Lord Haggleton's men would be coming to burn down our inn because it was obvious that we had helped you. He also said that I would definitely be hanged for helping traitors and accused of robbing the tinker, and that Moll and the others would be transported to the colonies. We needed no second telling, we were away before dawn the next day."

Moll gave a great sigh. "If it hadn't been for Noah," she gave a little shiver.

"When we left we looked back and could see the blaze from our Merry Fiddler. They'd lost no time in burning it down. We made our way north before turning west, and in this way we were able to avoid the militia. That was Noah's idea. He met up with us again near the Mendips and told us of your meeting with the militia above Lyme Regis. Later he sent us a message about you staying too long at a farm, and he hoped to get you moving west again." She smiled at Lucy.

"He's kept a close watch on all of you and kept you safe. He's a good man, and very brave."

"So why must he always wear a mask?" asked Uncle Jack. "It doesn't make sense."

"It makes very good sense," said Nathaniel, sucking hard on his pipe. "Very good sense if you're a wanted man by Lord Haggleton. You've seen what he can do to a young lad," he pointed to Alfie. "Just think what he might do to a sworn enemy."

They fell into a silence and Benjamin stood up to throw another log onto the fire. "As far as I'm concerned," he said in a low voice. "Noah is the best. He saved my family from transportation, and for that alone I shall always be in his debt."

Lucy turned to Silas. "So where do you come from, sir?" she asked politely.

Although Silas did not speak much it had become obvious to Lucy and the others that he spoke with a very different dialect and accent. He smiled. He had the whitest beard Lucy had ever seen and his long hair fell gently to his shoulders. He had weather-beaten cheeks, and his deep, dark eyes seemed to know everything and see everything.

"I'm a shepherd; little Charity and I come from the north," he said, "high in the Dales and not far from Mickle Fell, though I don't suppose that means much to you. It has been a very bad winter and a following spring. It's been so cold that the lambs, bless them, have frozen in the fields. No matter how hard we tried, how hard we dug into that snow, we couldn't save them. I've never seen so many lambskins on sale. My poor dog, he died trying to dig out one of the ewes. They had to drag me out too, it were so bad, so vicious." He fell silent.

Moll continued his story. "Silas's wife died many years ago, so he lived on his own in his shepherd's hut on the moors."

Lucy thought back to their escape and the night they spent in the shepherd's hut back in Sussex. That had been a cold night but nothing like the nights Silas had described.

"Silas's son and daughter-in-law lived close by, but a few years ago they were robbed and killed by bandits. So Silas had to bring up Charity on his own. It has been very hard for them both, but this last winter he decided to come south and to look for work down here."

"I've been a shepherd all my life," he said, puffing on his pipe. "I reckon I've got a few skills that might be of use to someone down here. Don't you think?"

"I do, I do," said Lucy firmly. She had taken quite a liking to this quiet, kindly man. 'Now this is what a grandfather should be like,' she thought. 'Not like Lord Haggleton.' She gave a shudder.

"It's getting late and a bit chilly," said Moll. She'd noted Lucy's shudder. "Tomorrow we'll make our way towards the next town or village and then we can show Lucy and Alfie how we earn our living. Don't you worry, Uncle Jack," she added, seeing his puzzled face. "I'm sure we can find some work for you too!"

40

Morgan looked worried. The sergeant of the militia had returned at last. Most of the men, who had been with him, had deserted.

"I'm sorry, sir," he said. He had just drunk a pint of ale, quicker than a swift skimming a pond. He had had nothing to eat for two days, so the effect of the drink soon became apparent, it made him feel bold and full of bravado.

"If Lord What's 'is name had bothered to send us our wages, or even sent us some food, then I might have been able to keep the men together. Out of sight, out of mind, that's what the lads said, no one cared about us, so why should we care about them? Answer me that then, Mr Hoity-Toity, answer me that?"

He grabbed hold of Morgan's jacket to prevent himself from sliding onto the tavern floor. Morgan lifted him up by the scruff of his neck and threw him into a high-backed chair in a dark corner of the room.

"Now, you listen to me," he hissed into the unfortunate soldier's ear. "Your task was to find those three escaped prisoners. I don't care what you did when you found them, but what I want to hear is that you did find them, and that you dealt with them. Did you or didn't you?" He grabbed the front of the man's coat and all but strangled him. The sergeant slowly shook his head.

"No," he mumbled. "We was close to them at Lyme Regis, and then that phoney captain sends us on a wild goose chase. We nearly caught 'em in Devon but somehow they got a warning, we nearly—"

"NEARLY! NEARLY!" shouted Morgan. He hit the sergeant so hard around the head that the poor man collapsed across the table. Several of the regulars paused in their drinking and looked towards them.

The sergeant wiped his bloodied nose. Despite his pain, he gave a rueful grin. "You'd best be careful, sir, or you'll get everyone interested in our conversation and I'm sure you don't want that, do you? What would his Lordship say?"

Morgan looked him straight in the eye. "He'd say that transportation would be too good for you." He sat down opposite the sergeant, and turned to glare at the other drinkers. They all hastily turned away.

"But he doesn't have to know, does he?" replied the sergeant. "Couldn't you just tell him that everything has been accomplished like he wanted. I can get paid, and he'll be none the wiser and then we can all get on with our lives. Couldn't you just say…?"

"No, I couldn't," said Morgan, in a harsh tone. "These were spies, sergeant, French spies. If word got out that you let them escape from under your noses, well, it could be classed as treachery. At the very least you could lose your stripes, perhaps even your life."

The sergeant wasn't stupid. He hadn't earned his stripes by giving in to bullies, and his next statement took Morgan a little by surprise.

"Let's look at it another way, sir," he said. "Me and the lads, well, we never thought they was spies. A young girl, and a lad, half beaten to death by you, and a well-known local doctor." He began to raise his voice and so attracted the customers' attention once more. "Yes, a well-known doctor. A more honest and generous doctor as ever anyone here would want to meet." There were murmurs of agreement from some of those at the bar. The sergeant lowered his voice and leant towards Morgan. "So how about paying me a little, sir, on account like, and I'll carry on looking for them quietly. His Lordship will be none the wiser."

Morgan studied the sergeant's face. Despite the blood, he could see that this was a man after his own heart, what's more, he reasoned that he might be of some use to him in the future. It was becoming clear to him that Lord Haggleton was besotted with the idea of capturing Lucy, and he could see that this might easily get in the way of his other more lucrative business, namely the trading of people into slavery. He couldn't allow his Lordship to waste all that money which they had both built up over many years, he had to make certain that, at least, his own fortune would be safe.

"Very well," he said slowly. "I'll see to it that you are paid, and that you have a decent meal and a bed for the night, but you must swear that you will be ready to do what I ask, when I ask. Is that a bargain?"

The sergeant spat on his hand and offered it to Morgan. It was a short curt handshake.

41

The next few weeks of Lucy's life passed in a sea of greasepaint and travelling. The doom-merchants found that, despite their warnings, the world did not destroy itself, no hand descended from the heavens and plucked up all the righteous, nor did the Devil come riding through the villages and towns to collect his followers. It was a quiet time, when folk bent their backs in the daily struggle for survival, but underneath it all, there was the ominous threat of Napoleon and his armies. Would he invade? Was this to be this generation's Armada? French spies were seen everywhere. Lucy and her friends were relieved to be with Moll and her husband's travelling players.

It was Nathaniel's idea that the best place to hide was in a crowd.

"You stick out like a boil on a beauty's nose," he said early on in their encounter. "The best thing for all of you, is to travel with us and use your talents on the stage." He paused and grinned. "In some of my plays," he added.

So that's what they did. Lucy and Alfie on stage, Uncle Jack behind the scenes. It turned out that Silas was a fine fiddler, and could also play the whistle pipe well. Little Charity was keen to show Lucy her own skill of clog dancing. She was so light and nimble on her feet, Lucy had never seen anything so perfect as Charity's dancing to her grandfather's playing. The need to travel west seemed to recede. It appeared as though the militia had stopped hunting them. The posters for their arrest had been torn down by unknown persons or had just rotted in the bad weather, but times were hard, and it was not easy getting their wagons along the muddy tracks but they kept on the move. The months began to slip by.

"Do you know?" said Lucy, one quiet October evening when they were all gathered in the wagon of Moll and Nathaniel's. "I think that today is my birthday, and if I'm right, I am fourteen."

Uncle Jack took a long pull on his pipe. "Oh my," he spluttered. "I do believe you are right, Lucy. Was it really fourteen years ago that I brought you protesting into this world? It doesn't seem possible."

"She's always protesting," laughed Alfie, fingering his soft, new growing, beard. "Just like all women."

Moll gave him a gentle cuff around the ear. "You're not too big yet, my lad, to give you a smack," she said.

"Well," he said ruefully. "No one bothered about my birthday back in March."

"And what about Charity?" asked Uncle Jack.

"And Rowan and Heather?" asked Benjamin, pointing to his two children.

"We've all been so busy, we've not marked any of the children's birth dates."

"Then tonight we will," said Moll, moving to the back of her wagon and bringing out a flagon of dandelion wine which she had been storing for a special occasion. "We'll all drink their health and ours."

"And I'll recite to you one of my monologues suitable for such moments," said Nathaniel, in such a solemn tone that everyone groaned and then burst out laughing.

They all had such a happy evening that they didn't hear the rain on the canvas nor take any notice of the gusts of wind.

In one of the quiet moments Lucy turned to Uncle Jack. "You know, I can hardly remember my father's face, it's dreadful. I try to bring his face into my mind but sometimes it won't come."

"Your father?" queried Moll gently.

"I know you keep telling me that my father was a violinist, that his name was Maurice Duval, that my mother was called Margaret, but I'm sorry I cannot understand it. To me, my father will always be Amos the Apothecary and my mother was Rachel, who died of smallpox when I was little. I just cannot believe that that wicked, ugly Lord Haggleton is my grandfather." She shook her head. "It's too horrible to think about."

"Then don't think about it," said Alfie firmly. "Tonight we are celebrating our birth dates, so let's just think about good things and drink some more of Moll's delicious dandelion wine."

"Oh, no you don't, my lad," said Moll chuckling. "You've had enough already. Don't think I haven't been watching you tipping it back, and besides it's getting late, we have to be up early in the morning to move on."

Everyone reluctantly agreed, it had been a good evening, but it was time to stop.

Uncle Jack was one of the last to leave, he looked at Moll. "She is in denial," he said. "It is not surprising, but how will we ever persuade her to think otherwise?"

"Give her time," replied Moll. "Noah will explain it to her when the time is right, you'll see."

"Noah!" exclaimed Uncle Jack. "I had all but forgotten about him. Where is he now? We haven't seen hair nor hide of him for months. Has he given up on us, do you think?"

"He knows exactly where we are," said Moll, with a knowing smile. "And for the moment he believes this is your safest course, to stay with us, but sooner or later we will all be travelling deep into the west, deeper into Cornwall."

A yell from outside brought them quickly out of the wagon. Silas and his granddaughter were busy grappling with the canvas of their wagon. A sudden gust had broken one of their ropes and the whole top was in danger of ripping off. To add to their problems the rain was being driven horizontally into their faces. Lucy felt as if her face was being pierced by hundreds of little needles. Children and adults worked together to bring the canvas under control. The only light came from their storm lanterns, and as they swirled about they gave the wagon a supernatural appearance, like a giant dragon with wings tethered trying to take off. All the time Silas's belongings were being soaked by the heavy rain. It took some time to stabilise the whole thing. The wagon was declared unusable for the night and so Silas, Charity and Uncle Jack were bedded down in Moll's wagon.

The only problem they sadly reflected on was that there was no more dandelion wine left.

42

William was happy. He looked around the house for Morgan and found him in the library.

"I will not have to marry the Duchess of Woolbeck after all," he said gleefully biting into another apple. "So what do you think of that, eh Morgan?"

Morgan slowly closed the book which he had been about to read and leant back in his chair. "Now, Sir William, what makes you imagine that?" He had one of his supercilious smiles on his face. William controlled the urge to hit him.

"I have been given the task which you have so lamentably failed to complete over the last few years," replied William grandly. "I am to capture the highwayman known as Noah, if I do this, then I will not have to marry the Duchess."

The emotions which contorted Morgan's face changed from anger, at the words 'lamentably failed', to incredulity and then gave way to sheer mirth. His laughter filled the room, it changed from great guffaws to uncontrollable giggles. He pulled a large handkerchief from his pocket and began dabbing his eyes. William looked perplexed and began to worry about the man's sanity, then he became angry as he realised that Morgan's laughter was directed at him.

"What do you find so funny, Morgan?" he asked crossly. "I will catch this ruffian, you mark my words. We are in the nineteenth century, there cannot be that many highwaymen wandering our roads anymore."

"Sit down," commanded Morgan, and pointed to the chair opposite him. William did as he was told.

"You have about as much chance of catching this Noah as you have of sitting on the moon," he said, wiping the tears from his face. "Don't you think I have followed this man's 'career' closely over the years? He is regarded as a present day Robin Hood. The only treasure he seems to take is from Lord Haggleton and his friends. He steals money and property."

"Property?"

"Well, people then, for they are his Lordship's property."

William gave an involuntary shiver and bit hard into his apple.

"It's no good you being squeamish, William. This is how your family makes their fortune. Without the slave trade you would be nothing. Noah is trying to stop that, and we have to stop him, but he is no ordinary highwayman. Sometimes I think he must be in league with the Devil."

"Or the angels?" offered William timidly.

Morgan snorted. "I tell you he has strange powers."

"How?" asked William.

Morgan looked furtively around the library as if expecting some of the characters in the books to leap down from the shelves and attack them. He leant towards William.

"A few years ago, I shot him at point blank range."

"And?" William leant towards Morgan so that their noses were almost touching.

"The bullet made him reel back in the saddle but there was no blood, and although he could have killed me, as he too had a pistol, he didn't. He just laughed, turned his horse and rode away; however, one of his followers decided to do the job and shot me in the shoulder. Luckily he had a poor aim, it was but a graze."

"I remember," replied William. "You made quite a fuss about it at the time."

"Not nearly as much fuss as your continued whimpering about your bruises, when you fell off your horse," retorted Morgan.

"Well, they hurt so much," said William feebly. "It's a long way to the ground from the top of a horse."

"If you hadn't have been drunk you wouldn't have fallen off," replied Morgan.

A stony silence took hold.

Eventually William said, "Did you really shoot him?"

Morgan nodded. "By rights he should have been killed but he wasn't. He was up to his usual tricks the next week. So, as you can see, his Lordship has given you an impossible task." He stood up and made his way to the door. Without looking back he added, "I predict that you will be marrying the Duchess before the year is out." He left and William could hear his laughter as he made his way along the corridor.

William picked up the book abandoned by Morgan and threw it with great force at the closed door.

"I will never marry that woman," he muttered.

43

Fu Yong Song was very happy. He had lived with Mr and Mrs Nimble for many months and during that time he had taught them many things, and they, in turn, had been willing and grateful students. The residents, too, had learnt and developed a variety of skills. Some of the men had become excellent carpenters, one had become a blacksmith, many enjoyed learning about gardening with Thomas, but other pursuits also came to the fore. Among them they found potters, sculptors, painters, poets and musicians, for, as Fu Yong Song said, "Why should the arts be only found amongst the rich? Everyone is born with a talent, one just has to find it, and believe in it."

It was after one of their musical evenings, when they were all gathered around a log fire in one of the larger rooms that Fu Yong Song asked a question which had puzzled him for some time.

"Tell me, Horatio, why are you here? What was this magnificent house before it became this way?" He waved his arms around indicating the broken, flaking plaster which clung to the walls, the cracked stucco and the trailing black cobwebs.

Horatio Nimble looked at his wife who nodded. "You might as well tell him, Horatio," she said. "There is no real shame in it."

Horatio cleared his throat and looked at the assembled company.

"Many years ago, Eliza and I fell upon hard times. I made some bad investments and Lord Haggleton decided to call in our debts. Despite my wife being heavily pregnant with Thomas we were sent to a debtors' prison."

A knowing sigh came from his audience.

"The gaolers were shifty men, open to bribes and deceit, anything to make more money on the side, for they weren't far from poverty themselves. The dreadfulness of it all caused dear Mrs Nimble to have our little baby prematurely."

He reached out and held her hand. "There were no midwives, in fact," he said proudly, "I delivered Thomas myself."

There were cries of "Well done!" "Yes, we did that!" Mr Nimble waited for the comments to ease before continuing.

"Well, when a midwife eventually arrived, she was drunk and incompetent. She dropped the baby, Thomas, on his head. He nearly died, as did my wife from a bed fever caught in that filthy place. I was desperate that I might lose them both. It was when I was at my wits' end that Morgan arrived."

A very audible groan came from the listeners.

"He gave me an offer that I really could not ignore. He said that Sir Haggleton, as he was then, was willing to pay off all my debts if I would move with my family to this house, just north of the city. How could I not agree? I admit I was amazed when I saw it. The size, the enormous rooms, the grounds, it filled me with foreboding. I asked if I was to be just a caretaker, and all Morgan said was, 'For the time being.' They gave us clothes, clean bedding, a room of our own and even food, but it was very strange and somewhat eerie as all the other rooms were vacant. It was obvious that it had once been a grand home, but of the previous occupants, there was nothing."

"Surely you could have found out about the house from the local vicar?" said one of the listeners.

Mr Nimble shook his head. "Anyone who had previous knowledge of the house and its occupants had been removed, or were too petrified to speak. No one wanted to come near us. After a few weeks, when I was beginning to think it was a hideous joke, an army of men arrived with furniture, such as beds and bedding, cupboards, and utensils for the kitchen. It was all placed in the house just as you see it now. Morgan then took me to London to meet Sir Haggleton, I was worried about leaving my wife and young son, but he said I had no choice, no harm would come to them and, if I valued their safety, I had best do as I was told."

"You must have been scared, missus," said Granny Murphy, with heartfelt sympathy.

Mrs Nimble nodded.

"So what did the monster have to say for himself?" asked one of the men.

"He was so civil, I was terrified, his voice could have cut through a man-o-war at twenty paces. He made it very clear, we were to run this 'house of work', he called it, a private workhouse where some of the poor, but mostly criminals, were to come."

An angry mutter went through the group. Mr Nimble looked embarrassed and awkward but continued.

"That is what we were told," he said hastily. "It didn't take long for us to realise that this was untrue. My wife and I were to run this place until Morgan came and took folk off to a better place, then new inmates would arrive. I asked his lordship who had owned this place and he went into a dreadful rage. I thought he was going to kill me, but Morgan intervened and whispered something in his ear. It seemed to calm him down. He told me that it had belonged to a very wealthy family who had fallen upon hard times and so had decided to live in Italy. They had left behind their house in payment of their debts."

"Did you believe him?" asked Fu Yong Song, who had been silent for some time.

Mr Nimble shook his head. "No," he answered. "Something bad had happened in this house, of that I have no doubt. My wife could sense it. What it was I cannot say, but it is a house of tragedy, that's for certain."

"And where did you think they were sending us after you had 'fattened us up'?" asked a woman sitting at the back, and holding her little daughter close to her.

Mr Nimble sighed. "At first I truly thought that you were going to go to better places, where you had the opportunity for work and that the little ones would be cared for. I began to have my doubts just before the arrival of the apothecary, Amos, and Lucy, his daughter. I also saw the toll it was taking on my wife. In order to cope with her feelings of shame and remorse at our work, she began to develop a new persona. She became a hard woman, and this I didn't like."

Mrs Nimble burst into tears.

"It was the arrival of dear Mr Fu which brought us to our senses."

A great cheer went up.

Fu Yong Song held up his hand. "We must not condemn Horatio or Eliza for their actions. How many of you here can honestly say that you might not have acted as they did? Pure evil can come in many forms. It can steal in quietly as a snake into a rabbit burrow, it can appear benign and persuasive to achieve its ends. It does not have to be loud and dramatic, it merely has to play on our fears; fears of torture, of untimely death, of starvation, to name but a few. So unless you are certain of your own reactions, it is wise to give this some thought before condemning them. We should be sorry for them, for here in this great house they are just as much prisoners as if they had stayed in the debtors' prison."

Several older ones nodded their heads.

44

Over the next few days, the three wagons trundled slowly across Devon and even drifted back into Somerset. They presented their travelling show to villages and small market towns, all the time, however, keeping a watchful eye out for possible spies from Lord Haggleton. Their show was very successful, Silas's fiddle playing was always cheered, especially so when Charity donned her clogs and began to dance. Nathaniel's plays were usually farcical comedies and Lucy was very popular as the coquettish maid who always managed to drop everything.

"A bit like real life," teased Alfie.

Lucy liked the market towns; suitably disguised, she was able to wander around the stalls admiring the wares on sale. Silas always made his way to the pens where the sheep were gathered together to await their fate. It was when Lucy was admiring some embroidery that she noticed Silas in earnest conversation with a gentleman standing by a small flock of sheep. They were stocky, heavy-looking sheep with large curly horns, the man talking to Silas seemed to get very animated. Suddenly he shook Silas's hand and turned away, leaving the old shepherd standing there looking somewhat bemused.

That evening, after the show, Moll called them all together.

"I've had some serious news," she said quietly. "It appears that word had got around about us, and that some of Lord Haggleton's friends wish us to perform at Rippleham Manor next week, as part of some birthday celebrations. Lord Haggleton may attend."

Her remarks were greeted by a stunned silence.

"I knew it couldn't last," said Uncle Jack. "We'll leave first thing tomorrow, Moll. You don't want to be accused of harbouring French spies."

"No," replied Moll. "Nathaniel and I have talked about this. "We will take you west, as Noah has advised." She turned to the others. "Sara, Benjamin, you and your children may come with us, if you wish, or you may make your own way elsewhere with Silas. It is your decision."

Before Benjamin could answer Silas gave a cough and stood up.

"If you don't mind, dear lady," he said. "Charity and I have something to say." He gave another cough.

"You may have noticed that whenever we gets to a market, I always goes to look at the sheep. I miss 'em, you see. Today I been speaking to a man what owns hundreds of Dorset Horns, lovely looking creatures they are, quite different from our Wensleydales, which are also lovely, I might add, in fact…"

"Grandad," said Charity kindly. "Just tell them, it'll be all right, you'll see."

"That was the man you were talking to at the pens today," said Lucy, remembering the scene.

"It were indeed, my dear," answered Silas. "His shepherd has passed away, has no family, no one to follow on. He's offered me the job of being his shepherd, and I'd like to go. Travelling around like this is no life for Charity. We should be settled and she should go to school, there's only so much I can teach her and—"

"It's all right," interrupted Nathaniel gently. "We understand. We will miss you very much, but you must do what you think is right for you and for Charity. We all wish you both the very best for your future life. I hope your new master is a good man."

"From what I have heard," replied Silas. "People tell me he is very fair and gives an honest wage for an honest day's work. He will also give me a small cottage on his estate. I've never had a small cottage of my own, not since my poor wife, God rest her soul, passed away many years ago."

"And what about you, Sara?" asked Moll.

Sara looked at Benjamin who nodded.

"We've decided," she said, "to come with you. We'll travel west, like Noah says, and hopefully get away from his Lordship and start anew."

Lucy gave Charity a big hug. "I'll miss you," she said. "Take care of yourself."

Charity couldn't answer for fear of crying.

"Might I suggest we leave at dawn tomorrow," said Uncle Jack. "As soon as it's known that we're not turning up at Rippleham Manor, then Lord Haggleton and his friends will start suspecting something. If, on the other hand, we just move off in the early hours, they may think we've just gone off to the nearest town for awhile."

The others agreed.

"We'll pack away now," said Moll. "We can then leave at first light. We'll miss you, Silas. God speed."

They all said their farewells and then began preparations for a speedy departure in the morning.

45

"It's good to be travelling with other people, isn't it?" said Lucy.

She was sitting at the front of the wagon quietly marvelling how Alfie was coaxing the horse through a sea of mud.

"So you'd rather be with Moll and the others than just poor old me and Uncle Jack, is that it?" teased Alfie.

"No, no," Lucy blushed. "I didn't mean that at all, what I meant was…"

"It's all right, Lucy," laughed Alfie. "I was only teasing you, but I'm not teasing now when I say that I think Peg could do with a bit of help at the front. This mud is really slowing her down, she's struggling. You take the reins and I'll lead her."

"No, it's all right, I'll do it," said Lucy, and jumping down from the wagon she very nearly slipped under the front wheel.

Moll came alongside, she'd been helping Sara whilst Benjamin and Uncle Jack were trying to sleep, they had taken the early shift with the horses. Nathaniel had gone on ahead to check the road, well, what was left of the road, the winter rains were gradually washing it away.

"It's no good," she said. "Peg needs a rest. This long climb will be the death of her. We'll have to stop awhile."

"Does it ever stop raining in the west?" asked Alfie. "All we ever seem to do is push carts and wagons through a sea of mud."

"These are the winter rains," replied Moll. "They can be very bad and we're lucky they haven't yet turned to snow. It'll come soon, mark my words."

"That's all we need," grumbled Alfie.

"Ah, but when the sun shines, then these hills and tors can become the most beautiful place on earth, you wait and see, my lad," she said with some feeling.

"Have you been here before?" asked Lucy, sensing the pride in Moll's voice.

"I was born in Cornwall," said Moll. "I would never have left but for Nathaniel, now there's love for you." She laughed.

Just then her husband returned, and seeing their predicament agreed with Moll that the horses needed a rest. They pulled off the track and unhitched both of them.

"It's not far now, Moll," he said. "I've seen the sign, just as we left it. I don't think anyone has been along that track since we last came, two years ago."

"I expect Noah's used it but you would never know," she replied. "He always covers his traces. Like a ghost in the night, he comes and goes."

"Who is Noah?" asked Lucy once more. "And why does he always keep that mask on? I know he has a scar because I've seen a bit of it peeping out from under his mask. Is he badly disfigured?"

"What a lot of questions," replied Moll. She gave Lucy a smile. "It's no use you asking me that, my dear, I am sworn to secrecy, he'll tell you when he's ready."

Benjamin and Uncle Jack woke just before midday, it was already getting dark. Nathaniel told all of them that the next part of the journey would be hard, and that they must do what they could to help the horses over the long climb. There was little talking, all of them helped to push the wagons through the mud, even the smaller children.

"Well done, Heather," said Lucy, encouraging the little girl by her side, who was panting with the effort. "We're nearly there."

At the top they paused.

"Oh my," was all that Alfie could say.

The view was overwhelming and there, in the distance, was the unmistakeable grey, silver strip of the sea.

"No stopping, I'm afraid," said Nathaniel. "I want to be at the mine before the sun sets, we have about another two miles to travel but the road is much kinder this way."

"What mine?" asked Lucy, looking at Alfie. He just shrugged and shook his head, he had no more idea of where they were going than she did.

Winter daylight is scarce and the last mile was difficult, but Nathaniel was sure of the way and that gave the travellers confidence. He led Peg by the head, coaxing her every step of the journey, she trusted him and the following horse, Mars, was happy to pull his wagon behind her. Lucy pointed out the sign as they turned right at the last fork. They could just make out the words; *To the West Mine*. Underneath someone had written; DanGer Do nOt Enter.

"This way," called Nathaniel.

Lucy was completely confused. Why would they be going to a disused mine, and one that had a warning of danger? They moved along in silence, only the jingle of the harnesses and the clunk of pans were audible. Suddenly Nathaniel held up his hand for them to stop.

"We're here, Moll," he said quietly.

Moll slid down from her seat and held her lantern high. It swung back and forth casting great shadows of light. There in front of her loomed giant, cavernous, iron doors. They were securely padlocked, though the padlock itself and the chain looked ancient and rusty. Nathaniel produced a key which turned sweetly in the lock, its age was an illusion. He beckoned to Uncle Jack and Benjamin and together they pulled away the chain and lock and began to push open the giant doors. Although everything had been made to look old, it soon became obvious to Lucy, and the others, that all the mechanism was in perfect working order. Behind the doors was a portcullis which Nathaniel was able to winch up on his own. He then signalled Moll, who quickly urged Peg and the wagon into the entrance, she was immediately followed by Sara driving Mars.

Nathaniel turned to Moll. "I shall go back a little way to make certain that we have not left any tracks. You take everyone through to the others. I'll follow on as soon as possible."

"Be careful," warned Moll, as she gave him a kiss.

"Don't worry, old girl," he said fondly. "We're safe now."

With that he left them.

Lucy looked around the dark, vaulted entrance. Apart from Moll's tiny lantern everything was dense blackness.

46

Alfie couldn't help it. As soon as the portcullis slid down he let out a whimper. He realised the sound must be coming from him because, at the same time, he couldn't stop his body from shaking. As the great iron doors began to close he felt an uncontrollable panic rise up inside him. He fell against Lucy who was standing by the wagon wheel.

She gave a gasp as his full weight pushed her against its rim. "Whatever is it, Alfie?" she asked.

Uncle Jack was quickly by his side, the others hadn't noticed, they were too busy lighting tar torches from the one precious lantern.

"Breathe slowly, Alfie," he commanded, "slowly and deeply. Come on, lad, you can do it, slowly and deeply. Fan him, Lucy, find a cloth, anything that you can use to waft some air towards him."

"What's happened to him?" she asked anxiously.

"We mustn't forget that when you and I were thrown into Lord Haggleton's prison, Alfie had already been held a prisoner there for several days. Held in the dark, Lucy, and only taken out to be tortured and beaten by Morgan. The sudden blackness in being confined here has triggered those memories. Keep moving that cloth, Lucy. Can you hear me, Alfie? Nice and calm. Slow breaths. Nice and calm."

At this point Moll and the others came to the side of the wagon carrying their torches and lanterns. A yellow light shone all about them, whilst their shadows crept up the cavern walls.

"Are you all right, Alfie dear?" asked Moll. She felt his forehead, it was very damp.

Alfie took another deep breath and nodded.

194

"I'm sorry," he said, looking at all their anxious faces. "I didn't mean to worry you. I just couldn't stop myself. It brought back all those feelings and…"

"No more," said Uncle Jack kindly. "You're amongst friends now, and you'll never have to face that monster, Morgan, ever again. I give you my word on that," he added grimly.

"There are many of us who have scores to settle with that creature," said Moll. "But," she added with a grin, "I think Noah is the one who has the biggest claim to settle it. Now listen everyone…"

They all gathered around her, keeping close to the light, for despite Nathaniel's words earlier, that they were all now safe, none of them felt that way. The high, dark walls of the cavern glistened in the light of the torches. Water dribbled down the sides, forming puddles on the floor before draining away into some obscure underground stream.

"This cave entrance started out as a tin mine but was quickly abandoned because men refused to work here. There were a series of accidents, people were killed in explosions, and the floor of one of the sections gave way, because no one realised that it had been undermined by the sea. That section is now sealed off," she said hastily, seeing their worried faces.

"Now," she continued. "I know my way through these tunnels. Noah and his friends used them, and extended them, so as to make an escape route for those poor souls being hunted or condemned by Lord Haggleton. I will lead the way with this torch. You, Alfie, can drive my wagon, Lucy sit with him. Uncle Jack, you walk with me with the lantern. Benjamin, you walk ahead of your wagon with the second torch, and, Sara, you drive. Rowan and Heather, you must stay in your wagon and on no account must you try to get out. Do you all understand?"

Everyone nodded.

195

"It's going to take us two maybe three hours to make our way through these tunnels. It's not going to be easy, but we'll get there, you'll see. There can be rock falls, so be on the watch and don't make too much noise. Watch Mars, Benjamin, he may not take kindly to the dark, Peg has done this trip many times, I have no fears for her. Now, everyone, let's have a quick drink before we set off on the final part of our journey."

They all took a swig from the flagon which Moll passed around and then wishing each other good luck they took up their positions. Lucy climbed up next to Alfie and suddenly gave him a great hug and a kiss on the cheek.

"You're not to worry," she whispered. "I'll be here for you."

Despite his earlier fears, he couldn't help smiling at her.

"Thank you," he said, and kissed her on the forehead.

Slowly the two wagons rumbled their way along the uneven floor. The drivers keeping their eyes securely fixed on the leading torch bearers. Every now and then Moll, would point out a rockfall which they would have to skirt or a particularly strong flow of water cascading down the rocks, but all the time the torches burnt they were safe. Moll unerringly led them past dead ends and false trails, without her they would have been lost.

They had been travelling for over an hour when Moll held up her hand for them to stop. Throughout their journey they had become used to the moaning of the wind, which at times seemed determined to extinguish their torches, but this was no ordinary moan which they now heard, it was more a roar followed by a thud, as if something was pounding a flat drum.

"It's the sea," called Moll, pointing to a shaft on their left. "The tide must be up and the sea is being driven into the borehole. Take care of the lanterns, the wind may well blow out our torches."

And she was right. No sooner were they level with the shaft than a great wind roared through, sending the flames in a horizontal direction. The torches failed and now their only light came from the two small lanterns. Lucy gripped Alfie's hand.

"It's all right," he whispered. "I'm here."

She withdrew her hand. "I'm supposed to be caring for you," she replied indignantly, and they both laughed.

Once past the roaring wind tunnel, Moll stopped so that they could relight their torches from the lanterns. "It's not far now," she said.

And it wasn't.

Suddenly, in the distance, they could see other lights coming towards them and soon they could hear voices. One sounded remarkably like Nathaniel.

"Well done, everyone! Well done!" His unmistakeable deep voice boomed out.

"Well done indeed," said the second man.

It was Noah.

47

They emerged from the tunnel with the cliff face towering on their right-hand side, and on their left, a steep drop down into an agitated sea. The path before them wound its way down into what appeared to be a village. It was hard to make out, they had exchanged the darkness of the tunnel for the turbulence of the night. A full moon had dragged in a sea tormented by the wind. Clouds flew past the moon like witches rushing to a coven, the slapping of ropes on masts resounded round the bay as if applauding their flight, and all the time the waves boomed as they hit the rocks. Lucy had never heard anything quite so terrifying. The horses panicked, and it took all of Nathaniel and Noah's skills to calm them down.

"Jack!" shouted Nathaniel, as he unharnessed Peg. "You lead her down the path. Just keep to the right of the path, you can't go wrong. Ben, unharness Mars and follow on."

Both men nodded.

Moll was already tying down some of the items in her wagon, and she signalled Sara to do the same. Lucy and the others quickly helped. When all that could be tied down was deemed secure, they sheltered in the entrance to the tunnel and waited. No one spoke, partly because of tiredness, and partly because it was futile to try speaking above the noise of the storm. Alfie was, probably, the only one present who found the whole experience exhilarating. The smells, the sounds, all brought back deep memories of his father and grandfather. He had no doubt that this was where he belonged, close to the sea.

As their eyes became accustomed to their surroundings, Lucy could make out two giant shapes slowly approaching them up the steep path. Voices of several men could also be heard, including that of Uncle Jack. An occasional spark seemed to flicker from the path as these monsters approached. Two enormous shire horses emerged from the dark.

Nathaniel went straight towards them and stroked their heads. "Ah, my gentle giants," he said fondly. "It is so good to see you again."

"Peg and Mars would never have made the descent with our wagons," explained Moll to Lucy and Alfie. "But Atlas and Hercules are used to it, they're always travelling up and down these hills with heavy loads. They'll get it all down safely with a little help from the men."

The men, who had come up with the horses, began to loop ropes around the wagons. Noah was quietly giving them instructions. It was obvious that he was their leader. When the horses had been made ready, Noah called to the men to take the strain so that the wagons could begin the journey into the village below. Nathaniel drove one wagon, Noah the other. On such a stormy night even great shires like these found the steepness difficult to negotiate, sparks rose into the air as their giant feet bore down on the cobbles. By the time they were half way down the hill, everyone was taking the strain on the ropes, even Rowan and Heather. It was a long and difficult journey. All the time the wind buffeted them and the only respite came when, occasionally, the path took a short turn away from the sea in order to cope with the gradient. As they neared the first of the cottages, it became apparent that the path was only just wide enough for such wagons as these to pass through, those men holding on to the sides had to move to the back. Nathaniel and Noah could be heard encouraging the horses to pull their heavy loads through these narrow gaps. At one point it was thought that the lead horse, Atlas, would be unable to pull the wagon through, so small was the path between the cottages, but some careful handling by Nathaniel and extra pushing from the men gradually freed everything up and they were able to resume their journey. The offending house was left minus a windowsill.

At last they reached the bottom and the path opened out into a wide cobbled square. Here they made a welcome stop. Several women suddenly appeared from the shadows, and Lucy and Alfie heard voices that they had almost forgotten.

"Lucy! Alfie!" came the sounds. "Is it really you?"

It was Nelly Mere closely followed by Polly Sneed.

"You've come at last," said Nelly. "You've taken so long. We'd almost given up hope."

"I was so worried about you, Alfie, even though Noah kept telling me that you would be all right," said Polly, flinging her arms around Alfie, much to his embarrassment.

"Lucy!" A third voice broke through the general hubbub, as a diminutive figure launched itself upon Lucy. It was Alice.

"The others will be so pleased to see you, Lucy," she said, hugging the older girl so hard that Lucy gave a gasp.

"I told you to stay in bed, Alice," said Nelly with mock sternness. "You should be asleep."

"Oh, Mrs Mere," sighed Alice. "You don't mean that, do you?"

Nelly laughed. "No, I suppose not." She turned to Lucy. "Now you and Alfie, plus Uncle Jack, are to come back with me for what is left of the night. Moll, dear, you and Nathaniel are at the inn as usual, and Sara you and your family go with Polly. We'll meet up at noon."

Everyone agreed, and it was only then that Lucy realised that the wagons had moved away, as had some of the men.

The cobbled square suddenly seemed quiet, even the storm seemed to have calmed down, and the clouds of witches had finished their crazy ride across the moon.

"Where's Noah?" she asked peering into the dark.

Moll laughed. "He's long since gone, my dear," she answered. "No doubt we'll see him again when he's ready."

48

Lord Haggleton was angry, was there ever a day recently when he wasn't angry? Today, however, he was distraught with anger. Firstly, William had flatly refused to marry the Duchess of Woolbeck, and no amount of persuasion or threats would move him. Secondly, Morgan had apparently sent three men to the Nimbles to find out how or why they were disobeying orders. There had been no movement of people to or from that establishment for many, many, months, which seemed preposterous. The three men had disappeared off the face of the earth, nothing more had been heard about them. Thirdly, his sergeant-at-arms had let it be known that he was now in the employ of Morgan, which was outrageous. He never did trust Morgan, the man was too fond of his own self-importance. As far as Lord Haggleton was concerned there was, and could only ever be, one person in charge of this whole venture, and that was himself. He decided to forget the problem with William, that could be dealt with later, but the sergeant was a different matter. He decided to visit him at the local tavern.

The woman behind the bar spat on the glass and wiped it with a dirty cloth. She eyed the stranger up and down. Toffs like this didn't normally frequent her establishment unless they were after something other than drink.

"So how might I help you, sir?" she asked, trying hard to be coquettish.

The stranger snarled at her. "Forget it, you old hag. You're way past your prime and most likely riddled with lice. I understand a sergeant is staying here, take me to him."

The woman looked angry. No one spoke to her like that and certainly not in her own establishment. The stranger only had one companion with him who looked very nervous, she gave a nod and two of her cutthroats appeared from behind the bar.

"I think this geezer needs to be taught a lesson, boys," she said nodding towards the stranger.

Lord Haggleton gave a sigh and threw back his hood. "I think this apology of a woman needs to mind her manners, and answer my question before I decide to have her transported."

The woman gave a gasp and fell to her knees. "Oh forgive me, your honour. I meant no harm. I can't just divulge the names of my guests to strangers. I was only protecting my customer. You do believe me, don't you?"

Lord Haggleton threw a gold sovereign at her. "Now where is he?"

She snatched up the coin and pointed up the stairs. "Back room."

Lord Haggleton followed her directions hastily accompanied by his footman, who followed, more out of fear than as a protection for his Lordship. They made their way up the wooden stairs, an abominable stench of alcohol and vomit filled their nostrils.

"Oh, m'lord," sniffled the footman. "Is it wise for you to be taking in such dreadful odours?"

"Probably not," came the curt reply. They had reached the end door and Lord Haggleton raised his boot and kicked hard, the door flew open. The smell in here wasn't much better. The sergeant lay sprawled on his bed, the money given to him by Morgan had not found its way out of the tavern, sadly he had decided that his thirst was greater than his hunger. Somehow he realised that he was in the presence of a stranger. At first he thought it was Morgan but then, as his vision began to clear, he saw that it was His Lordship. Slowly he staggered to his feet, clumsily trying to button up his tunic at the same time.

"Oh, my gawd," he slurred. "It's you."

Lord Haggleton looked at him in disgust. "Did I not give you the task of finding the three spies?"

The sergeant nodded.

"And did I not say that you were to report to me personally about all your findings?"

Again the sergeant nodded.

"So why have my informants told me that you were seen here making a deal with Morgan? When were you proposing to tell me about it? Do you know where the spies are? No, of course you don't, you've been wasting your time here, carousing with women and other like-minded vermin."

"It weren't like that m'lord," pleaded the sergeant. "Morgan made this proposition to me. You see we, your militia like, we hadn't eaten or slept for some time, we was desperate, he gave us money—"

"Which you promptly spent on drink," interrupted Lord Haggleton angrily.

The sergeant fell to his knees. He could sense that this was a dangerous moment for him. Disobeying orders had never been part of his life, but he had known from the beginning that the three absconders had not been French spies, and he had felt all along that he and his men were being used to carry out a secret vendetta on that little girl. It was then that he made a mistake.

"What is the girl to you, your Lordship? Why is she so important?"

Lord Haggleton turned his back on the sergeant and signalled his footman to leave the room. The footman hesitated.

"Wait outside," he commanded. "This is private business, make certain no one is listening." The footman obeyed.

Without turning back to face the sergeant, he said softly, "Stand up, man, you're a soldier not a snivelling wretch. Brush yourself down and straighten yourself up. You should take a pride in your appearance. Of course you want to know about the girl, a pretty little thing by all accounts."

He could hear the sergeant struggling to stand up and making an effort to tidy himself up. Suddenly he swung round and looked the sergeant straight in the eyes.

"But sadly you will never get the opportunity to know," he said softly, and plunged his dagger deep into the sergeant's heart.

It all happened so quickly that the sergeant had no time to even call out. He fell to the floor with barely a sound, a look of surprise upon his face. His Lordship carefully wiped the blood from the dagger onto the sergeant's tunic.

"I cannot abide a traitor," he said quietly, as he kicked the body towards the bed.

The footman was waiting nervously outside as requested.

"Are you all right, m'lord?" he asked anxiously.

"Never better," replied Lord Haggleton.

They left quickly.

That night he called for Morgan to come to his library to talk and perhaps have a glass or two of ale with him. William was not about.

"Ah, Morgan," he said benignly, indicating that he should sit by the fire with him. "We haven't had much of an evening together for some time, have we? I thought tonight would be a good time to go over one or two of our business deals. What say you?"

"Very good, m'lord," replied Morgan. He had learnt over the years that when his Lordship was in these moods it was always best to agree.

"Have you heard any more about the three idiots you sent to the Nimbles?"

"No, m'lord," replied Morgan, a little uncomfortably. "I am very angry about it, but I plan to send a young man, another Chinaman, there as a spy. As you know, it has been reported that the Nimbles have acquired a Chinese friend and, I thought that perhaps the sight of a fellow countryman might take him off guard. What do you think, m'lord?"

"An excellent idea, Morgan, excellent," replied his Lordship. He held up his tankard as if about to examine its contents. "Now how about my militia, what has happened to them and to their sergeant?"

Morgan paused. "I regret to say, m'lord, that I believe they may have absconded. There has been no news of them for some time now."

"Really?" replied Lord Haggleton, suitably surprised. He stood up and gave an exaggerated yawn. "Well I must away to my bed." As he reached the door he paused and turned to face Morgan. "By the way, there's a little job I have for you, tomorrow will do. It has been brought to my notice that the woman who runs the local tavern has murdered someone. Please check that out, Morgan. I understand that the body is in the back room, and the woman has also stolen a gold sovereign from that unfortunate man. I have made certain that nothing is moved until you go there tomorrow. Goodnight."

49

Morgan paused by the kitchen door. He leant against the woodwork, took out his small dagger and began to clean his nails.

"Oiy!" shouted the cook, she was afraid of no one. "Don't you go doin' such things in my kitchen. You may be the bee's knees with his Lordship but in my kitchen you ain't!"

"Be quiet woman," he retorted. "I'm thinking."

"Oh," she answered, mockingly. "That must be all the screechin' and clankin' I can hear. Yer brain's not used to such work." She gave a chuckle as she continued making her dough.

Morgan ignored her. That morning he had been to the tavern. The mistress had left in the night. She wasn't silly, she knew that his Lordship would be back as soon as she discovered the body of the poor unfortunate sergeant in the back room. Lord Haggleton had placed guards on the door, but there wasn't a secret passageway that was unknown to her in this inn. She hadn't worked there for ten years for nothing. She made her escape that night, taking her gold sovereign with her.

The buzz of the flies and the stench was almost more than even Morgan could stomach, but he did his job, everything was cleared away, posters were displayed stating that the woman had killed the sergeant, and had robbed him of his money. Nothing was left that might incriminate Lord Haggleton, but Morgan realised that he, too, could be on sticky ground. The young Chinaman would be the answer.

Out loud he said, "I must release the Dog Master."

"Release the what?" asked William. He had just entered the kitchen via the courtyard door. "Hello, darling cook," he said, giving her a hug. "Have you got anything for me?"

"Oh, Master William," she blushed and pretended to be shocked. "Whatever would his Lordship say? Here you are, you naughty boy."

She handed him a large chunk of bread which had been dipped in a generous amount of dripping.

"Disgusting," sneered Morgan. "You should know better."

"So who or what is the Dog Master?" asked William, chewing on his bread, and making sure that nothing dripped onto his fine clothes. "It sounds rather fun. Is it to do with dog racing? I fancy a bet or two this week."

Morgan looked at William with contempt. The boy, he still thought of William as such, might be stupid but he could prove useful if things went bad with Lord Haggleton. On the spur of the moment, he decided to take him into his confidence.

"Come with me," he said curtly.

William hastily ate the rest of his bread and dripping.

Morgan took William out into the yard where he called a coachman to come and take them, in the unmarked coach, to the docks. There was no point in advertising the fact that he was about to take William into the East End of London. Once there he ordered the driver to stop outside one of the more derelict warehouses where several unpleasant looking men were lounging around the entrance.

"It's all right, lads," he said. "He's with me." They parted and let them through.

"Are these your men, Morgan?" asked William, trying to sound suitably impressed.

Morgan merely nodded and strode into the warehouse. It was very dark inside and William found it hard to get his bearings. The windows were so caked with cobwebs and grime, very little light could get in or out. Against a side wall were railings indicating a staircase going down. Morgan made his way towards it, and accepted the lantern given to him by a burly, bald-headed man who had suddenly stepped out from the gloom. No words were exchanged. William followed.

The smell of the tide ran through the basement and sea water swirled around their feet. William had never been to this place, in fact he had had no idea of its existence until this moment, he was certain that they must be walking below the river level. They had walked only a few yards when he heard the howling and barking of dogs, someone was trying to calm them, there was no shouting, just a quiet voice speaking in a foreign language.

"I'm coming in," shouted Morgan. "Keep the dogs under control if you know what's good for you. I've brought a friend with me."

With that he pushed open the door which confronted them. It was heavy, like a prison door and had a minute hole covered by a thick grating. The smell of dogs which had urinated and defecated all over the floor caused William to retch. He hastily placed his silk 'kerchief over his nose and mouth.

"You'll need a stronger stomach than that, William, if you're going to be of any use to me," snapped Morgan. "Look, behold the Dog Master!" He uttered a cruel laugh.

William could just make out the figure of a small, thin man huddled in one corner and surrounded by dogs of all kinds. It was difficult to guess his age, he looked so gaunt and emaciated, but William guessed he could be in his mid-twenties.

"Do you know who this is?" asked Morgan, as if he was about to uncover the greatest scientific conundrum ever known to man.

William shook his head.

"This is the eldest son of Fu Yong Song, the annoying little Chinaman who is helping the Nimbles to disobey your father."

At the sound of his father's name the young man growled and all the dogs joined in.

"Quiet!" shouted Morgan. "I am going to return you to your father. I knew you were going to prove useful one day."

"But why are you bothering to return him now?" asked William haughtily, not taking his eyes off a particularly large dog which seemed to be getting closer all the time.

"Ah, William, I can see that you are really one of us, you'd like us to keep him. He is very good in the dog fights, I must agree," said Morgan, misunderstanding completely William's question.

William gave a quiet shudder.

Morgan guided William out of the room. Such a wailing and barking followed them that they could not speak until they were out in the fresh air. Morgan stopped and spoke to one of the men, who gave a nod of agreement.

Whilst they were returning home in the coach Morgan explained. "He has been with us for over ten years. Lord Haggleton wanted me to throw him overboard like his brother but I decided to keep him. I felt he could be useful one day. We found that he had a natural way with dogs, he can calm them and they will do anything for him, so he became known as the Dog Master. He doesn't speak any English and he believes that his mother is still alive, and the only way she will stay this way is if he does as we say."

"Is she alive?"

"No, of course not, but that doesn't matter as long as he believes it," snapped Morgan. "Now his father, Fu Yong Song, is on a mission to find his eldest son. And this is the clever bit." Morgan gave a chuckle at his own brilliance. "When someone is on a mission and it succeeds, what do they do? Well, they go off on another one, don't they?"

William nodded.

"I'm betting that when Fu Yong Song gets back his son, he'll be so overjoyed that he'll stop playing silly games at the Nimbles, he'll take his son back to China with him, and leave the Nimbles, and that's when we move in."

"I'm sure you are right, Morgan," replied William, thankful that the coach was now entering his home courtyard. "I wish you well in your venture, if it succeeds then his Lordship will be delighted, but please do not ask me to go there again, the smell is vile and," he added looking down at his shoes in horror, "I think I have trodden in something equally vile."

He scrambled down from the coach.

"Oh my," he exclaimed. "This is appalling. My shoes, my stockings, they've all been ruined. Oh and the smell! I must have a bath and rid myself of these clothes."

He stumbled towards the door to the kitchen, thought better of it and made his way to one of the servants' entrances, leaving Morgan congratulating himself on what he believed was a brilliant plan. William, he thought, would be much easier to control than the present Lord Haggleton.

50

"And so, you expect us to believe that you wish to leave the employ of Lord Haggleton and come to live and work with us?" Mr Nimble sat back in his chair and stared at the three dishevelled men standing before him. They all nodded.

"By rights, we should return you to the authorities," continued Mr Nimble. "But I have to agree with Mrs Nimble that there is no point in doing that, as everyone is in the pocket, or terrified of, his Lordship. But how do we know that we can trust you?"

"You can, sir without a doubt," said the tallest man. "We have no stomach for the work which Morgan and Lord Haggleton now expect from us. We cannot understand why his Lordship hounds that young girl, nor why the local doctor has been forced to flee the area."

"If you will allow us to stay, we'll work 'ard for our food and lodgings, that's for certain," said the small, slightly stout, man. "It's a long time since we 'ad a decent meal."

Mr Nimble looked at Foo Yong Song who nodded.

"Very well," said Mr Nimble. "Go with Granny Murphy to the kitchen, she will find you something to eat."

"This will be your last free meal," warned Fu Yong Song. "You must work hard for the rest."

As the men left the room he turned to the others. "That means we have three more fighters to add to my three compatriots who joined me from London. It is good."

"Do you really think we will have to fight, Mr Fu?" asked Mrs Nimble.

"You forget, dear lady," he replied. "We have already fought and won one battle. I believe another is inevitable."

Before the others could respond one of the children ran into the room.

"Come quickly!" he shouted. "Hurry! A strange man with savage dogs is coming towards the house."

Fu Yong Song hastily picked up his staff and followed the boy. The sight which greeted him was strange indeed. The wretched creature was staggering along the gravel path, every now and then he fell onto his knees, but no one dared approach him because of the dogs. Each time anyone tried to help, the two dogs growled and savagely bared their teeth. They were large broad-shouldered hounds used to hunting and fighting.

Fu Yong Song approached them cautiously and shouted an order in Chinese. The effect on the dogs was amazing, they immediately stopped their barking and sat down on the path beside their master, who upon hearing a Chinese voice collapsed to the ground. For a moment the two men just stared at one another in silence. In fact all the onlookers also became silent, they could sense that something very special was taking place. Fu Yong Song spoke very quietly, but the young man's voice was agitated, several times he tried to stand only to collapse with exhaustion. Suddenly to everyone's astonishment, Fu Yong Song burst out laughing and rushed to gather the young man up in his arms. He turned to face the others.

"Everyone must celebrate," he announced. "For this is my son, Li Yong. This is my son!"

*   *   *   *

There was indeed much celebration that night. Son and father had been reunited. Mrs Nimble could hardly stop crying, she was so happy for them. Li was given a bath and new clothes, and a little food, for as Fu Yong Song warned, he had not had a real meal for such a long time, his stomach had to become used to food again. Thomas took charge of the dogs, after Li had told them that he was a friend. He bathed them and fed them, they had been full of fleas and other vermin and were quite emaciated. All work was suspended and everyone joined in the happiness of father and son, but it soon became obvious that Li was very tired, though he and his father could not stop talking, laughing and crying together. He was given a room of his own, though his two dogs would not leave him.

When Li left for bed everyone else began to drift away, several of them patting Fu Yong Song on the back and congratulating him on his good fortune before they left. Moments later all was quiet, just the Nimbles and Fu Yong Song were left sitting by the fireside. It was the Chinaman who broke the silence.

"It will take some time," he said. "My son is very weak. What he has told me about his life since his capture is bad, very bad." He shook his head as if to throw such thoughts from his mind.

"Well," said Mrs Nimble quietly. "You told us at the very beginning that you had travelled half way round the world to find your son, and now you have found him."

Fu Yong Song smiled. "You are thinking, I believe, that this is the moment when I will tell you that I will return to my homeland."

"We cannot expect you to stay," replied Mr Nimble sadly. "You must take your son home to safety."

"My son and I have discussed this already," replied Fu Yong Song. "Such is our anger towards Morgan and Lord Haggleton, if you will permit us, we would like to stay and help you in your fight for justice."

"Permit you!" said Mrs Nimble in amazement. "We need you, we would love you to stay, you dear kind man."

With that she promptly threw her arms around the bewildered Chinaman.

Then she looked so embarrassed that Mr Nimble roared with laughter and Thomas could only marvel at the strangeness of his parents.

51

Life at Porthellen, as the village was called, gradually began to take shape. Moll and Nathaniel took over the running of the only inn and renamed it, The Merry Pilchard. It was only right, explained Moll, that this should be its name, as the main fish landed were pilchards. The previous owner of the inn was delighted to leave and return to his main love, his small trawler. Alfie was so happy to be near the sea, as he kept telling everyone, the sea was in his blood. To him, Porthellen was paradise.

As for Uncle Jack, he was welcomed with open arms. There had been no doctor in the village and, when everyone knew of his calling, they quickly found him a cottage in the centre of the village, helped to clean it and set it up as a home and a surgery. He was soon known as Dr Jack by all, and it made him feel good.

Lucy, in the meantime, went to live with Polly and Nelly and soon found herself teaching in the local village school, Alice was there too helping with the very little ones.

Everything at Porthellen was at a slower tempo but it could never afford to disregard the wiles of the sea and the vagaries of the weather. Much of the villagers' necessities were transported to them by sea as there was no passable road down to them. The track was only wide enough for a single horseman. Occasionally, however, the tunnel through which Lucy and her friends had travelled, was opened, but this was mostly at night. Lucy knew this must be so, as in the morning new pale and tired faces would be found in the village. These would be men, women and children who had been saved from the gallows or from transportation, people who had been unjustly sentenced in Lord Haggleton's courts.

"But where will they all go?" asked Lucy. For even she had worked out that after a while the population of the village would grow beyond its capacity to care for everyone.

"Noah has other villages throughout the country," explained Polly. "He has places hidden all along the south, and I believe some in the north. Not everyone stays, some want to return to the large towns, others go elsewhere to seek their fortune, but all are grateful to Noah for saving their lives."

"How can he possibly do all that?" asked Lucy in amazement. "And where is he? We have been here for many months and we still haven't seen him."

"You may not have seen him," replied Polly. "But he has surely seen you. He knows that you and your friends are now safe from Lord Haggleton and that evil Morgan. He will come soon, never fear."

It was several months later and they were approaching the season of winter storms, by now even fifteen-year-old Lucy could read the signs. The sea had long since changed its colour to a dark metallic grey, gulls were swooping in and complaining loudly that it was too rough. Boats scurried in to harbour to find shelter, sailors were warning that a great storm was coming, and the wind moaned and roared around the little streets. Some fishermen decided to leave port and try to ride out the storm, they remembered the last time, when vessels were smashed against the small harbour wall that was supposed to protect them. At that time some boats had been driven onto the land, and up the streets by the force of the wind.

It had been a rough night, so when Lucy looked out of her window that morning, she saw a group of men staring at a damaged boat leaning against the harbour wall. The tide was out and the men were gently lifting off a body from its decks. The tall figure of Noah was there helping them.

Gathering up her things she rushed from the cottage to greet him.

"Noah! " she called.

He turned and caught her as she leapt at him.

"Steady, little one," he laughed, catching her in his arms. "My how you've grown. We'll talk later but first we have to put this poor soul to rest and then prepare for a great storm to arrive."

She felt ashamed and silly that she had interrupted this sombre event, yet she had been so happy to see him. He could sense her embarrassment.

"There is something important you must do for me," he said. "You must go to all the houses, everyone must come, we must get as many boats, as possible, up into the streets away from the harbour. The storm will come in on the tide, we only have a few hours to get this done. Those boats which can moor soundly, we can leave, but the others must be brought in for safety. Now go as quickly as you can and get as many able-bodied folk to come with you."

She ran, thankful to have something positive to do.

All day the whole village worked hard. Moll brought food and refreshments out to everyone, but few stopped for a rest, they all knew that this work was vital to their existence. Noah was constantly giving orders and working as hard as possible alongside of everyone, and all the time his mask stayed securely in place. Lucy marvelled that no one ever asked him to remove it or questioned why he wore it. The sky was so dark it was difficult to tell if the day had given way to night, but as the tide turned and the waves began to rush in, so the wind grew to a roar and the boats left in the harbour began their crazy rocking.

"We must all get to high ground," shouted Noah, above the roar.

"All taken care of, Noah," shouted back Moll. "Nathaniel and the vicar have taken food and bedding up to the church.

We'll all be safe there or half of England will be under water!"

"All the women," called Noah. "Go now! Take any children with you. The men and I will stay to secure these last two vessels. Doctor, please go with the ladies, some may need help, we will follow on shortly."

Lucy didn't want to leave, she could see the look on Alfie's face when he was included in 'the men', she wanted to stay to help but, nevertheless, did as she was asked. It was only when they were back at the church that the women looked at one another and all burst into laughter.

"My, my," said Nelly, laughing. "We do look a bedraggled bunch." And she was right, they did.

The women gathered up their children, and very soon they had all been fed, and, after a great deal of protesting, were ready for bed. The vicar had prepared a corner of the church where all the children could sleep together, but many of the little ones decided to cuddle up to their mothers.

All this time the wind was rising. It shrieked and screamed around the church and over the little cottages huddled against the cliffs, but the most terrifying noise came when it began to growl. They knew that the growl had started far out to sea, it was as if a terrifying beast had been let loose from the depths of the ocean and was rushing towards them. There was no stopping it, it just seemed to increase as it came closer. It grew so much that when it reached the church it felt as though the wind wanted to suck the very air from the aisles. Some of the children tried to scream but nothing came out. The candles were extinguished and then Lucy heard the strong voice of Moll begin singing a hymn which everyone knew. Soon they were all joining in and singing all the hymns that they knew, and slowly the children calmed down and fell asleep, and only then did the mothers sleep. The fathers took turns to stand watch, but as the tide turned and dawn came, so the storm passed over.

Alfie and Lucy sat huddled together and eventually fell asleep.

52

The next morning the villagers awoke to a scene from hell. The streets were littered with seaweed and all manner of flotsam, including lobster pots, bits of rope and twine, and planks of wood and timber from some of the vessels. Such had been the force of the storm that a large splinter of wood was found embedded in the door of The Merry Pilchard. Windows of those cottages which lacked shutters, were broken or smashed to pieces.

It was the harbour, though, which suffered the most. One boat was no longer seaworthy, whilst another had been lifted on top of a smaller vessel. Much to Lucy's amazement, the villagers all agreed that the damage had been less severe than the storm two years back, owing to the fact that they had been able to get some boats out of the water and up into the streets.

The day was spent with everyone working hard to clear the mess, Moll, with the help of some of the other women supplied all with food and drink. Lucy and Polly organised the children in collecting the seaweed and running errands for anyone who needed them, but by midday the men were looking anxiously at the smouldering sky, it seemed as though the heavens were still angry. The wind began to shift as it drove the clouds back towards the land.

"The storm's cummin' back," muttered one of the men. The others agreed. They had worked hard all morning securing their fishing boats, but now their attention turned to bringing more up into the streets and battening down their homes more securely. The vicar and Dr Jack prepared the church again and boarded up those windows which had been damaged in the night. Everyone was working as hard as possible, they knew it was a race against time.

"It won't be as fierce as last night," reassured Noah, looking at Lucy. He mopped his brow. It had been exhausting work moving that last boat up into the street, and it was obvious that he had found his mask uncomfortable.

"Why don't you take your mask off now?" asked Lucy. "Surely here you are amongst friends and can trust everyone."

Noah shook his head. "That is not the reason," he replied. Then seeing her frown, he added, "It is not time yet for me to remove it, but soon it will happen, you'll see."

By late afternoon with the incoming tide, the waves began to drive forwards, white horses filled the air with their spray, the storm was on its way back. Somehow folk seemed a little more relaxed, after all, they told themselves, they had done all this before and survived, they were ready for whatever nature could throw at them. Some of the men took turns to keep watch outside, as it did appear that this second storm was not going to be as fierce as the first. It was in the early hours of the morning, just past midnight when Nathaniel entered the church.

"There's a ship out in the bay in distress," he announced. "She's fired a rocket, her sails are ripped and it looks as though she's lost her steering. She's headed for Ginn Bay."

"God rest their souls," said one woman.

"Where's Ginn Bay?" asked Alfie.

"The next bay on," replied Noah. "You passed by it when you came through the tunnel. It's also known as The Devil's Teeth because of the rocks, and the dangerous currents to be found there."

"She'll end up being smashed there," said someone.

"Could be good pickin's tomorrow," said another.

"But what about the people on it?" asked Alfie. "Shouldn't we see if we can help in some way?"

221

One or two shook their heads. "What can we do?" "No point in riskin' ourselves" "Foolhardy".

"I'm prepared to try," said Noah. "Will anyone come with me?"

Several of the men came forward including Nathaniel, the doctor, Alfie and Benjamin. Moll, Lucy and Nelly stood up too.

"There might be a poor woman on board," said Moll defiantly, seeing the look of concern on the men's faces.

They set off collecting poles, sacking and lanterns to take with them.

"How will we get to the bay?" shouted Lucy, above the screaming wind.

"Back through the tunnel, if we can get the doors open in this wind," shouted back Moll. "There's a turning on our right which will lead us past the bore hole and down into the other bay. When the tide's low, and on a good day, you can walk there from this bay, but, of course, that'll be impossible tonight."

They pulled their shawls about them, the men buttoned down their thick coats. There was no way they could hurry to these poor stricken souls, whoever they were. The wind tore at them as they battled against it to climb the pathway up to the tunnel's entrance. Each step was an effort, sometimes the wind was so strong that it was impossible to make a step forward. Lucy bent down, she felt as though she was pushing at a brick wall, several times she was almost blown off her feet. Eventually they reached the rock face where the giant, iron doors concealed the entrance. After much fumbling with the key, all the men leant their weight against them and slowly they were pushed open, there was a sudden rush of wind as it forced its way through.

"Close up the doors!" shouted Noah. They all took the strain as they did as he asked.

Lucy felt as though the wind sounded like a monster trying to batter its way into the cave. She looked about her, everyone had a grim face, they knew the seriousness of the next part of their journey, there was a certain determined look to the group made surreal by the pale yellow glow which swung back and forth from their lanterns.

"This way!" called Nathaniel.

They made their way down a narrow tunnel which led to the bore hole, the noise of the wind and the thud of the waves made Lucy pull her hood even tighter around her ears. On one side of them towered up the damp cave wall, whilst on their right, the side wall had disappeared and Lucy looked down into an abyss. Something dark was twisting and writhing down there, she began to realise that it was the sea cleverly carving yet another tunnel into the rocks. Now the screeching wind was remorseless, it was as if it was trying to push them back, trying to prevent them from rescuing any poor souls who might be trapped aboard that stricken ship.

'What if we get there,' thought Lucy, 'and there's no one on board.'

As if reading her mind, Alfie took her arm. "They could all have been washed overboard," he said. "But we've got to try, Lucy, we've got to try."

She nodded too tired to answer.

The path took a sudden pitch downwards. The gravel beneath their feet became small and loose, it was hard to keep their balance on such a wet slippery slope. Then suddenly they were out in the open, they had reached Ginn Bay.

53

Now they could see exactly what they were about to tackle. Although the tide was beginning to turn, the waves were still thundering in and hissing their way back down the beach. It was hard to keep one's footing, Lucy found that either her feet slowly sank into the pebbles or she was sliding towards the waves. It was as if some invisible thread from the sea was drawing her in. It was made all the more horrific because it was so dark. The wind was in control of nature, waves and clouds did its bidding, but every now and then they could see the horror unfolding before them.

The vessel had been hurled against the Devil's Teeth, there it was wedged between two jagged rocks, its sails already in shreds, its timbers slowly breaking up. A blackened skeletal image of what it had once been, this lovely ship was dying. Then came the moment that Lucy would never forget. As if held up by time itself, the mainmast splintered and slowly plunged down onto the deck, half on the ship, half claimed by the sea.

Moll let out a groan of despair, but Nell shouted, "Look!"

There at the foremast of the vessel stood two men and a woman. The smaller man was helping the other one to get the woman onto the rocks, he signalled the taller man to follow her, but when it came to his own turn a cruel wave hit hard and he was flung into the white cauldron.

"We must try to reach them," shouted Noah. He began unravelling one of the ropes and began to tie it around his waist. Alfie did the same.

"No!" Noah tried to stop him. "It's too dangerous Alfie, you can't come too."

Alfie looked him straight in the eye. "Can you swim as well as me?" he asked defiantly.

"He's a brilliant swimmer," said Lucy, holding onto Noah's arm. "I've seen him dive and swim under the water. He's marvellous, Noah."

Moll gave Lucy a sideways glance. Now was not the time to ask Lucy how she knew all this. That could wait till later.

Noah knew there was no time to argue. "Come on then," he said. "You help the man, I'll try to save the woman."

The ship was about fifty yards out, stuck on the rocks, although the tide was endeavouring to drag it out to sea once more. The two of them waded into the sea as Nathaniel and Benjamin took the strain on the ropes.

The shock of the cold sea almost took Alfie's breath away, but once he had overcome this he was able to give his full attention to keeping his balance. Several times they were both knocked off their feet but managed to scrabble upright again. By now the water was past Alfie's waist and he decided to dive through the next wave and swim towards the rocks. This seemed to give him more momentum as the outgoing tide began to pull on him. Now his problem was to control his movements towards the rocks and not be flung against them like so much flotsam.

The man had seen Alfie and Noah swimming towards them, he began to encourage the woman to make her way to the edge of the rocks, so that it would be easier for them to reach her, but she was reluctant to leave him. Suddenly Alfie found himself lifted by a wave and thrown against a jagged stone, it really hurt, and he felt as if his ribs had once more been broken. Noah appeared beside him and held on to his arm firmly. Alfie nodded and managed a half grin to show that he was alright. With some difficulty Noah and Alfie coaxed the woman into the water beside them, her voluminous skirts did not help. Noah held on to her securely and allowed Nathaniel to drag them both in to shore. To Alfie's horror the young man jumped into the raging sea, as if to follow, but was soon in difficulties. Alfie had to dive under the waves and grope for the man's body, luckily he felt his hand grasp a coat, and with all his might he began to drag him to the surface but the man began to struggle and so pulled Alfie down again. With a great effort Alfie dragged him back up and then hit him as hard as he could in the face which knocked him out, then he was able to signal to Benjamin to pull them both in.

On the shore the others were watching the events unfold in horror. Several times they thought they had lost both the rescuers and the rescued. Once Noah staggered up the shore with the woman, Moll and Nell took her and laid her gently on the stones. She was just alive.

"Dr Jack!" called Nell. "This woman is going to have a baby very soon!"

Immediately Dr Jack moved to help them whilst Lucy, Noah and the others began to pull in Alfie and the young man.

"Oh, Alfie," cried Lucy, as he collapsed on the beach.

His face and hands were cut and a large bruise was appearing on his right cheekbone, an ominous trickle of blood oozed from the corner of his mouth.

"We did it, Lucy," he gasped, and promptly collapsed.

Lucy began feverishly to untie the rope from around his waist, she looked up and saw Noah watching her. His mask had come astray and he hastily turned his back on her, but not before she had seen. Somewhere, somehow, she knew she had seen that face before.

54

Mrs Nimble looked about her. Standing here alone in the garden, which Thomas had created, she felt pangs of guilt that she had never given him the praise which he had so rightly deserved. How did she let that happen? She couldn't help but think how life could be so strange and have such twists and turns. Some learned people, she knew, talked about life's patterns, but as far as she could make out, there seemed to be no pattern about any of the recent happenings in her life.

She remembered how she and Mr Nimble had been so happily married until that fateful day when all their money had been lost by, as the bank manager had said, a 'poor investment'. Their world quickly fell apart and they were flung into a debtors' prison with little ceremony, even though their first child was on the way. Then no suitable midwife could be found, and so Thomas had suffered as a result. That was the moment when all the bitterness of the world seemed to descend upon her. It did not leave her, even when they were given the opportunity to leave and set up home as caretakers in this vast house.

They were to run a Holding House, a Workhouse, for Lord Haggleton. It became a living nightmare. If they didn't meet their schedules, they were sent less food and victuals for everyone. She had felt herself changing, she knew she was becoming an embittered woman, but she couldn't stop herself. It was the only way she could survive.

When the girl arrived with her father, Lucy Apothecary she had decided to call her, yes, when she had arrived, well that was the last straw. Mrs Nimble sighed. How could she have been so cruel to such an innocent child, who had only ever wanted to help others. Slowly she had been changing into a monster, upholding all those things which she abhorred, greed, deceit, anger and cruelty, and all because she feared the consequences, the wrath of Lord Haggleton.

After Mr Nimble's dreadful beating, her whole world had begun to collapse; if it hadn't been for the Chinaman, she shuddered to think of what might have happened. Now here he was, helping them and reunited with his son, Li and, what was more, five more Chinamen had arrived to help. Somehow they had heard of the Nimble's plight and of Fu Yong Song and his son, and had decided that their services were needed. It was indeed remarkable how well they had fitted in and built defences, trained the younger men in martial arts, and even worked with Thomas and his friends in the gardens to produce their own food.

The only puzzle was that, like Mr Fu and Li they often talked of Noah and how he had said that the time was coming. That everything would be righted soon. 'Who is Noah?' she asked herself. Is he a man or a special prophet of theirs? When she asked this question of Mr Fu he just smiled and said all would soon become clear.

55

The journey back from the shipwreck was hard. The men had carefully placed the man and the woman on two makeshift stretchers. It was difficult getting these up the beach to the cave entrance, with every step the shingle shifted and slid away from them. This combined with the relentless wind driving the surf and rain, made the journey treacherous. Both the rescued strangers were unconscious as the four men slowly carried them up the beach to safety. Lucy could only admire the strength and determination of Noah who was helping to carry one of the stretchers. She hoisted Alfie's right arm over her shoulder whilst Nell supported his left side, together they half carried, half dragged him up the beach, Moll was anxiously walking by the side of the woman's stretcher.

As they reached the cave's entrance they heard a mighty crack, like an explosion, then came a deep roar and looking back they saw the ship rise as though lifted by an invisible hand.

"She's going," shouted Benjamin above the screeching wind. "Her back's broken!"

Lucy looked in horror as the ship reared up before plunging down hard on the jagged rocks. It seemed to cry out in pain as what was left of its masts smashed into the Devil's Teeth, this followed by a low groan of capitulation. She had never seen a ship die before, it was a sight she never wanted to see again, it was as if a beautiful creature had suddenly come to the end of its life. She turned away, tears streaming down her face, she didn't want to witness those last dreadful moments. Together, she and Nell, managed to drag Alfie into the shelter of the cave's entrance.

At least for a while they would be away from the worst of the storm.

Once inside the men lowered the stretchers and took stock of the situation.

"Moll," said Noah gently. "You must go on ahead. No, no protests. You'll be able to travel much quicker than the rest of us. Get down to the village and round up a few of the others to come and meet us and help with the carrying. See if you can get others to make ready some bedding or clothing for these wretched souls."

"There's no problem about that," replied Moll. "You must all come to The Merry Pilchard. There'll be warmth and clothing there. Just be careful carrying these stretchers past the bore hole, it'll be very slippery there."

She gave Nathaniel a quick kiss. "You be careful too, my love," he whispered, as she made her way alone through the tunnel. The glow from her lantern soon faded from sight.

Noah looked at the small weary group left behind. "Now," he said, "this will seem a much longer journey going back. We will have to take frequent rests and hope that Moll is able to find some volunteers to meet us and help with the carrying. Will you be all right with Alfie?"

This last question was directed at Nell and Lucy. They both nodded.

Alfie muttered. "I'm not dead yet, it's just that my legs won't work."

The others laughed. "It's the cold, you were in the water a long time, Alfie," answered Dr Jack. "It's good for you to keep moving as much as possible, and, Lucy, don't let him fall asleep!"

Lucy nodded. "We won't. Did you hear that, Alfie? You're to stay awake!"

Alfie merely grunted.

The first part of the journey was very hard, the path sloped upwards towards the tunnels which led down to the bore hole. The noise seemed to have lessened this time, a

230

combination of the tide turning and the storm receding. Despite the steep path, Lucy kept up a constant banter to Alfie, urging him to stay awake and to try to keep his legs moving.

Nell laughed. "You two sound like an old married couple," she said.

Lucy blushed, and Alfie muttered, "If this is what it's like I shan't bother."

This only made Nell laugh even more.

They made several stops, and slithered and slid their way past the bore hold until, eventually, they came to the more even path which they knew to be the last section before the great doors leading to the village. Once here Noah signalled them to make another pause. He was panting hard, the rescue, plus carrying the stretcher, was beginning to take its toll.

Dr Jack looked at him carefully, "You're going to overdo it, young man," he said solemnly. "We need to have longer rests."

"But these people need help, Doctor," he replied. "We can't afford to wait about too long, especially so as the woman is pregnant. She needs to be in the warm and dry."

"At the moment she's fine," replied the doctor. "She's unconscious, and it's best she remain that way for a little longer."

"Look," said Nathaniel. Down the tunnel there suddenly appeared a glow which gradually turned into several small, bobbing glows. The villagers were coming. A great cheer resounded along the tunnel when they saw the small band of rescuers. The four men looked relieved. At last they had some additional help. Two of the villagers had also brought another stretcher and, despite much protesting, Alfie was placed on it and covered with a blanket. In fact they had additional blankets for all the rescuers, which was just as well as Lucy was beginning to feel the cold seep into her bones.

At last they reached the iron doors and made their way down the slope into the main part of the village. Dawn was beginning to break, and seagulls, pleased that the worst of the storm had passed by, let out a raucous chorus of bravado, swooping down and around the harbour.

As they approached The Merry Pilchard so the young man began to move and fidget on his stretcher.

"Keep still," warned one of his carriers. "We won't be able to hold the stretcher if you keep on moving."

The man tried to sit up, he was searching for the young woman.

They were just going through the doors of the inn when he suddenly saw her being taken on a stretcher into a side room. He called out trying to attract her attention. *"C'est ma femme, ma femme, Nicole!"*

One of the men looked at him in horror. "Blimey!" he said. "He's a ruddy Frenchie, he's a Froggie!"

56

Despite her protests, Lucy was led away to Nelly's home. Alice was there and welcomed them with a warm drink of milk.

"I've been awake all night worrying about you," she said. "I couldn't stay in the church with the others. I thought you must have died or even been attacked."

Nelly smiled. "We didn't die nor were we attacked, young Alice," she replied. "In fact due to the bravery of Noah and Alfie we were able to rescue the poor folk trapped on that sinking ship."

"But not the man who fell overboard," muttered Lucy, grasping her mug in both hands. She was so cold that the warmth from the mug set her into a fit of shivering.

"True," replied Nelly. "God rest his soul and all the others who must have been on board at some stage."

"What happened?" asked Alice eagerly.

"Not now," answered Nelly, seeing Lucy shaking and giving a great yawn at the same time. "We're all going to try and get some rest. There'll be plenty of time for chatter later in the morning."

With that she ushered the two girls into bed and settled back in her comfy chair to have a short sleep herself.

*　　*　　*　　*

Dr Jack was having a hard time persuading some of the local men that it was right and proper to treat the Frenchman and his wife.

"But we're at war with France," said one. "It don't seem right to give 'em medicines nor to look after 'em. They's the enemy."

Dr Jack peered round the smoke-filled room. It was crowded with anxious, tired looking people. Moll had been handing out free rum to warm them up and a log fire blazed in the hearth. They'd all had two restless nights because of the storm, some had lost their boats and most of their belongings during those dreadful nights, and here he was offering help and comfort to two foreigners, and enemy foreigners at that.

He could understand their fear and their concerns.

"Listen," he said quietly. "This poor couple were left on that ship. Somehow they were deserted by the crew and abandoned to their fate. The woman is at this very moment having her baby, she has shown great courage and determination. For goodness' sake, they are fellow human beings and entitled to our help, surely you can show them some kindness. Those of you who fish for your living, would you want your wives out in such a storm? How would you feel? Now I must also leave to help Alfie, who has risked his life helping the young man."

There were a few mutters, when one of the poorest women suddenly said, "She'll be wanting some clothes for her little one, no doubt. I'd best go and find her some, my lad has outgrown his."

Others followed muttering things about dry clothing until most had left the bar. Dr Jack swiftly left the room and went upstairs to see the woman.

"It's all right, Doctor," Polly smiled at him as she opened the door. "The young lady has just presented us with a beautiful little boy, and both are well."

"Amazing!" He gazed in admiration at the woman holding her newborn child. "After all that you have been through, well, I'll be jiggered!" With that he left her in the capable hands of Polly and the local midwife to attend his two male patients.

Apart from a few bruised ribs and various lacerations on his body, the young man, whose name was Frederic, was in no danger. He had swallowed a fair amount of sea water and consequently had been very sick, which the doctor considered a good thing. He allowed himself a small smile when Frederic complained of a very tender jaw and wondered if it was broken. He decided that it would serve no good purpose to tell him that the cause was the blow delivered by Alfie. Frederic had no recollection of the punch.

Alfie, however, was a different case altogether. He had been so badly beaten by Morgan that it had left him in a much weaker state then any of them had realised. He had kept much of his pain to himself. Fortunately the doctor found that the blood from Alfie's mouth was not due to his earlier broken ribs but to the fact that he had bitten his own tongue quite badly; nevertheless, his whole body was covered in deep bruises, especially around his chest where the rope had been tied. His hands and feet were badly cut from being hurled repeatedly against the rocks in his endeavours to hold on to Frederic. He was developing a fever. Polly left the midwife looking after Nicole, and she came to sit by Alfred's bedside and gently mopped his brow.

"I'll not leave him, Doctor," she said quietly. "I'll stay until this dear boy comes through this."

The doctor threw another log on the fire. "He's no longer a boy, Poll," he said quietly. "Tonight he proved himself to be very much a man. He mustn't die, he's become like a son to me, a son I've never had. We'll pull him through, Poll, we must."

He left the room to find Noah. How had this extraordinary man fared, he wondered?

Noah was with Frederic, they were having an earnest conversation.

"How are you?" asked the doctor.

Noah grinned. "A little bruised," he replied. "But otherwise no problems. More importantly, how is Alfie?"

"Not good," answered the doctor. "But, with the help of Polly, I have every hope that we may pull him through."

"He is a very brave young man," said Frederic, in perfect English.

The doctor looked surprised.

"I have many good English friends," explained Frederic. "In fact my brother married a beautiful English lady, and that is why we have made this journey. I will tell you…"

"No you won't," replied the doctor firmly. "You may go to see your wife and then you must come back here swiftly and get some rest. That is an order. Whilst you are gone I will have a short discussion with Noah, but I shall expect you back shortly!"

Frederic gingerly rose from his bed and, much to the doctor's embarrassment, kissed him on both cheeks. "Thank you, thank you," he murmured gratefully. Then he left the room as quickly as his injuries would allow.

"Now let me look at you," said the doctor to Noah.

"It's nothing," replied Noah, trying to wave the doctor away.

The doctor took no notice and lifted Noah's shirt. To his horror across the highwayman's back was a very nasty gash, which needed his immediate attention, but most interesting of all were the old whiplash marks. Scars criss-crossed his back and had obviously been there for many years.

57

Lucy slept through the whole of that day and into the next. It was Alice who cared for her. Nelly had left her in charge. Alice was growing into a very confident young lady and, being bright, often helped in the village school with the younger children. She and Nelly had grown very fond of one another, she looked upon Nelly as a long-lost mother.

"I've been asleep too long," said Lucy, becoming agitated when she knew a whole day had gone by, she tried to sit up in her bed. "You should have woken me. I must go and see Alfie."

"There's no hurry," replied Nelly gently as she came into the room. "He is being well cared for. The doctor and Polly are there. They haven't left his side."

"That means he must be very ill," said Lucy, fearfully. "They wouldn't be there all the time if it wasn't so. He looked so bad, so white, when we brought him back to the inn. There was blood from his mouth. Is he dying?"

"He's a very strong and brave young man," said Nelly, carefully avoiding a straight answer. "Dr Jack is a marvellous physician, we are so lucky to have such a man here. If anyone is to bring Alfie back to full health then it will be our doctor, but you must understand, Lucy, that Alfie had suffered dreadfully at Morgan's hand. We must just pray that he will make a full recovery."

"I can do more than just pray," answered Lucy defiantly. "You forget, I am an apothecary's daughter, there are many herbs that I can find which might help Uncle Jack." With that she pushed back her bedcovers and made ready to put on her clothes, but she was very unsteady on her feet and almost fell over.

"You can't go traipsing down to the village just yet," said Nelly holding on to her. "You're still too weak."

"I am not too weak," replied Lucy angrily, as she held on fast to the bedpost. "I am going down to The Merry Pilchard to see Alfie and to help him get better, and you can't stop me."

"I'll go with her," said Alice, seeing the worried look on Nelly's face. "I'll make sure she doesn't keel over, don't you worry."

Nelly sighed. "We'll all go," she said. "I want to see Polly anyway. Come on then, Miss Obstinate, let's help you dress and we'll go down to see your Alfie."

When she heard Nelly call Alfie, 'your Alfie' Lucy felt herself blush, especially so, when she heard a little giggle from Alice.

She heard herself say, "He's just my dear friend, that's all."

This made the other two laugh aloud.

The walk down the cobbles to The Merry Pilchard was one that Lucy would never forget. The storm had gone and left all its detritus behind, but very little was going to waste. Everywhere people were gathering up what might prove useful to them. On the east side of the harbour she could see small empty wagons being pulled by tired horses, or equally tired villagers, up the sloping path to the iron gates which concealed the tunnel. From there they made their way down to the beach where they collected large pieces of wood and other objects. They dragged all this back, past the bore hole and placed their findings in the carts to bring them back down to the harbour. It was like watching a giant group of ants going back and forth.

"What are they doing?" she asked.

"The ship that was wrecked has broken up and much of it has been washed ashore. So everyone is collecting the flotsam, it is of no use to anyone else, least of all to the poor man they found washed up on the shore this morning," replied Nelly.

"Do they know who he was?" asked Lucy.

Nelly shook her head. "But I daresay that the young Frenchman at the inn will be able to tell us."

The Merry Pilchard was bubbling with people and conversation, but when the three women entered it suddenly went very quiet. Then someone began clapping, and a voice shouted, "Well done! Bless you child!"

Lucy looked around in bewilderment, Noah was nowhere to be seen. From out of a side door came Moll, and when she saw Lucy she threw open her arms, almost suffocating her in her embrace.

"Come with me, my darlin' girl," she said, and beckoned the other two to follow.

She led them along a corridor behind the bar and up a staircase, they stopped outside a bedroom door, worn and battered from centuries of use.

"Noah has had to leave," she said. "But he says that you are to listen very carefully to the Frenchman and his wife. They have much to tell you."

Lucy wanted to ask about Alfie, and Moll seemed to sense this. "You can see Alfie after you have talked to these people. He's not going anywhere for a while, but," she put her fingers on Lucy's lips, "he is past the worst of it and making a slow recovery. He'll be pleased to see you later. Now in you go."

With that she took the other two away with her and left Lucy staring at the closed door wondering what on earth could be on the other side.

58

Morgan looked perplexed. "Are you *certain* you want this carried out, m'lord?" he asked, with great emphasis on the word 'certain'.

"Have you ever had reason to doubt my judgement, Morgan?" replied Lord Haggleton in a threatening tone. "If so, when? Out with it man."

"No, never, sire," returned Morgan hastily. "It's just that, well, it's just that it seems so dangerous, sire, and so final."

"Sit down, Morgan," replied Lord Haggleton, in the smooth tones which, over the years, Morgan had learnt to mistrust.

Morgan sat in the formal seat opposite his Lordship, who was seated, as so often in these type of one-sided discussions, behind his enormous desk. The chair had the effect of making its occupant feel even smaller in this high vaulted room with its portraits and enormous casement windows.

"I am tired, Morgan," continued His Lordship. "Tired of the Nimbles and their inability to do the simple job of caring for the people I send to them. They have a free roof over their heads, I send them money to feed these people and then I take them off their hands by removing them to places where they can spend productive lives. Is that too much to ask?" He didn't wait for Morgan's reply. "I have had enough of their incompetence. Therefore they must all be removed and the house, which has always been a sad reminder to me of times gone by, must be razed to the ground. I don't care how you do it. Blow it up, set fire to it, but destroy it."

"And the occupants, m'lord?" asked Morgan, quietly. "What will become of them?"

Lord Haggleton gave a deep sigh. "Haven't you been listening to a word I've been saying, Morgan?" He leant forward across his desk. "Get rid of them, all of them, the Chinaman included. It will be very tragic, Morgan. They will all perish in a great fire. Such a great loss, but I am tired of them and their petty ways."

"I cannot undertake all of this on my own, m'lord," Morgan considered his words carefully. He had no intention of taking the blame for arson and the deaths of so many. "I will need to use your militia."

"No!" Lord Haggleton's reply came out like a shotgun. "You must use your own men, or take a few from the local jail. You may offer each of them two golden sovereigns for their trouble and then arrange for them to have a free crossing to the New World." He gave a low chuckle. "There will be no witnesses to our little plan, Morgan."

Morgan stood up, not too certain if he liked the sudden change to 'our plan'. "Very well, m'lord." He gave a slight bow. "It will take me a few days to gather together such a group of men, but I daresay, I can have this whole venture completed within the next two to three weeks."

"Splendid, Morgan," replied Lord Haggleton, rubbing his hands together in satisfaction. "Let me know when you decide to leave, but do not on any circumstance bring any of the men here, you understand?"

Morgan nodded.

Lord Haggleton drew on his pipe. "Now I can get down to the more taxing business of William's forthcoming marriage."

Morgan left the room. Whatever thoughts he had he was keeping well to himself.

A few days later the Corporal of the Militia stood before Lord Haggleton, just as Morgan had done earlier. He, however, stood to attention.

"Relax, Corporal," said Lord Haggleton. "I have a great problem and I need your help most urgently."

"How may I be of service to you, m'lord?" The young man had never been in such a vast room before, and Lord Haggleton could see that he was very much in awe of the whole place. He knew this would be a relatively easy fish to land.

"I am aware, and indeed, much in your debt already, of the manner in which you have undertaken the onerous tasks and duties of our murdered sergeant. I sincerely hope that those responsible will soon be brought to justice for their heinous crime against such a valiant soldier. I intend to promote you to his position as soon as possible, when, of course, your wages will be increased."

"Thank you, m'lord," muttered the corporal, and attempted an awkward salute.

"What I am about to tell you," continued Lord Haggleton, "must remain a secret. It is vital that these instructions are not discussed with anyone else. I only divulge them now to you because of your increased status as a sergeant. You understand?"

The young man nodded, thrilled at the prospect of being privy to such a secret, whatever it was.

Lord Haggleton glanced around the room as if expecting an eavesdropper to suddenly appear from behind the curtains. "I understand," he said, leaning forward and adopting a conspiratorial tone, "that a band of cut-throats is about to descend upon my old country residence, a place very dear to me, and where, as you know, we tend to the needs of the less fortunate. My information is that they intend to kill the occupants, ransack the building and burn it down. I require you and your men to do your best to prevent such a happening. Mete out any punishment there and then, these men are not worthy of the hangman's noose."

"I'll send a rider immediately, m'lord, to warn the occupants," said the corporal eagerly.

"No, no," replied Lord Haggleton hastily. "Your rider will only serve to warn the cut-throats. We must catch them all red-handed. Tragically it may be that a few may die in order to save the many. Any ill-gotten gains or monies you may find about their person, you and your men may keep."

"Thank you, m'lord."

"There is one other minor problem however," said Lord Haggleton.

'This is it,' thought the corporal. Out loud he said, "Yes, m'lord?"

"My great friend and companion, Morgan, has somehow let himself become involved with these men. Try to save him, but if it…" he tailed off and waved his hands in the air. "I know you will do your best, Corporal, I know you will try to save him, but if it proves impossible… I will understand."

"We will do our very best, m'lord," the corporal gave a short bow.

Lord Haggleton gave a curt nod and the corporal was quick to see that his interview had ended. He left the room.

Lord Haggleton leant back in his chair and placed the palms of his hands together. It was all proving to be so easy. He smiled.

59

It did not take long for Morgan to recruit his small band of men. The promise of money and freedom had them almost queuing up for a chance to take part in this venture. The fools! He gave them a contemptuous look, huddled as they were in the back of the wagon, swigging back as much ale as he had been able to muster for them. Full of bravado, but bereft of a single brain cell between them. A hotch-potch of life's losers, two of them looked quite old, and he had been surprised to realise that they were no older than himself, and a young boy, no more than thirteen years destined for transportation. The only man he had enlisted from his own band of followers was Swithun.

Swithun had worked at the house for as long as Morgan could remember, he didn't say much, he couldn't read or write, but he was always there in the background, watching and waiting. To tell the truth he sometimes made Morgan feel a little uncomfortable but, over the years, Morgan had found him to be reliable and always there when needed. So it was to Swithun that Morgan turned when he needed someone to drive the wagon, Morgan rode ahead on his own horse, scouting out the potholes and making sure that very few people saw them as they made their way north and out of London towards Essex.

He once asked Swithun how he had acquired his name. Swithun had looked surprised at the question, as if everyone knew the reason.

"Cos I were born on 'is day," he'd answered solemnly. "Ma said it never stopped rainin' from the moment I cum."

Morgan had merely nodded. It was obviously not a subject which Swithun wished to discuss further.

A few days before they set out on their journey Morgan called Swithun to meet him in the stone outbuilding, which he used as his home and his office. Not many were invited into this sanctuary.

"Sit down, Swithun," he said, in a tone which he hoped carried as much weight and authority as that of Lord Haggleton. "I want you to know that we are being sent on a special mission by his Lordship."

Swithun nodded.

"There is something about this trip which bothers me and, therefore, I have decided to take you into my confidence, do you understand?"

Again Swithun nodded. "You'm goin' to tell me a secret," he muttered.

Morgan smiled and opened the top drawer of his desk. He withdrew a roll of parchment. "I have written down some very important facts on this scroll, Swithun, and if things get bad where we are going, or if I get killed or captured, I want you to make your escape, leave me, then come here and retrieve this scroll which I'm going to lock away in that chest over there." He indicated a large box in the corner of the room.

"Do'm you want me to give it to his Lordship?" asked Swithun, in a matter-of-fact tone.

"No," replied Morgan swiftly. "You must go into the city and find the Prime Minister, Mr Pitt, and hand it to him personally. On no account must Lord Haggleton know of its existence. On no account must you let him know what is inside this chest or written on this parchment."

"You'm know I can't read nor write," muttered Swithun.

"That's one of the reasons why I've chosen you," replied Morgan sarcastically. "You won't want to try to read it yourself. Now swear an oath that you will carry out my wishes, or I'll make it my business to haunt you all your miserable days."

"I swear." Swithun's face had turned pale. "There's no need to be troublin' yourself when you be gone. You enjoy yourself when you're dead, don't you bother none about me."

That had been four days ago and now they were outside the grounds of the Nimbles' house. The men had become very quiet. Morgan rode to the back of the wagon and lifted up the ragged cover. One or two of the men looked a bit worse for drink.

"Now," he said brusquely, "we must first send in some scouts to see what sort of reinforcements there may be."

"What are you talking about?" demanded a big burly man. He looked as if he could snap a neck with one hand. "You told us that there would be no trouble. Straight in, do the job, and straight out again."

Morgan had deliberately left out any mention of Fu Yong Song or his son.

"My latest information," replied Morgan, sitting high on his horse. "Is that these people may have employed one or two mercenaries to help them, but as I told you before, they are all criminals. They have broken the law by entering his Lordship's home, and stealing his property. You, on the other hand, have his Lordship's full permission to drive them out, burn them out if necessary."

"And all we get is two miserable gold sovereigns for tackling some mercenaries. Why ain't his Lordship using his own militia? What's to stop us taking our money from you now and runnun' off?" asked a weasel-faced looking man.

"These," replied Morgan, pointing two loaded pistols at them.

"And these," added Swithun, who had got down from the wagon and was now standing in the shadows of the trees, also holding two pistols.

"There's not much moon," continued Morgan. "And it must be turned midnight. You two," he pointed at two on the edge of the group, "go through the graveyard, see if

246

they've appointed any guards and get back here quickly to tell us what you've seen."

After some muttering the two left.

It was all going too easily and Morgan was uneasy.

Suddenly there was a bloodcurdling scream and one of the men came rushing back into the group. His clothes were torn and his face one of horror.

"There are black devils in there!" he screamed. "They came from the graves and set their hounds from hell upon us."

The second one staggered back, he had been a little braver and had stood his ground for a few more seconds. His shirt was ripped and his eyes stared wildly into the night.

"The Devil himself is in there!" he shouted, before falling to the ground.

At first the others greeted all this in silence, and then a great panic consumed them as they tried to leap from the wagon and escape.

"Stop!" yelled Morgan. "This is nonsense. They're nothing but a bunch of old men, women and children. All you have to do is to torch the place and get rid of them. There's no Devil in there, no hounds from hell!"

The men stopped. "What do you mean?" asked the burly man. "Old men, women and children? What do you mean?"

"No one ever mentioned children," said another.

"Nor old women. You said they was criminals."

Morgan was saved the trouble of answering because a sudden volley of shot passed over his head and, as he turned, he saw Swithun talking urgently to a masked man. It was Noah. He turned back to his men who were rushing to take cover. Swithun ran towards him.

"We must get out, Morgan! Get out quickly! It's the militia. You'm been betrayed! We must go!"

Morgan looked back into the shadows, the masked man had gone, he leant down and pulled Swithun up behind him. Without a further glance at his men he rode hastily away.

The ragged band of men was left to its fate. Only one, the young boy, would be able to enjoy his promised freedom.

* * * *

Noah gazed down at the merriment in the Great Hall and smiled. From his position in the shadows of the gallery he could watch without being detected. It had been a close thing, but he had had just enough time to warn Swithun and so save Morgan. Why he had bothered to save Morgan, he had no idea but it had seemed the right thing to do at the time. He had also been able to save the young boy, and that was pleasing, but it was really Granny Murphy who had saved the day and he was relieved that his gamble had paid off.

Whilst the soldiers had been busy rounding up Morgan's gang, Noah had quickly rushed the young boy into the house, there he had met Granny Murphy armed with nothing more than a soup ladle. A few words in her ear and to everyone's surprise she bravely strode outside. Soon they could all hear her shouting.

"Freddie Murphy, you should be ashamed of yourself! What would your dear, departed, mother think of you bringing all these soldiers here to shoot your own grandmother! Did I not bring you up and nurse you when she died? Shame on you, Freddie!"

By this time the soldiers had either captured the gang or dispatched them to a better world. They lowered their rifles in amazement at her words and the effect they had on their new sergeant.

"Granma?" The young man couldn't believe his eyes. Was this demented old woman, waving a soup ladle about her head, really his grandmother?

"Cease fire!" he commanded as he walked towards her.

It soon became obvious to all present that she was indeed his very own grandmother, and very much alive and well.

After much hugging and remonstrating, he ordered all his men to put down their arms. Mr and Mrs Nimble were quick to take advantage of this pause and invited all the soldiers into the house for a sup of cheese, bread and ale. Fu Yong Song and his men hid in one of the upstairs rooms, it was best, they felt, that the militia did not know of their presence. The gang had been easy to frighten but the soldiers might prove to be a little harder!

Satisfied that the danger was now over, Noah slipped away, but not before he had had a quiet word with Fu Yong Song.

"I think the days of Lord Haggleton's tyranny may be coming to an end very soon," he said to his friend.

Fu Yong Song gave a short bow. "I agree."

"Will you stay, or will you return to China?" asked Noah.

"My son and I will stay," he replied. "My friends will also remain, for if, as you say, Lord Haggleton's grip is waning, then who will own this house? Will it be his pathetic son, William, or the monster, Morgan? We will stay to help Mr and Mrs Nimble, whatever the outcome."

Noah nodded. Perhaps he should have let the militia kill Morgan. Was that a missed opportunity, he wondered.

60

Lucy tapped on the heavy, oak door.

"*Entrez!*" called a strange voice.

She pushed it open, it gave a tired screech as though the wet weather had seeped into its joints.

"You wanted to see me, sir?" She wanted to add, 'Why on earth should a Frenchman who's just been shipwrecked on the Cornish coast want to see me?' but good manners prevented such an outburst.

"Lucy," he said, and grasping her in both his arms he kissed her on the forehead.

Lucy let out a little squeal and jumped backwards.

"For goodness sake, Frederic," exclaimed his wife, who was sitting up in bed nursing her new son. "You will terrify the poor girl. You must explain yourself before she collapses with fright!" She spoke half in English and half in French.

"I am so sorry, Lucy," said the young man, bowing courteously to her.

"Please forgive me. Come sit by my wife and I will explain myself to you. It is all very simple."

"No, Frederic," interrupted his wife firmly. "It is not all very simple, you must tell it slowly so that the dear child may comprehend what you are saying."

"Yes, my dear," replied Frederic. "You are right as always." He gave her a little bow which caused Lucy to giggle.

"I'm sorry," she said, as she sat in the nursing chair by the side of the bed. "But I have never spoken to a Frenchman before. You seem to do a great deal of bowing. Oh dear, is that rude of me to comment so?"

"Not at all, *cherie*," he replied smiling. "We Frenchmen are very polite, especially to the ladies."

He walked over to the small bay window and for a few moments stared out at the busy scene below. Everyone was working hard to clear away the mess left by the storm, even the smallest child scurried here and there collecting debris, and anything that could be used as fuel. Suddenly he turned, took a deep breath and began his story.

"I am Frederic Duval, my brother was Maurice Duval, a promising young violinist, destined, many thought, to become a great violinist. All in our family are, or were, musicians, our parents were opera singers, my first cousin is a wonderful flautist – I, myself, am a pianist of no mean ability." He gave a short bow and Lucy felt she was obliged to give a small clap of appreciation.

His wife sighed, "Oh, Frederic, you do go on so!"

He ignored her and continued. "My brother toured Europe, he gave recitals in fine houses, and the great Tartini himself said that he had a wonderful future ahead of him. It was whilst he was performing for some of your Royal family that he met and fell in love with a beautiful young woman called Margaret Haggleton, the daughter of Sir Daniel Haggleton." Lucy gave a little gasp as Nicole reached across the bed to hold her hand.

Frederic continued. "Sadly Sir Daniel did not approve of their liaison. He wished for Margaret to marry some elderly, but very rich, duke. The young lovers decided to run away together and they were secretly married in a little French church in Brittany. They were there but a short time for, I am sad to say, that in France, an English wife was not welcomed at that time, so they returned to this country. Margaret, I think, hoped that Sir Haggleton would relent."

Lucy grasped Nicole's hand so firmly that it was the turn of the young French woman to gasp.

Frederic continued. "He did not relent, even though his daughter was expecting his first grandchild. Then one night, after Maurice had given another recital, he was attacked and killed, murdered." He paused as though visualising the dreadful scene. "His body was found in the River Thames a few days later, the tide had carried it away. Margaret went into hiding but she could not live on her own. The cook, of that dreadful house, helped her all she could, but the shock of her husband's death caused the baby to arrive early. The servants brought Margaret into the house, hoping that Sir Daniel Haggleton would change his mind, but it was no use. My dear sister-in-law died, and the little one was given to an apothecary and his wife to bring up as their own."

He paused again and looked at Lucy.

"I do believe, *ma cherie*, that you are that child, and that I am your uncle."

Lucy went to stand up, but her legs buckled under her and she fainted.

How long she was unconscious, Lucy had no idea, but when she awoke a very anxious Frederic was busy fanning her face with a small towel, whilst Nicole was gently stroking her head.

"I told you that you should wait, Frederic, the news was too sudden, too much, too soon," she scolded. "You forget she was there the night our ship sank. She has been through much these last few days."

He nodded. "Yes, my dear," he replied. "You are right as usual."

Lucy sat up and sipped the tea which Frederic was offering her.

"But I don't understand, sir," she said after awhile. "How did you come here, to Cornwall? What made you journey to this part of England?"

Frederic smiled. "I have been searching for you, Lucy, ever since we learnt of the death of my brother. This is my third visit to England, and each time I have been able to gather more information. On my last visit I learnt that you and your friends had been cast as French spies, and were travelling to the west of the country. I found a captain who was willing, at a price, to drop me on the shores of Cornwall. Not an easy task even in the best of weathers," he smiled. "But this time my dear wife insisted on coming with me, despite being very pregnant. The crew were very unhappy about having such a woman on board, they considered it bad luck. When the storm started they were convinced it was my wife's fault and they mutinied, leaving the captain and one other to complete the journey. Sadly they both perished, and if it had not been for the daring of your friends, Noah and Alfie, undoubtedly we would both have perished too."

Lucy looked at him in amazement. Was this effervescent man really her uncle, the brother of her real father?

She looked down at the baby, serenely sleeping in Nicole's arms. Her mind in a turmoil and not knowing how to respond, she asked, "What will you call him?"

Nicole smiled. "He shall be known as Alfred Noah Frederic Duval," she answered proudly.

"Alfie will be pleased," said Lucy. She sighed before adding, "I do wish Noah was here, I have so much to ask him."

"He will return as soon as possible, *cherie*," replied Frederic. "He has much to do, but hopes that much may be resolved when he returns."

'What could be so important that he had to leave us now?' thought Lucy.

61

Morgan was beside himself with anger. He kicked open the door to the library with a vicious savagery. It was 2 a.m. in the morning, he knew that Lord Haggleton was elsewhere. His Lordship had let it be known that he would be attending the Duchess's Ball, and might very well not return until the following day.

He threw his heavy top coat across the room, unbuckled his sword and carefully laid it on the polished surface of the table, which ran virtually the whole length of the room. Crossing to the sideboard he poured himself a large brandy and downed it in a single swallow. He poured another one, and walked slowly to the armchair beside the log fire. The embers were still glowing, so he threw on a log, and, using the bellows, he soon had enough flames to add a few more to the fire. Settling down in the armchair he found that his pistol was causing him some discomfort, so he placed it on the small table by his chair and alongside his brandy. At last, feeling comfortable, he began to relax and to think through the evening's events.

It was inevitable, he reasoned, that his long service to Lord Haggleton should be coming to an end. He had had a good run but undoubtedly Lord Haggleton had decided that the time had come for a change. Morgan was in no doubt that his Lordship had killed the sergeant, and had also been the one who had betrayed him and sent the militia looking for him at the Nimbles' house. Well, he was no weakling, Lord Haggleton would rue the day that he had decided to abandon him. He had already put in place his insurance policy in the form of the scroll which was hidden in his room. He felt certain that if anything did happen to him, then Swithun would take it to the authorities. Once they knew of its contents then Lord Haggleton might very well end up on one of his own transportation ships. The irony of that, made Morgan smile for the first time that evening. He took another gulp of the brandy.

He held the glass up at eye level and, slowly turning it around, he thought carefully. He was forgetting William, if he could turn that puny boy (he still thought of him as only a boy) against his Lordship then all was not lost. Yes, that was the answer. William was ready for more responsibility and, with Morgan to guide him, would be no worse than Lord Haggleton and perhaps even better, as he, Morgan, would have greater control over events. He smiled, it was a malicious smile, one that could chill the soul and spread panic amongst the weak. William was weak, Morgan drank some more brandy, it would not take long to terrorise William into believing that Morgan would be his saviour. He settled back in his armchair. The warmth of the fire and the effects of the brandy began to take effect, he was soon fast asleep.

*　　*　　*　　*

Very slowly the panel by the side of the great fireplace slid open. It had been well oiled over the years. A lone figure crept silently into the room, born of necessity William had often used this entrance when returning late to the house. Not even Lord Haggleton knew of its existence, it was his own secret passageway which he had discovered when only a small boy trying to hide from punishment meted out by Morgan or Lord Haggleton. The passage led from this room underneath the house and came out in the shrubbery at the back of the garden. There was even a side tunnel which went behind the cells where Lord Haggleton sometimes kept certain prisoners, such as Alfie, Lucy and the doctor. Carefully William closed the panel and turned to cross the room. He gave a quick intake of breath when he saw Morgan. A few snores and it became obvious that the man was asleep. William smiled, he noted the sword lying on the polished surface of the long table, the smell of brandy was strong. Instead of leaving Morgan, William decided to have a brandy himself. As he brought it back to the warmth of the fire, he saw the pistol by Morgan's side. He carefully placed his brandy by the opposite armchair and, before settling down, he made up the fire with more logs. Soon he had a good blaze going. He was tired and the fire was warm, so he settled down for a short nap.

It wasn't long before they were both snoring by the fireside.

62

Morgan woke first. Stealthily he picked up his pistol and pointed it at William, who began to stir.

"I say, Morgan," mumbled William, slowly stretching his legs and carefully sitting up. "Don't point that thing at me. It just might go off."

Morgan gave a short chuckle and placed the pistol back on the table. "Force of habit, William," he said. "What brings you here at this unearthly hour?"

William tapped the side of his nose with a finger. "A bit of a long night at the tables, Morgan," he answered. "I didn't want to wake his Lordship, so I sneaked in here for a spot of brandy before going up to my room. Came in through the kitchen, y'know, Cook has always been very good to me, but don't let his Lordship know."

"Lord Haggleton is not at home, William," replied Morgan, settling back comfortably in his chair. "He is probably spending the night at the home of the Duchess."

William looked shocked. "Not the same Duchess that he wishes me to marry?" he asked.

Morgan grinned. "I do believe it is, William."

William gripped the sides of his chair. "That's dreadful," he said. "To think that my own father could stoop so low as to court the woman he wishes me to marry."

Morgan took in a long slow breath, and stared hard at his glass of brandy. After what seemed an age, he said slowly. "Your own father would not stoop so low, William, but Lord Haggleton might."

There was a silence, before William said, "I don't understand. What do you mean?"

Morgan carefully placed his brandy back on the table and seemed to contemplate the logs in the fire.

"I said," said William impatiently, "I don't understand your meaning, Morgan. What do you mean by 'your own father would not stoop so low'? Why talk in such riddles?"

"If I tell you this, there will be no turning back, William," replied Morgan. "Our relationship will change for ever. Do you understand?"

"No I don't understand," said William crossly. "So please stop being so melodramatic, and just explain yourself."

Morgan smiled. The brandy was making him feel bold, he picked up the pistol again and laid it on his lap.

"You won't remember your grandfather, he died before you were born. Sir Robert Haggleton's one aim was that at least one of his sons should marry well. The Haggletons were poor, in those days they were the poorest part of the dynasty, even though he was a knight of the realm. Sir Robert had a weakness, like you, William, he gambled, and, like you, William, he usually lost. On one of his journeys around the country, in Yorkshire as it happened, he chanced to meet a very wealthy merchant who had a most beautiful and charming daughter, called Elizabeth."

"My mother," interrupted William. "Everyone says I get my good looks from her."

"Be quiet," commanded Morgan, waving the pistol in William's direction.

William glared at him but didn't take his eyes off the weapon. He didn't trust Morgan.

"The merchant wanted his daughter to marry into the aristocracy. So the two men struck a bargain, in exchange for a title, the Haggletons would get the money. Fortunately, Elizabeth fell in love with Sir Robert's eldest son and he with her, they were a perfect match. So it was not long before Elizabeth married John and the dynasty was saved."

William sat bolt upright. "I don't know what you mean," he said. "Who is John? My father's name is Daniel, is it not?"

258

"I told you to be quiet," growled Morgan. "I am telling you the truth, something that you have been denied all your life." He paused and gave a short sigh. "Of course, it may be that, after I tell you everything, I have to kill you, but at least you will go to your grave knowing the truth."

He didn't notice the change in William's demeanour. Suddenly the laid-back dandy, the man-about-town, had gone, in his place sat a very alert and attentive listener.

"Jonathan Haggleton was your father, William. Your parents were very happy, and, with the enormous fortune brought to your family by Elizabeth, your father built up a fine fishing fleet, plus ships trading in wool and coal throughout the world. One thing, however, he would not do, and he and Elizabeth were adamant about this, he would not entertain the slave trade. Many times he was asked to join in this lucrative trade but always he refused. Daniel, on the other hand, wanted to branch out on his own and was quite happy to join the slavers, but he couldn't do this easily because Jonathan had control of all the money."

"I could never understand how my mother could come to love a man like his lordship," muttered William. "So she was not his wife, he has lied about that too?"

"She was his wife," growled Morgan. "It happened like this… The two brothers had had a big quarrel about the running of their company. Everyone thought that, that was that. Then several months later, Daniel came to apologise for his behaviour, and the brothers resumed their friendship. They even began going on fishing trips together again. There is a large lake at the old property…"

"The Nimbles' house," said William quietly.

Morgan nodded. "You're quick, William, yes the Nimbles' house. It was originally known as Scolus. They often enjoyed an afternoon's fishing on the lake. On that particular afternoon, Jonathan fell into the lake, and despite all of Daniel's efforts he became entangled in weeds and drowned." Morgan paused. "Well, that was the official verdict, but I knew otherwise."

"What did you know?" asked William, shifting in his chair, but not taking his eyes off Morgan.

"I saw what was happening. As a young lad I'd do a bit of poaching on and off and I was there, that afternoon, tickling trout. I saw the two men arguing in the boat, then one stands up, it's Daniel, he hits your father a mighty blow across the head with his oar. Of course, Jonathan immediately falls into the lake, whereupon Daniel jumps in and holds him under all the time pretending to be saving him."

Morgan paused as though the retelling of the events had made him out of breath.

"I ran for help, but I didn't say what I saw," he said quietly.

"Why ever not?" asked William.

"Who would have believed me, a skinny urchin, that had been out poaching? Sir Daniel knew I'd seen him and seemed to know that I was going to prove very helpful to him in the future. He gave me a job straight away as his personal assistant. I was fifteen at the time."

"Fifteen?" William exclaimed. "Didn't anyone think that Sir Daniel's actions were strange?"

"If they did, well, they didn't say, and in any case everyone was too concerned about what had happened and what would become of the company." Morgan took another sip of brandy. "Sir Daniel was good to me in those early days, told me I was like a son to him. He had me tutored in reading, writing, number work, and even sent me to a good academy to learn the art of sword fencing," he gave a malicious smile. "For, as you have found out, William, I am a master swordsman."

William merely nodded. "How old was I when all this was happening?" he asked.

"You were barely two years old," replied Morgan. "Your sister was just thirteen. I must admit that, at first, I imagined Sir Daniel was grooming me, so that I could marry Margaret, but as you are aware that did not happen."

A hiss of anger came from William which only caused Morgan to laugh.

"How did my mother come to marry this fiend?" he asked quietly.

"Well, as I said earlier, your father had built up a large company and, after a suitable time had elapsed, Sir Daniel put it to your mother that your future, and that of your sister's, could only be safeguarded if she married again. It would be best, he explained, for all concerned, if she were to marry him. Keep it in the family, so to speak, and before you ask, you had just passed your third birthday."

A silence descended on the room only broken by the odd crack and spit from the fire. The flames were dancing on the logs as though enjoying this outpouring of truth.

Morgan continued. "Of course, Sir Daniel promised most faithfully that he would not entertain any idea of the company becoming part of the slave trade, but unbeknown to Lady Elizabeth, he not only entered it, but he also had his own version."

"You mean...?" began William.

Morgan nodded. "Yes, all those who came before his courts often found themselves part of that trade and later they were sent to Scolus. As the enterprise grew, so Sir Daniel realised that he needed someone to manage the property on a daily basis, and that's when he employed the Nimbles."

"So why did we leave Scolus? If that is the old family home, why leave?" asked William.

"There was a terrible 'accident'," replied Morgan. "Put that large log on the fire, William, there's a good chap." He indicated the log by pointing the pistol at it.

Inwardly William was seething, but he wanted to know the truth. Occasionally Cook had hinted at a dark past, and even Swithun had alluded to it, but he had never been able to find out all the facts. He threw the log onto the flames and settled back into his chair.

"I don't know why you keep waving that pistol about, Morgan," he said. "You know I'm not going anywhere, I'm intrigued by this whole story."

Morgan grunted. "It's not a story you idiot," he fairly spat out the words. "This is the truth and because it is, I need some insurance, like this." He waved the pistol up and down again.

"Well, what sort of an 'accident' was it?" asked William sulkily.

"It didn't take your mother long to find out that Sir Daniel had broken his word and was moving the company into the slave trade. One day she challenged him about it, and a dreadful argument ensued. He followed her out onto the balcony above the Great Hall. I was there. I looked up and saw him place his hands around her neck, she fought him but it was no use. He threw her to the floor, but they were at the top of the flight of steps, it only needed a small kick and she fell the whole distance. She just lay there, her neck was broken. She must have died instantly. Together we made certain that everyone thought it was an accident."

William frowned. "But why didn't my sister tell me about this?"

"She didn't know how her mother had died, even though she may have suspected something. When you were four, she tried to tell you that Sir Daniel was not your father, remember she was thirteen when her real father had drowned. Sir Daniel made her watch whilst he caned you. This she was told would happen every time she tried to tell you the truth. So you were left in ignorance. Servants who might prove a problem disappeared, some were transported on trumped-up charges. We moved to London and took on new ones, and Scolus remained deserted until Sir Daniel thought up his idea of having his own private charity house, to help those poor and needy folk who had fallen on bad times." Morgan gave a snort of laughter.

William took a deep breath. "He is evil, Morgan, as are you," he said quietly.

"I was afraid you might say something like that," replied Morgan, with a reluctant sigh. "That's why I knew I might have to kill you. I can't risk you going to the authorities to tell them all, because even though you are stupid, I do believe that you have a good streak somewhere in you. Good people have no place in this house, William."

He raised his pistol and took aim.

63

It was an eerie sight. The two men sitting opposite one another, the only light in the room a small oil lamp and the soft flickering flames from the fire. It should have been a homely scene, perhaps of two friends enjoying a late night conversation over a glass of brandy, but an onlooker would soon see that one of them was pointing a pistol at the other. The atmosphere was one of foreboding.

"Before you shoot me," said William quietly, "I'd like to clarify one or two things."

Morgan nodded, a look of sheer hatred and contempt on his face.

"My uncle, Sir Daniel, is responsible for the death of both of my parents?"

"Have I not explained all this," replied Morgan impatiently. "Were you not listening?"

"Yes, yes," William held up his hand as if to ward off the forthcoming shot.

"And, as well as allowing my dear sister to die, you were also responsible for the death of her husband, and the disappearance of my niece, the young lady who came here about the same time as the lad known as Alfie."

"Correct," answered Morgan curtly. "But you know all this, William, you're just trying to waste time. Prepare to meet thy maker."

He laughed and fired.

Nothing happened.

Morgan couldn't believe what had just happened. He looked at his pistol as though it was a useless lump of clay. He heard a tut-tutting, the sound came from William who was holding a pistol.

"Now this one works," he said, with a sigh as if talking to a child. "When I came into this room, you were asleep and I couldn't help but notice the loaded pistol lying on the table beside your sword. It seemed to me a very dangerous thing to do. You asleep, the pistol loaded, anyone could have taken it. So I took the liberty of replacing it with another, one which was not loaded."

Morgan made as if to stand up but William signalled him to remain seated.

"What are you going to do with me?"

The room was full of shadows, the morning sun showed no sign of rising, the oil lamp provided the only steady light, but it was obviously not man enough to light such a vast room.

"Put some more logs on the fire, Morgan, there's a good chap," directed William with some sarcasm. "They will provide us with more warmth and light."

Reluctantly Morgan did as he was instructed. He wasn't going to argue with a man pointing a pistol at him, even if it was that dolt-head William. He piled the logs high and was rewarded with great flames as the draughts in the room rushed towards the hungry fire. He turned to look at William, half expecting these to be his last few moments, but William was nowhere to be seen. In his place stood the unmistakeable masked figure of Noah.

"You!" hissed Morgan. He looked for his sword.

Noah laughed. "Is this what you were looking for?" he said, holding up Morgan's sword. "It seems to me that you are becoming very careless, Morgan, first your pistol and now your sword. Whatever shall we do with you?"

"If I had a weapon you'd soon stop smiling," retorted Morgan. "What have you done with William? You'll definitely hang if you've harmed him in any way, I suppose you've done away with him, though how, I don't know, but, I do know I would have done the same thing if I had been in your place, a waste of space, a nothing man of no use to anyone. You haven't got the nerve to fight me, a real man, a master swordsman."

"Oh, Morgan you do rattle on so when you're worried. Here is your sword." He threw the sword across the room for Morgan to catch.

"And William?" Morgan peered into the shadows. "What have you done with him?"

"He's safe and well," replied Noah. "There is no need for you to concern yourself, Morgan. Well, shall we settle this once and for all?" He made great sweeping movements through the air with his sword.

"That's all very well for you to say," retorted Morgan. "You have a loaded pistol in your other hand. I don't doubt you will use it if things become difficult for you."

With that, Noah threw the pistol down the room so that it skidded across the floor and ended up under a large heavy sideboard.

"There," he said with great emphasis. "Will that please you? And what is more, this should satisfy you completely." He removed his mask.

"You!" Morgan spat on the floor in anger.

"Now that's not very polite," said William laughing. "I thought that as 'a master swordsman' you would be pleased to know your adversary. Come, Morgan, we know this has to end badly for one of us, and I think it only fair, as you said earlier, that you should know the truth before you die!"

Morgan let out a great howl of anger and hurled himself at William but he had already leapt on to the table and slid across to the other side.

"I might have guessed," Morgan said. "You wouldn't stay and duel like a gentleman."

"Words, words," retorted William. "Tell me, Morgan, how did a master swordsman like yourself come by that scar on your face?"

Morgan instinctively put his hand to the scar. He remembered only too well the duel he had had with Noah, and the moment when the sword had slashed his face.

"It was, it was…" he began. He let out another yell of anger and slid across the table to confront William.

And so the duel began.

64

How long the two men fought would be hard to say. One unable to control his anger, at times resorting to slashes and wild sweeps, which never stood a chance of reaching their target, the other, remaining cool, but using his sword with deadly precision. William was fighting for his sister, for his mother and father, and for his newly found niece. He knew it was vital to stay in control of all the seething hatred he felt for this man, vital that he stay alive so as to take his revenge on his uncle. How he hated them both.

The fire was beginning to die down but they both knew that it would not be long before the servants would rise and begin their morning tasks. Neither of them wanted to be found duelling. So intent were they that they didn't notice the door leading to the hall quietly open. A dark figure entered, slowly it raised one arm.

The noise of the firearm temporarily deafened William. Morgan dropped his sword, a look of surprise on his face, blood began trickling from his mouth as he fell into William's arms. He had taken the full blast in his back.

"Lord Haggleton certainly chooses his moments," he whispered, as William gently lowered him to the floor.

William looked towards the door to where his uncle stood, a second pistol ready to fire.

"How convenient," said Sir Daniel quietly. "You will die, William, knowing that you will be remembered as the brave young man who defended me against the treachery of one of my servants." He raised the second pistol and took aim.

William flinched, there were two explosions. One seemed to hit the floor just in front of him, the other hit Sir Daniel.

William saw Swithun standing in the doorway a smoking pistol in his hand.

"He would've shot you'm like he done Morgan," said Swithun grimly. "He were a bad man, an evil man… I suppose I'll 'ang for this." He looked so forlorn, that despite the seriousness of the situation, William almost laughed.

He gave both men a quick check, ironically they had both been shot in the back of the neck. So close had been their paths during life it seemed inevitable that they should die together.

"Give me the pistol," he said, getting up from the floor. "Quickly!"

William took the weapon from Swithun's hand and placed it in Morgan's.

"If needs be, I'll worry about how to explain that they were both shot in the back later," he said. "This will suffice the explanation to the servants when they all come rushing in. Come Swithun, come!"

Hastily he gathered up the swords and his mask, and half dragged and pushed Swithun to the hidden panel beside the fireplace. Just in time, it closed behind them as the first of the servants came rushing in. They could hear the calls and shouts as they made their way along the secret panel and out into the shrubbery deep in the garden.

"Where you'm think we be goin' now, Sir William?" asked Swithun, a little anxiously.

"Nowhere," replied William firmly. "If we leave or go on the run, then people are immediately going to think that we did the killings, Swithun. We must stay and let events take their course."

"But I did kill'um," said Swithun forlornly. "I shot his Lordship, I…"

"Stop," said William. "You saved my life, Swithun, for which I shall be eternally grateful, for if you hadn't done so, he would undoubtedly have killed me. Now, you and I have been out for an early morning ride, Swithun, you must go and rub down our horses in the stable, whilst I return to the house and look absolutely horrified by the scene which will confront me. Do you understand me, Swithun?"

Swithun nodded and set off for the stables to groom two unsuspecting horses, meanwhile, William buried the swords and mask in the undergrowth. He would return for them later.

65

Lucy had had much to think about during the past few days.

Why had Noah rushed off without saying goodbye? How was it that this strange Frenchman seemed to know so much about her past? She didn't even know that much herself. Why hadn't Amos told her the truth? Perhaps he was trying to, when he had been so ill at the end. Her mind was in turmoil. She couldn't talk to Alfie about it, he was too ill to be bothered with such problems. Not for the first time that week, she made her way past The Merry Pilchard, past some of the fishermen's cottages, along the cobbled street, and up onto the path which led round the cliff face and overlooked the harbour.

Up here she could sit on a rough bench which had been carved out of a large log. The sea was calm, it almost seemed as though it was mocking the little fishing port. 'Look I can be good, it seemed to say, but just be careful, I can always be angry again.' Shafts of sunlight played with the waves, making it hard to remember that only a few days ago the great roar of the wind had driven the sea into the village.

Lucy's head felt as if it was going to explode. Inside, her heart ached more than she could ever have imagined. She burst into uncontrollable tears. Hunched up on the bench, she gave way to all the pent-up emotions which she had battled with for most of her journey into Cornwall, ever since her escape from the Nimbles.

She owed her life to Noah, she had no doubt. If he had not found her when he did she would have frozen to death, but she had been certain that it had been her father's spirit that had guided her from that dreadful place. He had told her to follow the lane and make her way into the wood. It

271

was Amos, he was her father, not some unknown musician. Noah had saved them all from certain transportation, and again from the militia. It was… her sobbing would not stop, could not stop. So engrossed was she in her own misery that she didn't hear anyone come up the track behind, nor sit quietly on the bench by her side. Suddenly she felt an arm being placed gently around her shoulder. It was Alice.

"You have a good cry," she said quietly. "It does you good, seems to cleanse all your troubles out of your body. Moll reckons it's the best thing for anyone, better than all that medicine they give you."

Lucy gave a big sniff and tried to dry her eyes on her cape.

"Mind you," continued Alice. "As I tried to tell Moll, it don't mend a broken leg, do it?"

She looked so solemn that Lucy found herself beginning to smile despite all the tears.

"Oh, Alice," she said. "You're so kind." The two girls fell into one another's arms and just hugged in silence.

After a while Alice said, "Well, you was kind to me, I don't forget how you came back for me and Ellie when the Ark was burning. I've still got Ellie, y'know."

From a pocket in her cloak she pulled out a faded rag doll, hardly any of its features were left. She passed it across to Lucy.

"Here, you take her," she said. "She'll keep you safe and remind you of me."

Lucy gave a sniff and then said, as if addressing the doll, "Why, where are you going?"

"It's not me," replied Alice. "It's you. This French uncle of yours wants to take you home with him and look after you."

Unfortunately this had the opposite effect intended, causing Lucy to break into more sobs of despair.

"I don't want to go with him," she said between sniffs. "I want to stay here with you, and Alfie, and the doctor and everyone. I don't want to go away."

They sat together looking out to sea, their silence only broken by the occasional sniffs from both of them. The seagulls seemed to be laughing at them.

"I don't want you to go either," said Alice. "And I'm sure none of the others want it to happen."

"Whatever shall I do?" Lucy gave a big sigh.

After a while Alice gave a laugh. "It's simple," she said, gently cupping Lucy's face in her hands. "You mustn't do anything until Noah comes back. He has gone to London to find out all about you. I know this, 'cos I listened behind the door to Moll and Dr Jack talking about it the other night. They reckon he won't be back for at least six months, they also said it was too dangerous for you to travel to France at this time, 'cos of the war. So you must stay until Noah comes back. See I told you it was simple, I knew Ellie would help!" She gave the old doll a kiss.

Later when Lucy spoke to Frederic she was surprised how readily he agreed to wait, for as he said, he had no wish to cause his new-found niece any unhappiness.

66

There had been great consternation at the discovery of Lord Haggleton's body and that of his servant Morgan. Those who had aided and abetted his Lordship in his cruel ways, silently disappeared, knowing that their reign of terror was at an end. Many of Lord Haggleton's colleagues on the Magistrates' Bench were delighted by his death. They had never been happy with his dealings with offenders, but had not been in the position to prove any wrongdoing. After all he always said that he was giving the poor unfortunates a better life.

The funerals over, formalities sorted, some of William's closest friends were excellent lawyers, the House began to settle down into a happier state.

William sent for Sir George, Lady Helen and Sir Henry, the three who had helped him rescue Lucy, Alfie and the doctor. Swithun also attended their meeting. When Lady Helen heard of his part in saving William, it was all she could do to stop herself from hugging him.

"I intend to do what my father and mother were prevented from achieving in their lifetime," announced William. "I shall end my family's reliance on the slave trade. We shall not be moving any shiploads of people, we shall return to transporting goods, to trade in wool, coal, timber and cotton, but no human cargo."

"At last," said Sir George.

"I know you have fought against this diabolical trade for some time, George," said William. "I would therefore ask you to journey to our overseas stations to inform them of my decision, and to make certain that they obey my instructions. I will give you a body of trustworthy men for this undertaking. Will you see to its organisation, my friend?"

"With pleasure," replied Sir George. "You will certainly give a great example to others who may be dragging their feet on this. There is, however, one thing that might cause you some problems."

"Only one," said William with a wry smile.

"You may be withdrawing from the trade, but what happens to those plantations where slave labour is actually in use?"

There was a short silence.

"You will need more men, and women too," replied William firmly. "We will free these people and teach them how to run their own plantation. I only own one plantation in the West Indies, but at least on that one I can begin to redress the balance. I will not own another human being as long as I live. No man has the right to own another."

The others cheered.

"And where are you sending me, William?" asked Sir Henry with a smile.

"You, my friend, will be going north," replied William.

"How far north?" asked his friend. "Oh, thank you, Swithun." Whilst they had been talking Swithun had poured each one of them a small tankard of ale, even Lady Helen.

"To the coal mines and to the cotton factories," replied William taking up a position by the fireplace. "I want to build proper homes for those who work for me. I have heard it said that some owners supply their workers not only with homes but with schools. I want to do the same and even to have a proper doctor close by. I have just the person who can help me organise that. Will you undertake the building of these homes, Henry?"

"I'd be honoured," replied his friend.

"And what about me?" asked Lady Helen.

"Oh, I have a very special job for you," replied William, with a twinkle in his eye. "But I'll talk to you about that later when we are on our own."

The others smiled as Lady Helen gave a short curtsey.

67

No one at Porthellen could ever have guessed that Noah would be absent for so long. It was two months before the first message reached them.

Moll broke the news.

Waving a letter above her head in The Merry Pilchard she announced, "Noah says to say that he will be delayed for some time. It appears that Lord Haggleton is dead."

There was a loud cheer from those present.

"He also says, that Morgan, too, is dead."

More cheers.

"So who will be the new Lord?" asked someone.

"It will be young William," replied the doctor, who was quietly puffing on his pipe by the fireside. He had taken to having his meals in the inn at night ever since he'd been attending Alfie and Nicole almost daily. Alfie was much improved and was enjoying a tankard with the doctor.

"He's a numbskull," said someone. "It won't take him long to gamble all his inheritance away."

There were nods of agreement and laughter.

"What else does Noah have to say?" asked Lucy, who had been helping behind the bar.

"Not a lot," replied Moll. "Except to say that, on his return, he hopes to have pardons for all who were wrongly threatened with transportation or imprisonment by the late Lord Haggleton. There's a message for you, Lucy and one each for Dr Jack and Alfie." She handed each one of them a separate letter. "He goes on to say that we should all remain calm and not to leave Porthellen until his return. These are dangerous times, we must be ready to defend our homes should there be a French invasion."

"Ise know you said 'not a lot', Moll," said an old man from a corner seat. "But Ise thinking you mun' mean there IS a lot. What you'm said seems a lot to me!"

Lucy went across and knelt by the fireside next to Alfie and the doctor.

"He's told me to wait for him to return, and not to go away with Frederic or Nicole. He says he will bring me more news about my real parents," she said quietly.

The doctor smiled and patted her head. "He's very sensible. You would be advised to do as he requests."

Alfie looked at her in horror. "Do you think he plans to ask you to marry him? He's much too old for you."

Lucy giggled. "I haven't ever thought of that," she replied, knowing that her cheeks were blushing bright red. Then she said teasingly. "Would it bother you?"

Alfie merely grunted.

The doctor chuckled. "He's asked me to consider a move from here," he said quietly.

"Would you?" Lucy and Alfie both looked worried.

"I'm not sure," Dr Jack replied. "I must give it some serious thought and know a lot more about his intentions. In the meantime there is much to be done here and I would need to discuss it with... others." He gave a short cough, and Alfie and Lucy exchanged a smile. Everyone knew that the doctor and Polly Sneed were reaching an 'understanding'.

"And you, Alfie? Has he a special message for you?" asked Lucy.

"Not much," he replied. "Just says that he hopes my health has improved and to carry on with my studies, and he hopes I'm still enjoying my love of the sea, and will one day have my own fishing boat. Very strange, he's never spoken that much to me about my wish to have a boat, but then, he's always been a bit odd."

"He's a very good friend," said Lucy firmly. "Without him we'd all probably be dead by now. He wouldn't say

278

these things without reason, Alfie. If he's got some plan for us, then I think we should listen. Don't you, Doctor?"

Dr Jack took a long pull from his pipe, the smoke whirled around his head before disappearing upwards. "I agree, Lucy," he said. "After all we're in no hurry. At the moment, I think, our priority should be to make certain that we can defend this little port from any possible invasion from Napoleon. We must trust that our Navy will prove invincible."

His words had a sobering effect on the group at the inn. Lucy wasn't the only one who was thinking of the little French family upstairs celebrating the birth of their first son. Could they really be her aunt and uncle? How dangerous could it be for them to be here? What would happen to them if there was an invasion?

"You mustn't worry so," it was as if Moll was reading her thoughts. She was coming round with a jug of ale and was filling up everyone's tankards. "All will turn out right in the end, you'll see, and as for that young couple upstairs," she added with a twinkle in her eye. "I've got just the right job for him."

A few days later through the tunnel came a strangely shaped parcel. It needed two or three men to hoist it onto a wagon and to bring it down to The Merry Pilchard.

Frederic was waiting there anxiously.

"Carefully, carefully," he said, wringing his hands in anticipation.

The men carried this strange shaped coffin into the inn and stood back as he lovingly removed the covers.

"What is it?" one of them asked.

"Oh, my friend," replied Frederic. "This is a pianoforte. Oh, Moll, you are indeed a wonderful woman."

Moll laughed. "I know," she said. "Not many people realise just how wonderful! I have to confess though, that it came from Noah."

Frederic pulled up a chair and gently lifted the lid. Slowly he ran his fingers over the keys, as if dusting the notes with his fingertips.

"Well, play sumthin' then," said one of the men. "We bain't carried it all that way just for you to look at it!"

"Of course," replied Frederic. He looked about him, several had gathered in the inn. News had quickly spread that a pianoforte had arrived, he knew he had to choose his first piece carefully.

As he played, the notes cascaded out of this slightly out-of-tune piano, no one cared, it was magic.

"I know this," called out someone. "My mother used to sing this with my pa! It's Roast Beef of old England!"

Everyone cheered and soon all were singing along. Frederic smiled as one by one people made their requests and he obliged. One hum through and he had the tune.

Moll chuckled. There was no need to worry about him anymore. He had a job for life!

68

A whole year had passed by the time Noah returned. It was a beautiful spring morning when one of the children suddenly rushed into the schoolroom.

"Noah's back!" she shouted. "Noah's back! There's lots of people with him!"

Lucy looked at Polly who smiled and nodded.

"Now be sensible, children," said Lucy. "You may all go down to the harbour to greet him." But even before Lucy had made her announcement the children had gone and, gathering up her skirts, she quickly followed. Such was the laughter and chatter in the village, it was as if a carnival had come to town. They all gathered around The Merry Pilchard.

"Come in! Come in!" called Moll. "Oh, Master George, it's you," she exclaimed as a tall young gentleman bent his head to enter the inn. "And you too, Master Henry. Oh and bless my soul, Lady Helen. Come in, come in all of you."

She sounded so happy and excited that all present caught her mood, even if they didn't know who these extra visitors might be.

By the time Lucy arrived at the inn everyone had entered. She could hear lots of laughter and talking. Looking around she noticed a solitary figure making its way along the harbour wall and up towards the cliff top. It was Alfie. Although she called out he didn't respond but continued on his walk. She was just about to enter when Noah appeared at the doorway and ushered her away.

"I need to talk with you," he said quietly, and, taking her by the arm, gently led her towards the little pack bridge which crossed the small river as it rushed into the inlet. They sat on the parapet as he carefully explained to her all that had happened; the night of her birth; how he had searched for her; all those things which had, until now, been rushing about in her head and had made no sense. At the very end he removed his mask and waited. He was not disappointed.

"Oh," she sobbed. "My uncle, my own real uncle." And there he held her whilst she cried, but this time it was tears of joy, of happiness and relief.

How long they stayed there, she could not say. He gave her his handkerchief to dry her eyes.

"I will always think of you as Noah," she said. He smiled and nodded. "And I will always think of Amos as my father. I will not say this in front of Uncle Frederic as such sentiments I am sure would hurt his feelings, you understand, don't you?"

"Yes," he answered, holding close his sister's child. "I too, have mixed emotions at this time. All my life I have thought Sir Daniel to be my father, in many ways it is a relief that it is otherwise, nevertheless, it is a strange feeling. It explains much about my life, you see, not once did he ever refer to me as 'my son'. I used to be very upset by this, but now it all makes sense."

Lucy suddenly remembered the lone figure of Alfie making his way to the cliff top.

"I must go and find Alfie," she said standing up. "Would you like to come too, Uncle?"

He smiled. "No you go without me." A sudden burst of laughter came from The Merry Pilchard. "I must go and make sure that George is behaving himself. Go and find Alfie and bring him back to join in the celebrations."

"I will," she called as she turned to leave, then pausing, she turned back and gave him a kiss on his cheek. "I am so pleased," she said, "that you found me, Uncle."

"So am I," he murmured.

*　*　*　*

She found Alfie sitting on the log bench staring out to sea. Every now and then he would pick up a pebble and throw it aimlessly towards the ocean. It didn't stand a chance of reaching the shoreline far down below. He didn't bother to look up as she approached although it was obvious that he knew she was there.

After a while he muttered, "So when's the wedding date?"

She pretended that she hadn't heard him. "I'm sorry, did you say something?"

He sighed, looked up and to her horror she realised that he had been crying.

"The wedding," he said gruffly. "When are you marrying him?"

She had intended to tease him but she couldn't bear to see him looking so unhappy, instead she said quietly, "I'm not marrying anyone... and I'm certainly not going to marry my uncle!" She waited for Alfie to take in what she had just said, for his realisation of the situation.

The corners of his mouth started to twitch and when he looked at her again he was laughing. "You mean..." he began.

Gently she put her fingers on his lips. "Noah is William," she said quietly. "He's my uncle."

And then she told him everything, all that William had told her, all that she could remember, and he listened in wrapped silence.

At the very end he said, "But you will marry one day, Lucy."

"That depends on who asks me," she replied coyly.

He kissed her gently on the forehead and they sat together until the sunset, quietly gazing out to sea. He knew he would ask her, and she knew that he would.

69

Such merriment became part of the legend of Porthellen. How would anyone ever forget the wedding day of Dr Jack and Polly Sneed? Somehow the Minister and Frederic set about repairing the old church organ, and, to everyone's delight, Frederic rendered each tune and hymn in so great a volume that they were certain it could be heard on the shores of France. Such dancing took place that no fishing boats went out to sea the next day. Even old friends came. Lucy and Alfie were delighted to meet Agnes and Hannibal again, plus their three children!

Once a month, Dr Jack would tour all of William's factories to check on the workers' health, and to discuss any issues with Sir Henry. Polly would go with him, and, whilst they were away, Alice would help a young trainee doctor who had come down from London to study with Dr Jack. Since Polly had moved out, Alice had gone to live with Nelly permanently, in fact she and Lucy took on the work of teaching all the young children. They even persuaded Frederic and Nicole to come to the school to give the children lessons in French and music. When it became obvious to Frederic that Lucy would not leave England, he and Nicole settled in a little cottage at the top of the hill. There, children would come for piano and singing lessons, or even more French.

In the meantime William sent Alfie to work with some of his finest seamen and captains in Dartmouth. Alfie was quick to learn, the sea was in his blood. On his twentieth birthday he was given his own fishing boat, and control of William's fishing fleet in the West Country. That was the same year he married Lucy.

For a short while, before her marriage, Lucy went to live with William and Helen on the outskirts of London, but it was no use. No matter how kind they were to her, she missed the sounds and sights of Cornwall, the beauty of the countryside, the smell of the sea, her friends and Alfie. She knew how kind her uncle was being, but she could not help herself. William understood. He found her a cottage at the head of one of the valleys and close to Porthellen. It commanded a wonderful view of the sea and harbour below. There she and Alfie brought up their four children, and welcomed their many friends to stay. William and Helen's children were adamant that Cousin Lucy held the best parties and had the best food in the area.

In the meantime, William worked hard behind the scenes, supporting Wilberforce, and others in Parliament, on the abolishment of the slave trade. Lucy was very proud of her uncle but she never did call him 'Uncle William'. To her he would always be Noah.

Readers might enjoy these books in the author's *Henrietta Trout* series:

Henrietta Trout – Golden Shifter

Henrietta Trout has a big secret! Her family have extraordinary powers. Highly trained, they can change their shape and infiltrate any objects – even computers and satellites! Known as shifters, they work for the elite Ministry of Inscrutable Shape Shifters, protecting the world from Gribblers – shifters working for criminals.

Henrietta's nearly ten when she'll also be a shifter, but she's secretly been practising already. She can even help put things right when shape-shifting goes a bit wrong – Uncle Alf has been a table lamp for ages, and Mrs Trout daren't say she feels like a cup of tea!

When the evil Gribblers' bizarre plot to use ice-cream vans to destroy the world threatens all the Trouts, Henrietta gets caught up in the most dangerous and mind-blowing adventures… Scary stuff, but brilliant fun!

Also:

Henrietta Trout
The Mythic Encounter

There's something afoot at Henrietta's school, something very unpleasant. First, a new boy turns out to be a horrid bully, then Year Six laptops go missing, but worst of all – Gribblers are planning a mass kidnapping of schoolchildren!

Still, Henrietta's a fully-fledged shifter like most of her family, so with her unique talents she's not afraid to do battle with Gribblers, those evil shifters intent on world domination. Now there's a new threat – an old evil that's been building up strength over the centuries, one of the most powerful and sinister shifters in the Universe – the Mythic!

Everyone is in deadly danger, what a nightmare! Henrietta has to think and shift faster than ever...

Another hugely entertaining and exciting adventure-awesome!

Lightning Source UK Ltd.
Milton Keynes UK
UKOW06f0431141116
287531UK00001B/23/P